D1004810

Frankenstein

FRANKENSTEIN

HOW A MONSTER BECAME AN ICON

*The Science and Enduring Allure
of Mary Shelley's Creation*

EDITED BY

SIDNEY PERKOWITZ AND
EDDY VON MUELLER

PEGASUS BOOKS
NEW YORK LONDON

FRANKENSTEIN

Pegasus Books Ltd.
148 W 37th Street, 13th Floor
New York, NY 10018

Compilation copyright © 2018 Sidney Perkowitz and Eddy Von Mueller

First Pegasus Books edition January 2018

Interior design by Maria Fernandez

Library of Congress Cataloging-in-Publication Data is available.

ISBN: 978-1-68177-629-3

10 9 8 7 6 5 4 3 2 1

Printed in the United States of America
Distributed by W. W. Norton & Company

Dedicated with love to my dear wife, Sandy, and to Mike, Erica, and Nora, just for being there. They are a great comfort, a great joy, and a great support when I'm writing a book and when I'm not.

SP

For my mom, and the love, support, and understanding that got us through all the Dark & Stormy Nights; and for all my Little Monsters: T., C., Z., and always and especially for K.

EVM

CONTENTS

INTRODUCTION

TWO HUNDRED YEARS OF *FRANKENSTEIN*

On a rainy night in 1816, eighteen-year-old Mary Wollstonecraft Shelley sat with her new husband, the celebrated poet Percy Bysshe Shelley, and their friends in a villa on the shores of Lake Como in Italy; among them, the poet and adventurer Lord Byron. To pass the time Byron suggested that each member of the company create a ghost story. In response, Mary Shelley drew on her imagination, her own life, and the science of the time to write *Frankenstein, or The Modern Prometheus*.

Shelley's tale about a tormented creature created in a laboratory by the fatally ambitious scientist Victor Frankenstein was published, at first anonymously, in 1818. The power of her story has never since waned. With the audacity of its central idea and the richness of its themes, *Frankenstein* has become a literary touchstone, a cultural phenomenon, and a global icon—and in its bicentennial year of 2018, this story still has lessons for us in the 21st century.

Few stories have reached the worldwide prominence that *Frankenstein* enjoys. It has been translated and adapted countless times, and versions of Shelley's novel have appeared in every possible medium and in every conceivable variation. The novel itself has not been out of print in nearly two hundred years and has appeared in about five hundred editions according to one source, perhaps more than any other work of fiction. It is routinely read by students from middle school to graduate school. Scholarly interest in the work is perennially high. Even a cursory look in Google Books or a university library reveals hundreds of books and articles in many languages devoted to literary and cultural analysis of Shelley's work, its milieu, and its popular forms. Its impact is undiminished in the digital age: in 2013, when reproductions of Mary Shelley's *Frankenstein* notebooks went online, the response was overwhelming. The site drew almost sixty thousand visitors from around the world in its first twenty-four hours.

Frankenstein has inspired a multitude of stage, screen, and television adaptations as well. The classic film version is the 1931 *Frankenstein*, directed by James Whale with Boris Karloff as Dr. Frankenstein's creature, which was a box office hit in its day. Now it is acknowledged as one of the 100 all-time greatest American films chosen by the American Film Institute, and contemporary critics give it a perfect 100% rating on RottenTomatoes.com, but it is only the peak of a mountain of Frankenstein films. These range from vintage (the earliest was a 1910 short from Thomas Edison's film company) to contemporary, including James Whale's follow-up *Bride of Frankenstein* (1935); *Abbot and Costello Meet Frankenstein* (1948), which, along with Mel Brooks's *Young Frankenstein* (1974), is listed by AFI among the 100 funniest American movies; and Kenneth Branagh's *Mary Shelley's Frankenstein* (1994), with Robert DeNiro as the Monster. Most recently, Haifaa Al-Mansour directed a new Mary Shelley biopic in 2017. A big-budget reboot of *Frankenstein* is on the way, slated for release in 2019.

One guide lists hundreds of *Frankenstein*-related films and television shows, many with only a tenuous connection to the original story. Another compilation, limited to versions that expressly attempt to follow Shelley's novel, still lists dozens of feature films and TV productions. Entering "Frankenstein" in a key-word search on the movie site IMDb brings up about one hundred entries since 1994 alone. The phenomenon is a global one: *Frankenstein* films have been made in the United States, the United Kingdom, Germany, Spain, Turkey, Japan, Canada, and Czechoslovakia. In addition to attracting audiences around the world, *Frankenstein* as a media property runs the gamut in terms of genre, budget, tone, and era, from cheaply made exploitation films to lavish period productions, from '50s teen-pics to racy "adult" movies in the 1970s. Indeed, almost no movement in the evolving art of the moving image is without its take on Shelley's timeless creation.

Clearly the ideas and emotions engendered by Shelley's story cut across decades and centuries and across cultural and national lines to find wide expression, partly because it has been continually adapted and reinterpreted. The text has been opened up to explore the many potential perspectives of the novel's rich cast of characters. For example, in Paul McGuigan's 2015 film *Victor Frankenstein*, the story is told from the viewpoint of Dr. Frankenstein's assistant; in a recent theatrical production in Newcastle, UK, titled *Dr. Frankenstein* (written and directed by Selma Dimitrijevic), the scientist who creates life is a woman, Dr. Victoria Frankenstein; and in 2011, Danny Boyle directed a well-received stage version of *Frankenstein* (written by Nick Dear) at London's Royal National Theatre, in which Benedict Cumberbatch and Jonny Lee Miller alternated the roles of Victor Frankenstein and his creature.

Manifestations of *Frankenstein* are just as prevalent elsewhere in popular culture. Beginning with the iconic image of Boris Karloff as the lurching Monster with electrodes in his neck from the 1931 film, they have continued nonstop. The phrase "Frankenstein's monster" is widely understood to represent a horrific, menacing, and shambling creature created by some other entity and used in every imaginable context; for instance, to cast slurs in the heated US presidential campaign of 2016. In another example, the very prefix "franken" has come to mean an ill-chosen collection of parts or something badly out of kilter. In 1992, Paul Lewis, an English professor at Boston College, first called genetically modified food "frankenfood." The name has stuck and is also applied to junk food. Then there is "frankenstorm" for violent weather and "frankenword" for awkward portmanteau words like "docudrama" or, self-referentially, "frankenword" itself.

Frankenstein has also been interpreted in less threatening ways for the younger set. Boxes of Franken Berry strawberry-flavored breakfast cereal for kids, sold by General Mills since 1971, come adorned with a pink cartoon version of the Monster. Or children can play with *Frankenstein*-themed dolls, action figures, and even *Frankenstein* "plushies." Described as making the Monster "more adorable than ever" for ages three and up, these stuffed versions come complete with soft electrodes. Kid-friendly versions of the Monster turn up on Saturday morning cartoons like *The Groovy Ghoolies* (1970–1971) and *The Drac Pack* (1980), and in animated features like *Hotel Transylvania* (2012) and books for young readers like Lola M. Schaeffer and Kevan Atteberry's *Frankie Stein*. And of course, Frankenstein and his monster both remain stalwart features of the annual Halloween masquerades in the United States.

Apart from its popular and cultural significance, and its impact on literature and the media, *Frankenstein* powerfully expresses the ethical issues raised by the relentless advance of science. After all its long history, the story's central premise—that science, not magic or God, can create a living being, and that the creators must answer for their actions as humans, not gods—is increasingly relevant as the modern science of manipulating DNA approaches the possibility of changing the biological nature of humanity and even of creating synthetic life. These ethical issues arise from the impact—for good or ill—of this kind of genetic manipulation on all humanity. Synthetic beings themselves would also raise ethical questions. In Mary Shelley's story, Dr. Frankenstein's artificial being keenly feels his own lack of natural parentage and blames his creator's rejection for his anger, his desire for revenge, and the lack of a moral structure that together drive him to murder.

Deeper still, Shelley's story raises compelling questions of conscience and consciousness—of how thinking beings understand and process their experience of the world, and the ways in which they try to share and use that experience. Part of the fear and fascination of Shelley's book comes from our following the characters on their respective journeys of discovery, as they confront the horrors their obsessions and desires have driven them to. As the subtitle *The Modern Prometheus* suggests, this tale touches the topical ethical dilemmas we confront not only on the ever-advancing frontiers of science but also in philosophy, morality, and myth. Small wonder that a tale conjured by a teenager that rainy night on the shores of Lake Como to send a shiver up her friends' spines still exercises such allure for scientists, scholars, artists, and curious minds the world over.

For all these reasons, the story of *Frankenstein* calls for new consideration on its two hundredth birthday. To provide that assessment, we have assembled leading scholars, scientists, and media experts and practitioners. They bring a diversity of voices and writing styles, from academic papers based on deep research, to interviews with media figures that express how their personal interactions with the *Frankenstein* story have inspired their creativity. The contributed chapters take a fresh look at Mary Shelley's marvelous creation and its global legacy by tracing how "Frankenstein" has developed from 1818 to 2018 and what the story means today. Like Victor Frankenstein's creature itself, stitched together from varied body parts, the different perspectives we present provide an integrated and, we hope, fully alive and lively view of this meaning.

To help you the reader categorize the great diversity of themes the story supports, these chapters are organized into three parts.

The Roots and Themes of *Frankenstein*. The origins of the Frankenstein story are varied and complicated. Besides Mary Shelley's own creativity, they include a deep intellectual heritage from her parents— William Godwin, a political philosopher and writer, and Mary Wollstonecraft, an advocate for women's rights and writer who died soon after her daughter's birth. This adds emotional overtones to Mary Shelley's story, which is, after all, about the "birth" of a new being and the defeat of death. Another thematic thread comes from the scientific beliefs of the time, which form the background of Victor's work in creating a living thing. One of its most important facets was the discovery of "animal electricity" by the Italian scientist Luigi Galvani in the late 18th century, thought then perhaps to be the animating principle for life.

These roots and more are addressed by our contributors. Catherine Nickerson, a literary scholar at Emory University, writes about the origins of the story, its emotional and intellectual themes, and how it reflects significant social, political, and ethical issues in 19th-century British society. Dwayne Godwin, a neuroscientist at Wake Forest University, and cartoonist Jorge Cham, who created PHD Comics, collaborate in an entertaining and scientifically accurate comic strip about how Galvani's work with animal electricity came to be associated with Frankenstein's creature. Laura Otis, who studies the interactions between science and literature, brings psychological and literary insight to discuss the emotional state of Frankenstein's creature as a being "born" without parents or family and rejected by its maker. Finally, Steven Kraftchick, a scholar of religion at Emory University who studies the meaning of trans-humanism, reflects on a different aspect of Frankenstein's creature, the meaning of its "monstrosity."

The Monster, the Media, and the Marketplace. After two centuries of extensive exposure, the *Frankenstein* story and its variants continue to engage audiences in every medium. Studying how it is presented in the media offers new insights into the evolution of its meaning over time and also into how the media deal with the story's scientific, ethical, and human questions. Our contributors tackle these issues as media scholars and as creative voices in the media, the writers and directors of *Frankenstein*-based stories on big and small screens.

Setting the stage, Evan Lieberman, a professor of cinema studies at Cleveland State University, surveys the *Frankenstein* myth as expressed on the movie screen from a broad perspective, examining the diversity of its adaptations from around the globe. Then Kevin LaGrandeur, who teaches English and the impact of technology at New York Institute of Technology, presents an interview with the celebrated director Mel Brooks about his beloved dark comedy *Young Frankenstein* (1974)."

Alexis Gambis, founder of Imagine Science Films, brings a different view as he writes about his vision for science in film, including his *Chimera* project to produce an independent film about hybrid artificial beings, and how that relates to *Frankenstein* on-screen. Jaime Paglia, cocreator of the *Eureka* series on the Syfy Channel, writes about how he and his colleagues probe the boundaries between life and death in the series, in homage to Mary Shelley's story. Then coeditor and film scholar Eddy Von Mueller interviews John Logan, creator and head writer of the *Penny Dreadful* Showtime cable series, and Stuart Beattie, director of the feature film adaptation of *I, Frankenstein*, about their takes on the timeless tale. In a second piece, Von Mueller traces the evolution of the Monster as an iconic figure in cinema, from the first version produced in 1910 by Thomas Edison's film company to more recent ones, such as Kenneth Branagh's *Mary Shelley's Frankenstein*.

Finally in a different vein but still within the world of popular culture, Carol Colatrella, professor of literature and cultural studies at Georgia Institute of Technology, writes about how the Frankenstein story has been absorbed into the world of toys, games, and costumes and what it may mean for childhood development.

The Challenges of *Frankenstein*: Science and Ethics. From the standpoint of how science and technology affect society, the most important aspects of Mary Shelley's story are what it tells us about the scientific possibility of seriously altering or re-creating humanity and the ethical considerations this raises. These questions are becoming more insistent as recent work in manipulating DNA brings us closer to changing the human genome in a controlled way and maybe building entirely synthetic versions of ourselves, a process whose first small steps have already been taken.

To begin addressing these questions, coeditor Sidney Perkowitz, a physicist and science writer, reviews what we can learn from *Frankenstein* and other fictional treatments of synthetic life, from early myth to today's media; then he shows where today's science stands in actually allowing us to radically change or remake ourselves, going on to discuss the resulting ethical issues looming on the horizon. Two other scientists, research chemists Jay Goodwin and David Lynn, explain how the contemporary scientific approach to understanding and duplicating the origins of life, including their own work on the molecular basis of life, echoes ideas expressed in *Frankenstein*. They end by noting the warnings for society that can be read in Mary Shelley's work, not only for new genetic technology but also for all the technological changes that along with their benefits threaten our own nature and the natural world we occupy.

In the same way that thinkers and artists can never exhaust the possible variations and interpretations to be mined from Shelley's story, even this diverse array of varied topics and writers cannot hope to cover every facet of what Mary Shelley's *Frankenstein* has historically meant and what it means today. We nonetheless hope that these selections will act as guides to the richness of the story and inspire further exploration from readers and students. To help those who wish to look more deeply into this classic work, many of the subsequent chapters provide references and guides to further reading and viewing.

Our book will have been a success if it makes readers appreciate the remarkable staying power of this cultural icon and helps them understand where modern bioscience may be taking us all, and what that may mean for society and humanity.

For their roles in helping to express these important issues, we the editors wish to applaud our contributors and thank them for their efforts.

Sidney Perkowitz
Eddy Von Mueller
Atlanta, Georgia

PART ONE

THE ROOTS AND THEMES OF *FRANKENSTEIN*

The world to me was a secret, which I desired to discover; to her it was a vacancy, which she sought to people with imaginations of her own.

> —Victor Frankenstein, describing himself
> and his foster sister and fiancée Elizabeth.
> Mary Shelley, *Frankenstein*

The origins of *Frankenstein, or The Modern Prometheus*, the novel, are almost as arresting and dramatic as the origins of the creature so famously brought to life by its title character. Mary Shelley, just eighteen years old, the precocious daughter of decidedly offbeat parents—her mother was the fiercely independent feminist Mary Wollstonecraft, who died when Mary Shelley was still an infant—is whiling away a dark and stormy night in a lakeside villa cooking up scary stories with her husband, the poet-philosopher Percy Bysshe Shelley, and their Bohemian pals. What occurred to the young woman during this casual exercise would become one of the most enduring works in the English language and would spawn two centuries of imitation, adaptation, and obsession.

Frankenstein, then, is a work both very much of its time, but also of our time. Our first group of essays returns to Shelley's celebrated novel, viewed through several different critical lenses, and explores where this remarkable story came from and why it speaks so eloquently across the centuries and generations.

Literary critic and scholar Catherine Ross Nickerson takes a closer look at the author and her times—the late 18th and early 19th centuries—to reveal some of the forces that likely influenced Shelley's sensibilities and storytelling: from the traditions of the Gothic novel and the Enlightenment thinkers she was exposed to at home to the traumas and complexities of her own unconventional domestic life and the iconoclastic ideas and ideals of her parents and her literary circle. Nickerson also cannily exposes the many ways in which the young author's life is reflected in the lives of her ill-fated characters, whose constellations of family relationships are nothing if not complicated.

On the lighter side (or the light*ning* side), neurobiologist Dwayne Godwin and cartoonist Jorge Cham remind us that Frankenstein's

Monster, like Victory, had many fathers: *Frankenstein* was written at a time of intense interest in "natural philosophy," when gentlemen amateurs, traveling showmen, and serious scientists alike were experimenting with, among other phenomena, electricity—creating the rich intellectual environment for the genesis of Shelley's story.

Laura Otis, with a background in science and a deep understanding of its many intersections with the humanities and the arts, sees in Shelley's novel expressions of emotional impulses and reactions relevant to any audience or era as Frankenstein, his creation, and their victims experience rejection, rage, yearning, and isolation. Otis's essay underscores both the timeliness and timelessness of this remarkable text, demonstrating how both the young writer's powerfully poetic use of language and contemporary psychological and sociological research resonate with the story's enduring themes.

Finally, biblical scholar and theologian Steven J. Kraftchick articulates the nuanced and complex ways in which Mary Shelley compels us to confront monsters and monstrosity, good and evil. His exegesis reveals how this now perhaps deceptively familiar story presents its characters on a moral spectrum along which nobility and compassion can be far too easily corrupted by ambition, cowardice, and intolerance.

A thread weaving through all these essays is that of unintended consequences: the myriad ways in which actions, ideas, and influences—personal, poetic, psychological, historical—ripple out through stories and through lives to give rise later to things wondrous, tragic, and new, like the tale born on that blustery night so many years ago, which, as we shall see, continues to echo throughout our scientific and popular culture today.

1

"HIDEOUS PROGENY": TELLING A TALE OF MONSTERS IN *FRANKENSTEIN*

Catherine Ross Nickerson

E ven if you have never read *Frankenstein, or the Modern Prometheus* (1818), you almost certainly know the story because of the book's status as a touchstone in popular culture. Mary Shelley's tale of ambitious folly and the unleashing of a resentful monster, has, as this volume attests, inspired many creative interpretations and adaptations. In this chapter, we will focus on the book itself: how it came to be, how its complex form highlights themes and issues in the story, and how it expresses the cultural anxieties of its day in the tale of a scientist who, in the process of creating a monster, makes himself into a kind of fiend.

This book about unhallowed beginnings has its own famous origin story. Mary Shelley wrote the original version of the tale as an entertainment for a circle of artists and writers, including Lord Byron and her husband, Percy Shelley, on vacation in Italy in the summer of 1816. They were staying together in a large house, and it rained a great deal. To entertain themselves, they started reading ghost stories aloud in the evenings, and when they ran out of published stories, they proposed writing their own. Shelley's first version of the story was created there, as a tale to be read aloud in a single evening. She continued to work on it, expanding it into a novel over the next two years, and publishing it in 1818. Shelley revised it significantly for a new edition in 1831, adding an introduction that sheds light on her own understanding of the novel. The introduction also discusses her intellectual history and background. She was the daughter of two intellectual radicals, Mary Wollstonecraft and William Godwin, both of whom were involved in revolutionary movements in the late 18th century. The way that they had grappled with the troubling characteristics of British social order in the period—the sexism, the racism, the disenfranchisement of the middle and lower class—clearly influenced Shelley and shaped the narrative of *Frankenstein*.

What most readers first notice is that the book takes a long time to get going. Indeed, the story as a whole moves rather slowly, with a good deal of time spent on the backgrounds of characters, descriptions of landscapes, and long philosophical passages. The slow pace of the story may seem counter to the needs of a classic horror story, but Shelley was working within an established literary tradition for writing about fear: the Gothic novel. Shelley's precursors in the Gothic tradition include dozens of popular novels, including Anne Radcliffe's *The Mysteries of Udolpho* (1794). A typical novel of this type features a young woman who has been orphaned or separated from at least one parent. She comes to reside in a strange house, a big and complicated structure. She undertakes, bit by bit, a quest to understand the mysterious people, sounds, and activities around her, but her investigations are thwarted in multiple ways. Metaphorically, the heroine is exploring the way the larger, patriarchal society works. Within the story, we continually encounter locked doors and windows, missing keys, candles that won't stay lit, people who cannot speak. This repeated highlighting of obstacles to knowledge and resolution is reinforced by the narrative structure of these kinds of stories, which Eve Kosofsky Sedgwick likens to a "Chinese box" (a puzzle of boxes within boxes with hidden springs and sliding panels that allow them to be extricated from each other). While the plot is quite different from other novels of this type, *Frankenstein*'s multiple stories-within-stories form a narrative structure inherited from the Gothic.

Frankenstein, the novel, is also distinguished by its multiple first-person narrators. Walton, the icebound captain of an exploration vessel, rescues Victor Frankenstein. The reader learns about Victor through letters Walton writes to his sister, and Shelley uses Walton's telling of Victor's story as a classic sort of "framed tale." In addition, within Victor Frankenstein's narrative, other characters speak: Elizabeth and Alphonse (Victor's adopted sister and his father) speak through letters to Victor; the monster speaks through the story he tells Victor about his escape and education. Furthermore, several stories that intersect with the main narrative are told in great detail: the life of adoptee and Frankenstein household servant Justine, before, during, and after her trial for a murder the monster actually committed; Safie's family history before coming to live with the De Lacey family in the cottage where the monster is hiding. In Gothic novels, the layers of narration serve as testimony to the power and frightfulness of the tale being told, as if it is a hot pan that needs to be muffled in layers of cloth so no one gets burned. Documents like the letters we see here offer a verification of the authenticity—a fake authenticity—of the story, indicating that the story has been heard and accepted by more than one person. In *Frankenstein*, there are stories within stories as well as stories, like Walton's, that frame the story. As a result, a reader can open the book in the middle and not be sure who "I" is. Is it Victor speaking, or is it the monster? That is clearly an intended effect, to enact in the narrative structure one of the main Gothic themes of the novel: that Victor and his monster are doubles for each other.

When we think about the differences between the novel and the films based on it, all the carefully constructed layers of narrative in the novel make a sharp contrast to the iconic, exciting "It's alive!" moment of so many of the films. In the novel, we have, instead of a literal or metaphorical lightning strike of triumphant genius, a report of the creature opening its eyes, taking a breath, and twitching, tucked into the end of a sentence, followed by Victor's direct address to the reader about the difficulty of telling this story at all: "How can I describe my emotions at this catastrophe, or how delineate the wretch . . . ?" (chapter 5 [chapter numbers refer to the 1831 edition]).

The novel represents the moment of animation not as a moment of thrilling triumph but as a moment of underwhelmed disappointment shading toward despair. Victor admits that he wanted his creation to be "beautiful," but instead, after two years of work, "the beauty of the dream vanished, and breathless horror and disgust filled my heart" (chapter 5). What is so horrifying about the creature is that it shows Victor to be a failure. Victor realizes that he does not instill life and vigor but rather deals in death and decay, which the nightmare he has immediately after reinforces. In it, he kisses his beloved Elizabeth and she morphs from a young woman in the "bloom of health" (chapter 5) into the corpse of his late mother, ridden with worms. He wanted to create a superior form of human; he realizes that what he has created is freakishly inhuman, a "miserable monster," more "hideous" than a reanimated mummy, "demoniacal," something even Dante, master portraitist of Hell, could not have imagined (chapter 5).

Undertaking this transgressive project has transformed Victor as well. He has isolated himself from his fellow students in a "workshop of filthy creation," and his obsessive ambition has led him to seek body parts from "the dissecting room and the slaughter-house"; he is filled with "loathing for my occupation," and yet he pushes on compulsively (chapter 5). He is made physically and mentally ill, he becomes secretive and cuts off communication with his family, he strays far from his own ideal of a life that does not allow "any pursuit whatsoever to interfere with the tranquility of [one's] domestic affections" (chapter 5). Even as he knows that his kind of overweening, brutal ambition leads to calamity, war, the destruction of empire, and the enslavement of people (chapter 5), he cannot stop himself from piecing together his experiment in defiance of the proper limits of human power. By his own standards, he has become a monster, too.

The creature, then, is born out of an unholy conjunction of male ambition and a belief that new scientific methods could hold the keys to the locked mysteries of the universe. In this portrait of Victor as a scientist seeking, without ethical constraints, to isolate and control the life force, the novel expresses the urgent anxiety growing in British culture immediately after the Enlightenment. Victor's education recapitulates the changing scientific paradigms and practices throughout the 18th century. When Victor's father refers to the work of Cornelius Agrippa, Albertus Magnus, and Paracelsus as "sad trash" (chapter 2), he is expressing a widely held belief among educated people that the age of alchemy was over and had to yield to modern disciplines like chemistry. Alchemy, which Agrippa referred to as "natural magic," appealed to the young Victor and his "fervent longing to penetrate the secrets of nature" (chapter 2). However, when he witnesses a massive oak tree near his home reduced to splinters by a lightning strike, he comes to feel that the mysteries of the natural world would always elude his understanding, and he turns to the study of mathematics instead.

At the university in Ingolstadt, Victor is taught that alchemy has been thoroughly discredited, and he takes up the study of chemistry with Waldman instead. But even as Victor learns something we can recognize today as a rational scientific method based on experimentation and observation, he is also under the spell of the charismatic Waldman, who proclaims that modern scientists "have acquired new and almost unlimited powers; they can command the thunders of heaven, mimic the earthquake, and even mock the invisible world with its own shadows." These words, which portray scientists as gods, are what set Victor on his disastrous course. He calls them "words of fate, enounced to destroy me" (chapter 3). In the moment, though, they awaken Victor; "soon my mind was filled with one thought, one conception, one purpose . . . I will pioneer a new way, explore unknown powers, and unfold to the world the deepest mysteries of creation" (chapter 3). Victor, the maker of monsters, is himself brought to life at this moment. We might even say that he is "galvanized," as a nod to the term Shelley uses in her introduction to the tale. He synthesizes the alchemists' pursuit of "boundless grandeur" (chapter 3) and the restless and relentless experimentation of the chemists and biologists. He is, in his own way, a frightening figure in the post-Enlightenment landscape, a pieced-together chimera of irrational motivations and rational methods.

How did poor Victor turn out so badly? He seems to lack the internal ethical gyroscope that would have steered him away from such a hideous, dangerous, and blasphemous project. The novel hints at a domestic source of the trouble. In the early 19th century, questions about the proper nurture of children and the best arrangements for family life were increasingly in the air. Victor attests that "no human being could have passed a happier childhood than myself" (chapter 2). And yet there are multiple anomalies in the Frankenstein household. The novel opens with an account of how Alphonse and Caroline, Victor's parents, came to be married: Caroline, left orphaned and destitute by her irresponsible father, was rescued by Alphonse, raised by a Frankenstein relation, and wed to him two years later. Theirs was not an entirely normative marriage: There is a significant difference in age, there is the way that Caroline went from being something like an adopted daughter to a wife, there is a complex web of emotional debts they owe and pay to each other, there is a kind of post-traumatic fragility in Caroline that draws Alphonse to hover near.

This pattern is then duplicated with Victor's intended. Elizabeth Lavenza, another orphaned daughter of an upper-class man, is adopted into the family because she is so pretty and charming. Victor tells us twice that she is "my more than sister," and we see another case of the blurred roles of women in the house, with patterns of intimacy different from what one might expect. The novel asks us to see Caroline and Elizabeth as twinned, or even interchangeable, in the way that Elizabeth comes down with scarlet fever and infects only Caroline, who dies; Elizabeth then takes on the role of mother to her younger brother, William (chapter 2). She also takes on the role of lover and bride to her older brother, Victor. There is also the complicated relationship that Justine has with the Frankenstein family; she has the dual role of servant and a sort of cousin. Her relationship with her rejecting, resentful biological mother is a grim mirror of the system of obligations that tie together the Frankensteins. Like Caroline and Elizabeth before her, Justine's proper role is to be "the most grateful little creature in the world" (chapter 6). All three women seem to be without larger ambitions, content to shape their lives to the needs of the Frankenstein household.

With these grateful women—all brought into the family by way of rescue—and an indulgent father, Victor does have an idyllic boyhood and is spared the difficulty of finding a mate, as Elizabeth is right there already, bound to him by the deathbed promise extracted by their dying mother. This irregular, structurally incestuous household, bound together by the "silken cord" (chapter 1) of a benevolent patriarch, seems to fail Victor in some significant ways. He complains that he feels "cooped up" and is eager to leave for university. But more fatally, all the attention and generalized gratitude focused on him by female kin allow his ego to grow to enormous proportions. His masculine grandiosity is apparent in his studies before the age of seventeen: he is attracted to the sweeping promises of the alchemists, hoping for the "glory" that would come with finding the elixir of life, and attempting incantations to raise "ghosts or devils" (chapter 2). These fixations of course foreshadow what he will accomplish in building his monster at Ingolstadt, but they also suggest that his excessive ambitions were cultivated in the hothouse of the Frankenstein home.

Victor himself is wholly inadequate as a "father." The monster is of course Victor's double, but he is also Victor's "hideous progeny," to borrow a term Shelley applied to the novel itself. He rejects his newly alive creation—twice that first night and on their second encounter, it reaches out to him with a "grin" on its face. He abandons the creature in a passive attempted infanticide and is relieved when it seems to have fled the premises by the next day. Victor is horrified by what he has wrought, but he doesn't think at all about what it might be like to be the monster. And as we learn later, the monster does indeed have subjectivity and an inner life. He has the intelligence to differentiate amongst his five senses, to understand pain, fear, misery, and delight, and, eventually, to acquire spoken and written language. In her narration of the education of the monster, Shelley is playing with the theories of Jean-Jacques Rousseau, John Locke, and other Enlightenment thinkers who were important to the Romantics. The monster is born into a state of innocence: it has an instinct for self-preservation, but also an instinct for compassion. We see that it knows to hide itself from angry, frightened villagers, but also that it is able to empathize with the De Lacey family, to see their sadness and suffering, and even to discern their "gentle manners." The monster longs for community, and it attempts to use its superhuman strength to help children in particular, but it is attacked violently every time it makes itself visible. The bitterness and cruelty and destructiveness we see later is all learned; the monster is fundamentally a moral creature, who says that while hearing narratives of human history, "I could not conceive how one man could go forth to murder his fellow" (chapter 13).

The monster's more formal education teaches it what it has been deprived of, which is to say the kind of idealized childhood that Victor enjoyed: it reads about "how the father doted on the smiles of the infant . . . how all the life and cares of the mother were wrapped in the precious charge . . . and all the various relationships which bind one human being to another in mutual bond" (chapter 13). Its ability to read strengthens its sense of deprivation: when it reads John Milton's *Paradise Lost*, it notes that Adam, unlike itself, is able to converse with his doting creator, and realizes that the envious, hell-banished Satan is its true entry point into the poem. By the time it discovers Victor's journal in his coat, it has a moral perspective on what Victor has done, on the "disgusting circumstances" of the creation of "my odious and loathsome person." It cries, "Why did you form a monster so hideous that even *you* turned from me in disgust?" (chapter 15).

With those words, the monster sums up Victor's profound failure. Victor's ability to bring a pieced-together creature to life does not endow him with the glory he sought as a child. He becomes instead a frightened, heartbroken man whose greatest accomplishment must be kept a secret. Even before we hear the monster's account of his first two years, there is little to admire in Victor. And yet, we feel Victor's agony and his fear as the monster launches the campaign of revenge that ultimately consumes everyone Victor loves.

One of the reasons that the narration works the way it does is the tension between the different kinds of fear that Shelley invokes. In an 1826 essay, "On the Supernatural in Poetry," Gothic novelist Anne Radcliffe made a famous distinction: "Terror and Horror are so far opposite, that the first expands the soul and awakens the faculties to a high degree of life; the other contracts, freezes and nearly annihilates them." Horror is what we and Victor and all the various villagers feel when we see the gruesomely animated corpse. Terror builds as Victor senses, instinctively, that his monster has killed his younger brother, William, has successfully framed Justine for the murder, and is out to get revenge in ways that Victor can only imagine, leaving him in "dread and misery" (chapter 20). Terror is about anticipation of something only partly known and is the element that advances the narrative momentum in this book of stories within stories. What will the monster do? we and Victor wonder. It is like us, it is partly human—but it is also partly other things.

When Victor and the monster meet after those two years, the monster comes off as the more rational of the two and exhibits a level of self-knowledge his creator has yet to attain. It explains, "I am malicious because I am miserable" (chapter 17) and "make me happy, and I shall again be virtuous" (chapter 10). Its proposed solution—that Victor create a mate for it—comes from its education in issues of what Enlightenment thinkers would have called "natural rights": "Shall each man . . . find a wife for his bosom, and each beast have his mate, and I be alone?" (chapter 20). For Shelley, and for her first audience in the early 19th century, the fantastical tale of a scientist who brings a corpse to life quickly connects to questions about the definition of personhood, natural rights, and the burning questions of the ethics, politics, and economic systems of empire and slavery.

Our monster subscribes to the Enlightenment formulation, repeated in the American Declaration of Independence, of the "self-evident" rights to "life, liberty, and the pursuit of happiness." The creature also uses the language and metaphor of slavery with ferocity. When Victor absolutely refuses to carry out the plan to create a bride for his monster, the monster roars, "Slave, I have reasoned with you, but you have proved yourself unworthy of my condescension. Remember that I have power" (chapter 20). The monster, which in the same conversation refers to Victor as a "tyrant and tormentor," evokes the turmoil of the current moment, as Britain is struggling with the profitable evil of chattel slavery within its empire; the specter of the being who is not exactly "us" rebelling and seizing control adds another note of fear to the narrative of *Frankenstein*.

In her introduction to the 1831 edition, Shelley tells us that her first image of the story that was to become *Frankenstein* was of the young scientist animating his creature, becoming horrified by his "odious handywork," hoping it will die, and being terrified when the creature comes to his bedside. That moment of origin is the center of gravity in this novel, what everything else leads up to or points back to. In the book, the moment is less cataclysmically dramatic than in many of the film versions; it is underwhelming because the creature itself is so disappointing to Victor. The real terror comes later, when Victor discovers that the monster he created to prove his own genius and power turns out to be capable of thinking, knowing, and plotting revenge for the crime of its own creation.

Victor thinks he is fulfilling his proper masculine destiny and achieving his ambition by creating a being, a new Adam, who will submit to his command. The attempt to steal the divine fire of creation is what gives the novel its alternate title, "The Modern Prometheus." But the actual product of this flawed ambition is the creation of conjoined demons—Victor and his monster. Both become versions of the Satan of *Paradise Lost*, "the archangel who aspired to omnipotence, chained in an eternal hell" (chapter 14). In the end they are twin monsters, locked in an "insatiable passion" (chapter 14) for their mutual extinction, utterly alike in their resentment, loneliness, and despair.

2

FRANKLIN TO *FRANKENSTEIN*

Dwayne Godwin and Jorge Cham

id Benjamin Franklin somehow inspire the novel *Frankenstein*? Perhaps he did not do so directly, but Franklin's experiments are said to have inspired Luigi Galvani's experiments in nerve conduction. That connection stimulated in turn the cartoon "Franklin to *Frankenstein*" (Figure 25, image insert) that is based on real history.

Around 1744, Benjamin Franklin's work in electricity was translated into Italian. Galvani was particularly intrigued with Franklin's results and demonstrated that muscle movements in the legs of frogs could be stimulated by electrical currents. Alessandro Volta later showed the conductive nature of nerve fibers, but it was Galvani who pushed the first domino that cascaded into our modern understanding of nerve function.

In a macabre turn of events, Galvani's nephew, Giovanni Aldini, took his uncle's discoveries to a new and gruesome level. Touring Europe, he demonstrated the postmortem movement of the bodies of recently executed criminals when they were probed with electricity. These spectacular demonstrations peaked in 1803 when Aldini electrified the body of George Foster, a recently executed murderer. Those who observed the demonstration remarked that it almost seemed as if the corpse was being restored to life. It's notable that Aldini's Foster demonstration came only thirteen years before Mary Shelley wrote her famous novel.

In the preface to the 1831 edition of *Frankenstein*, Shelley provided explicit insight into her conceptualization of her patchwork monster when she wrote, "Perhaps a corpse would be re-animated; galvanism had given token of such things: perhaps the component parts of a creature might be manufactured, brought together, and endued with vital warmth." Like a spark, a popularized scientific experiment had entered the public consciousness and inspired the imagination of a young woman who gave the world a tale that endures as the first science fiction novel, and a warning of the perils of scientific hubris.

3

FRANKENSTEIN: REPRESENTING THE EMOTIONS OF UNWANTED CREATURES

Laura Otis

Words that describe painful emotions suggest how physiology and culture combine to shape emotional experiences. Metaphors for the rage and self-loathing of rejected people convey the life forces of bodies trying to assert themselves but also the internalized hate of detractors who wish that the rejected didn't exist. Mary Shelley's novel, *Frankenstein*, depicts the emotions of an unwanted being in a way that can inform scientists and that few writers have matched. Accused of murder and bullied by her confessor, Shelley's character Justine laments, "I almost began to think that I was the monster that he said I was" (Shelley, 66). Like Justine, scientist Victor Frankenstein's abandoned creature sees himself as a monster—almost. One of the commonest words in Shelley's text is "wretch," used both by Frankenstein for the creature he has made and by the creature for himself. This double-edged word means both a 'despicable person' and a 'miserable person,' suggesting a vicious cycle (OED, 1245). "All men hate the wretched," says the creature, who feels wretched because he is unwanted and is unwanted because he is wretched (Shelley, 77). The pain, gall, ice, fire, and whirlwinds that represent his emotions reveal the forces acting on him, but also his fierce will to live. Shelley's *Frankenstein* stands out among literary works for its sympathetic depiction of an unwanted being. Even though the creature's rage and hatred lead to murder, Shelley represents his emotions as the products of natural and social forces that could work similarly on any deserted human being.

This brief study of *Frankenstein* examines the way that Shelley's emotion metaphors reveal the interplay of natural and social forces. It surveys the many forms that rejection takes in *Frankenstein* and the ways that the creature responds to being shunned. It draws on the psychological literature of attachment and abandonment, including John Bowlby's classic studies of the 1970s and more recent experiments assessing the capacity of revenge to bring pleasure after rejection. It analyzes patterns in Shelley's metaphors for the creature's emotions, focusing on spontaneous and learned components. Ultimately, this study aims to discover how unwanted people learn to hate themselves and others, and how their life-affirming impulses, which Shelley describes so eloquently, can be activated to overcome this hate. People feel anger and hatred for reasons, and *Frankenstein* encourages readers to seek these reasons in social treatment rather than flaws of character (Li, 16).

In Shelley's novel, the explorer Robert Walton retrieves Victor Frankenstein from an ice floe as Walton's ship is struggling toward the North Pole. In a long confession, Frankenstein tells Walton how his passion to discover the "principle of life" led him to animate a creature made of dead human body parts (Shelley, 33). Frankenstein describes how he fled his creature in horror rather than educating and nurturing him. Alone and regarded by most people as hideous, the creature educates himself and instinctively tries to help the humans he encounters. After increasingly violent rejections, however, the creature begins to harm the people who abuse him. Felix De Lacey, whom he has observed for months and from whom he has learned of human love, drives him off with blows; he later burns the De Laceys' cottage. When the creature learns that Frankenstein created and abandoned him, he focuses his anger on his "father," killing those closest to him so that his creator will feel as unloved as the creature does. At the time Walton encounters Frankenstein, the scientist has lost all those dear to him and is pursuing his creature with the aim of ending his "son's" life. After Frankenstein dies on board Walton's ship, the creature cries over his dead "father" and vows to burn himself to death. Walton, perhaps moved by Frankenstein's warning not to pursue knowledge relentlessly, heeds his crew's plea to return home.

Shelley wrote *Frankenstein* in three concentric layers so that readers would have three perspectives on the creature's making, abandonment, and revenge. In the outer layer, Walton encounters Victor Frankenstein and the creature he has made; Walton describes his interactions with them in letters home to his sister. Walton confronts the creature only after hearing Frankenstein's tale, so that his letters depicting the creature may be biased. Frankenstein's narrative provides the central, thickest layer, but the novel's most compelling section is the creature's story that forms its core. Here the creature describes his painful, solitary learning and offers a distinct perspective on the murder of Frankenstein's younger brother. Letters from Frankenstein's friends and family provide additional viewpoints. Shelley seems to have structured her novel so as to show its events from as many different angles as possible.

All three narrative layers resonate with their speakers' calls for sympathy. Walton writes to his sister, "I have no friend . . . I desire the company of a man who could sympathize with me; whose eyes would reply to mine" (Shelley, 8). By "sympathy" he means an ability to understand, share, and respond to his feelings and thoughts. He doesn't seek this sympathy in his officers or sailors but in Frankenstein, who comes from his own social class. Frankenstein is less vociferous in his desire for sympathy, but his desire for understanding and compassion drives his tale. Ostensibly he wants to warn others from repeating his mistakes, but he also says, "I myself have been blasted in these hopes, yet another may succeed" (Shelley, 186). Probably, like the creature, Frankenstein is narrating in order to *be*; he is enlisting another being as a witness to his life. Of the three narrators, the creature begs for sympathy most passionately. "Let me see that I excite the sympathy of some existing thing," he tells Frankenstein as he demands a mate. "My evil passions will have fled, for I shall meet with sympathy" (Shelley, 120–21). His heartrending plea carries a threat but also the message that love could transform his rage.

The creature's emotions aren't born but made. The novel's plot hinges on his rejection, and echoes of his abandonment resonate through the text. Walton's shipmaster is on his way to the North Pole because his fiancée preferred another man, and he gave the couple his entire fortune. Frankenstein's own fiancée and cousin, Elizabeth, was raised with his family because her father no longer wanted her after her mother died. Justine Moritz, also embraced by the Frankensteins, had to leave her family because her mother "could not endure her" and mistreated her after her father's death (Shelley, 46). The De Laceys, whom the creature loves, live in poverty because a Turkish merchant whom they aided in France refused to help them once he gained his liberty. The novel even sympathetically mentions Charles I, whose 1649 beheading might be seen as the ultimate rejection. Compared to most other characters, Frankenstein meets with good treatment, but he is stung when his father and Professor Krempe—his first potential academic mentor—dismiss the alchemy he loves as "sad trash" (Shelley, 23). Emotionally sensitive, he blames this intellectual rejection for setting him on the path toward "filthy creation" (Shelley, 36).

Unlike the creature, Frankenstein has experienced loving, nurturing guidance. He can't blame his failure as a "father" to his creature on a lack of role models. Frankenstein's own father "devoted himself to the education of his children" and continued to support him even when his son seemed to be a murderer (Shelley, 19). The loyalty of Frankenstein's friend, Henry Clerval, also contrasts with Victor's lack of sympathy for his creature. Frankenstein continually accepts his father's and Clerval's love without passing it on.

The flight of his "father" is only the first damaging rejection the creature experiences. Not only Frankenstein's actions but also his way of talking and thinking about the creature ensure that his offspring is denied repeatedly. "Unable to endure the aspect of the being I had created," he tells Walton, "I rushed out of the room" (Shelley, 39). When Frankenstein next sees the creature in the Swiss mountains, he calls him "the wretch, the filthy demon to whom I had given life" (Shelley 56). Every time he thinks about his creature, he tries to deny his connection to him by representing him as something evil. In his thoughts, Frankenstein becomes a god with a death wish, eager to "extinguish the spark which I so negligently bestowed" (Shelley, 77). Without the protection of a natural or divine father, the creature encounters violence everywhere he turns. He enters a village and is attacked; he rescues a drowning girl and is shot. He suffers most greatly when the De Laceys reject him after he has watched them for months and fantasized about being embraced. In agony, he recalls that "in a transport of fury, [Felix] dashed me to the ground, and struck me violently with a stick" (Shelley, 110). Any effort the creature makes to reach out to human beings results in a wounding attack.

With the De Laceys, the creature fails to find sympathy when he is on the verge of acceptance. Old, blind De Lacey tells him, "[I] cannot judge of your countenance, but there is something in your words which persuades me that you are sincere" (Shelley, 109). The creature has already learned that he is being rejected because of his looks—something he cannot help. The repeated attacks are all the more painful because they concern his stuff, his matter, his being. In a reading of *Frankenstein* grounded in disability studies, Amy Li observes, "Rage is not inherent to abnormal bodies, but rather arises in relation to a hostile world" (Li, 1). Only after the creature is shunned and learns how humans define beauty does he conceive of himself as ugly. He knows that he is hated because he looks different, and there is not a thing he can do about it. He tells Frankenstein, "I was, besides, endowed with a figure hideously deformed and loathsome; I was not even of the same nature as man" (Shelley, 96). Frankenstein's narrative affirms the creature's worst fears, since it grounds the creature's supposed evil nature in his ugly appearance. Frankenstein's "son" uses language well, but just when the creature has almost moved his "father" to compassion, Frankenstein reports, "When I looked upon him, when I saw the filthy mass that moved and talked, my heart sickened, and my feelings were altered to those of horror and hatred" (Shelley, 121). Frankenstein warns Walton, "His soul is as hellish as his form, full of treachery and fiend-like malice," although Walton shows signs that he can think for himself (Shelley, 178). The creature feels rage not just because he is being rejected but because there is no way he can change himself in order to win acceptance.

The emotions of rejection in *Frankenstein* follow a familiar logic: A creature who receives no attention through love will seek it through malice; if he can't have love, he wants power. In his plea to Frankenstein to create a female, the creature warns his creator not to ignore him further: "If I cannot inspire love, I will cause fear . . . I will work at your destruction, nor finish until I desolate your heart" (Shelley, 119). Telling the story of his life fans the creature's anger, since before he begins, he makes gentler arguments: "I am thy creature, and I will be even mild and docile to my natural lord and king, if thou wilt also perform thy part, the which thou owest me . . . I was benevolent and good; misery made me a fiend. Make me happy, and I shall again be virtuous" (Shelley, 77–78). The creature reminds Frankenstein that his "son" still has the potential to love, but his creator is not performing his *Erziehungspflicht*. This German word, which has no English equivalent, means a moral and legal obligation to raise a child that one has brought into the world. The creature's rage breaks through when he threatens, "If you refuse, I will glut the maw of death, until it be satiated with the blood of your remaining friends" (Shelley, 77). So runs the furious logic of rejection: If I am unloved, I will make sure that you are unloved; if I am alone and miserable, I will ensure that you are equally so.

As the creature indicates, the anger of rejection can be reversed, and Shelley's novel draws its potential energy in part from this possibility. If Frankenstein gave the creature the love he wanted, the narrative would lose its drive; there is a story to tell because instead Frankenstein first flees, then tries to kill his creature. The novel progresses with the creator's denials and the creature's increasingly intimate attacks. After the De Laceys reject him, the creature recalls, "My feelings were those of rage and revenge, I could with pleasure have destroyed the cottage and its inhabitants, and have glutted myself with their shrieks and misery" (Shelley, 111). His fury reaches its climax when he witnesses Frankenstein tearing up the mate that he promised to build. "I can make you so wretched that the light of day will be hateful to you," he warns. "You are my creator, but I am your master . . . You can blast my other passions, but revenge remains. . . . I shall be with you on your wedding-night" (Shelley, 140). In this threat, narcissistic Frankenstein perceives only the burning fury of rejection. As depicted by Shelley, the emotions of rejection also have a cold, businesslike aspect, as though the avenger were using a balance sheet. The deprivation of a mate will cost Frankenstein his bride, since the rejected avenger aims for a zero balance. There are reasons that Shelley describes the emotions of rejection through metaphors of fire and ice.

In the early 1970s, British psychologist John Bowlby found that children whose parents did not make them feel secure experienced fear and anger that affected relationships throughout their lives. Previous studies had shown that children whose parents had left them—either abandoning them outright, or just briefly to work or seek health care— no longer trusted their caregivers and tended to "cling" (Bowlby, 214). Bowlby observed that "the aggressive behavior of a child who has experienced a separation appears to be directed toward all and sundry," but in most cases, it was "plainly directed toward a parent" (Bowlby,

246). Depending on how abandoned children felt, they expressed either "the anger of hope" or "the anger of despair" (Bowlby, 246). If the separation was brief, children might reproach their parents, expressing anger in the hope that the adults would learn not to desert them again. Such disciplinary anger was functional, because it could reinforce a bond, but chronic anger aroused by "repeated, prolonged separations" was not (Bowlby, 247). Both children and adults often became angry after losses, either of a parent or an adult partner (Bowlby, 247). As Bowlby wondered about the evolutionary value of anger after losses, he reflected:

> Dysfunctional anger occurs whenever a person, child or adult, becomes so intensely and/or persistently angry with his partner that the bond between them is weakened, instead of strengthened, and the partner is alienated. Anger with a partner becomes dysfunctional also whenever aggressive thoughts or acts cross the narrow boundary between being deterrent and being revengeful. It is at this point, too, that feeling ceases to be the "hot displeasure" of anger and may become, instead, the "malice" of hatred. (Bowlby, 247–48)

Children abandoned by their parents, and partners deserted by their mates, could come to hate the people they loved because those people did not return their love as was their perceived duty. The most violent anger was likely to occur in children repeatedly threatened with abandonment (Bowlby, 249). Based on years of observations of children and their parents, Bowlby developed the term "anxious attachment" to describe the strategies of people who fear separation and scheme to stay as close to their attachment figures as possible (Bowlby, 253). Because separation arouses anger as well as fear, "love, anxiety, and anger, and sometimes hatred, come to be aroused by one and the same person" (Bowlby, 253). In the four decades since Bowlby published his research, numerous studies have confirmed his finding that children who feel deserted by their parents carry their fear and anger into adult relationships.

An inability to trust parents by whom one feels abandoned can cause lifelong instability in one's relationships and sense of self. In studies of adult attachment styles (secure, avoidant, or anxious/ambivalent), psychologist Cindy Hazan and her colleagues have noted that attitudes toward attachment are "highly stable over time" (Kirkpatrick and Hazan, 123). Her group's studies indicate that a person's social and romantic relationships, and even his or her definition of self, depend in part on attachment styles developed in childhood (Hazan and Shaver, 511). Psychologists Eugenia Mandal and Anna Latusek have found that "the lower the level of a secure style is, the lower is the level of interpersonal skills" (Mandal and Latusek, 185). People anxiously attached to their parents may develop "rejection sensitivity" (Norona and Welsh, 124). In a questionnaire study, psychologists Jerika C. Norona and Deborah P. Welsh noted that rejection sensitivity "develops early on in children who were raised by caregivers that failed to meet their needs for safety and security . . . For protection, these children become hypervigilant and readily expect rejecting behaviors" (Norona and Welsh, 124). Such individuals feel less satisfied in relationships (Norona and Welsh, 124) and may bring on rejections by anticipating them.

When rejected, *anyone*—regardless of parental treatment—is likely to feel angry. In a provocative study, psychologists David S. Chester and C. Nathan DeWall assessed the motives of rejected people who seek "mood repair" through revenge (Chester and DeWall, 1). Chester and DeWall dared to face the disturbing prospect that aggression and revenge can bring pleasure. Their study is limited in its applicability, since it involved online games in which participants were excluded from "cyberball" or "blasted with noise," then had the opportunity to stick pins into virtual voodoo dolls representing their fellow players (Chester and DeWall, 3, 5). The psychologists found that after taking symbolic revenge, "rejected individuals' moods were indistinguishable from [those of] their accepted counterparts" (Chester and DeWall, 15). Based on their results, Chester and DeWall proposed that revenge might be driven by a kind of emotional homeostasis (Chester and DeWall, 1, 15). Aggression seemed motivated not by negative feelings but by positive ones, or more precisely, the *anticipation* of pleasure (Chester and DeWall, 2). Chester and DeWall cautioned readers that their studies measured only short-term effects, and that after revenge, negative emotions might soon replace any positive surge (Chester and DeWall, 15). This is certainly the case with Frankenstein's creature, whose revenge against his neglectful parent only intensifies his misery.

When one reads 19th-century literature against 21st-century science, it is pointless to say that Shelley anticipated or disproved the results of scientists two hundred years later. Psychologists often find their hypotheses in stores of cultural wisdom and generate data supporting or disproving them. It makes more sense to say that careful observers of human beings at two different points in history noted a pattern and represented it in different, equally valid ways. People unloved and neglected by their parents may grow up to mistrust others. Depending on the degree of neglect, they may take out their anger as revenge against their parents or more "innocent" people they encounter. Learning whether these acts of aggression repair their feelings long-term will require further study. Shelley's novel indicates that revenge only increases unhappiness.

Through his acts of vengeance, the creature aims to eliminate each person who loves Frankenstein until his creator feels as isolated as he is. In terms of Bowlby's anger of hope, the logic might run, "when you are in the same position as I am, you may finally understand what I feel." Probably the creature acts more from hopeful than from desperate anger, since he communicates through his murders. He *wants* Frankenstein to know what he is doing and why. In the case of Frankenstein's younger brother, William, their father writes that "the print of the murderer's finger was on his neck" (Shelley, 52). Strangling is an intimate way to kill and often indicates an emotional link between murderer and victim. Readers learn from the creature's narrative that his first murder wasn't quite intentional. The creature comes upon William by coincidence, and only after the boy has insulted him and revealed himself as a member of the Frankenstein family does the creature act in an almost defensive way: "I grasped his throat to silence him, and in a moment he lay dead at my feet" (Shelley, 117). The creature's wording reveals his framing of Justine as more intentional, although he blames the humans who have taught him how to hurt: "I have learned how to work mischief," he explains to his creator (Shelley, 118). By placing on Justine's person a locket that the boy had, the creature makes it appear that Justine killed William; she is later put to death for the boy's murder. By the time the creature kills Frankenstein's best friend, Henry Clerval, his strangling technique has become more methodical, more communicative. Clerval is found with "the black mark of fingers on his neck," and Frankenstein gets the message (Shelley, 147). In an opium-induced dream, he senses "the fiend's grasp in my neck" (Shelley, 155). Frankenstein has understood only part, however, of what the creature is trying to say. Emotionally, the creature is spiraling in, killing people increasingly close to his creator. Frankenstein misunderstands the creature's strategy, however, because he misunderstands the nature of love. Frankenstein expects that his own murder is the creature's goal, but the creature wants to kill him emotionally. Readers never learn how the creature kills Elizabeth, but her "bloodless" state, loose hair, and body "thrown across the bed" suggest strangulation with a sexual intent (Shelley, 165). As represented by Frankenstein, the creature takes sadistic pleasure in his creator's pain: "A grin was on the face of the monster; he seemed to jeer, as with his fiendish finger he pointed towards the corpse of my wife" (Shelley, 166). If Frankenstein interprets his expression right, his momentary delight in the horror he has caused upholds Chester and DeWall's finding that revenge—at least temporarily—can relieve emotional pain.

In social as well as emotional senses, perpetrators of revenge conceive of their acts as homeostatic. Anger is physiological and visceral, but it is also linked to perceptions of injustice (Lakoff and Kövecses, 1987, 209). After rejection by the De Laceys but before the murder of William, the creature tells Frankenstein, "My sufferings were augmented also by the oppressive sense of the injustice and ingratitude of their infliction. My daily vows rose for revenge—a deep and deadly revenge, such as would alone compensate for the outrages and anguish I had endured" (Shelley, 116). Emotionally he experiences a tilted universe, and he wants to restore its balance. As Bowlby found with neglected children, anger increases when acts perceived as unjust are repeated and cries for justice go ignored. In her study of the creature's rage, Amy Li calls destructive, vengeful acts "the possible pitfall of rage . . . rage which goes unheeded, untransformed into a politics of attunement and affirmation: disillusionment and hatred" (Li, 16). When dismissed, the anger of hope can become the anger of despair, which is less inhibited in its destructive aims. In the novel's final segment, as Frankenstein shifts from hunted to hunter, he, too, seems driven by a desire to restore order: "I must pursue and destroy the being to whom I gave existence; then my lot on earth will be fulfilled, and I may die" (Shelley, 181). Frankenstein tries to enlist Walton to kill the creature for him, but Walton has his own ideas. His witnessing as the outer narrator lets readers see the failure of revenge as a means of emotional repair. Sitting over his dead creator, the creature feels the worst pain of his life. Walton reports that "every feature and gesture seemed instigated by the wildest rage of some incontrollable passion . . . The monster continued to utter wild and incoherent self-reproaches" (Shelley, 187). In the moment of the novel most likely to evoke tears, the creature bewails his creator's death. Revenge has brought him no relief, since what he wanted was love.

As a storyteller, Shelley describes her characters' emotions so that readers can feel them in their bodies. To make the creature's feelings palpable, she uses metaphors that convey emotions as natural forces and awaken her readers' senses. The creature's line "the bitter gall of envy rose within me" evokes a visceral heave that some readers can taste (Shelley, 105). As Terence Shih has observed in a study of *Frankenstein* and neurology, Shelley associates emotional pain with physical pain to the point that it is hard to tell one from the other (Shih). Science writer Giovanni Frazzetto has noted that "the relationship between physical and emotional pain goes beyond semantics," because both seem to involve some of the same neural mechanisms (Frazzetto, 117). As the creature becomes aware of himself and his surrounding world, he learns through pain. "I was a poor, helpless, miserable wretch," he tells his creator. "I knew, and could distinguish, nothing: but, feeling pain invade me on all sides, I sat down and wept" (Shelley, 80). His bodily hurt tells him that he exists when no living being will comfort him. The creature discovers the nature of fire when he "thrust [his] hand into the live embers, but quickly drew it out again with a cry of pain" (Shelley, 81). He learns his most excruciating lesson when he saves a drowning girl and is shot for his efforts. The English word "feeling" can refer to sensation or emotion, and when Shelley describes the creature's feelings, his physical and emotional pain merge: "Inflamed by pain, I vowed eternal hatred and vengeance to all mankind" (Shelley, 116). The creature's emotions, grounded in his unloved body, are painful in every sense.

In a cycle that increases his anguish, the lonely creature discovers his emotions in landscapes and seeks lands that look the way he feels. Shelley's emotion metaphors emerge from correspondences between the mental states of her characters and those of the world. Having learned the secret of his creation and realized he is alone in the world, the creature reports, "I saw, with surprise and grief, the leaves decay and fall . . . Nature decayed around me, and the sun became heatless" (Shelley, 106, 114). The creature finds himself attracted to the harshest climates where the fewest people live. "Am I not alone, miserably alone?" he asks himself. "The desert mountains and dreary glaciers are my refuge" (Shelley, 78). The creature is especially drawn to icy regions, where he feels emotionally at home. "Follow me; I seek the everlasting ices of the north," he challenges his creator. "We shall soon enter upon a journey where your sufferings will satisfy my everlasting hatred" (Shelley, 174). In representing her characters' emotions, Shelley places them in a deadly white environment that reflects—literally—what they feel for one another.

Probably humans have compared emotions to ice since the time that they had gestures. The pounding heart and blood flow associated with rage invite metaphors involving heat, but with time, anger can turn cold. Like water, anger can change its form and may be deadliest when it hardens and expands. Shelley uses ice literally and metaphorically to shape *Frankenstein* because of its potential to change. Ice can stop motion; it can kill by crushing; but it can also melt, and it can break. Shelley depicts ice so often, in so many different settings, that it acts almost as a character in her novel. *Frankenstein*'s outer narrative layer depicts an impossible journey into ice. Through Walton, readers learn of the ice's instability and crushing force before they meet Frankenstein or his creature. Like the rage and hate of the creature he is about to spot, Walton's ice works as an entrapping force. "We were nearly surrounded by ice, which closed in the ship on all sides," he writes to his sister (Shelley, 12). Walton's ship is "shut in . . . by ice," but "before night, the ice broke, and freed our ship" (Shelley, 12). Shortly thereafter, his men pick up Frankenstein. By stopping Walton's progress, the ice allows Shelley's story to unfold, because it lets Walton and Frankenstein meet. The ice's coldness, its hardness, its instability, and its potential to change form suggest the emotions of all three narrators.

Extraordinary descriptions of ice set the scenes for some of the novel's key encounters. Frankenstein marvels at the beauty of the "tremendous and ever-moving glacier" just before his creature confronts him and tells his tale (Shelley, 75). The creature's hot narrative works like the fire he lights on the glacier to warm his listening creator. Popular metaphors compare long-term rage and hate to ice because of their tendency to "freeze." Supposedly, emotions should flow as life proceeds, and long-term efforts to recall and redress grievances are pathological. Frankenstein and his creature may experience hate, but repeatedly, Shelley emphasizes ice's tendency to shift. She has chosen ice as a metaphorical vehicle more for its instability than for its hardness. As the creature moves northward, local people "conjectured that he must speedily be destroyed by the breaking of the ice" (Shelley, 175). Shelley's descriptions of ice suggest Walton's feelings as Frankenstein reveals his death wish and urges his rescuer to kill the creature. "I am surrounded by mountains of ice," Walton writes, "which admit of no escape, and threaten every moment to crush my vessel" (Shelley, 181). Hope returns—physically and emotionally—when "the ice began to move" (Shelley, 184). Walton and the triple narrative survive because he declines to attack the creature, or the creature spares him. In either case, readers may see that the hate has broken with the ice.

"Emotion" derives from the Latin words *ex* and *movere*, meaning 'to move out' (Harper). To represent the complex feelings of her characters, Shelley uses not just shifting ice but the more mobile forces of rushing wind and raging fire. The creature threatens Frankenstein that if the scientist fails to perform his duty, he will be responsible for an evil so great that "not only you and your family, but thousands of others, shall be swallowed up in the whirlwinds of its rage" (Shelley, 78). The creature describes his anger as a devastating wind, which, like Bowlby's anger of despair, wrecks anything it encounters. Wind and fire collaborate to destroy the De Laceys' cottage, and the creature's vision of their work conveys his inner state:

> The blast tore along like a mighty avalanche, and produced a kind of insanity in my spirits, that burst all bounds and reason and reflection. I lighted the dry branch of a tree, and danced with fury around the devoted cottage. . . . The wind fanned the fire, and the cottage was quickly enveloped by the flames; which clung to it, and licked it with their forked and destroying tongues. (Shelley, 113)

The creature's description emphasizes violent movement, but also insidious, satanic intimacy. Like the ice around Walton's ship, the creature's fire surrounds the lone cottage and presses up against it. As the creature recalls the De Laceys' rejection, he feels burned and crushed to death. At the novel's end, he plans to stage his suicide as he did his narrative, through a meeting of fire and ice. "[I] shall seek the most northern extremity of the globe," he tells Walton. "I shall collect my funeral pile, and consume to ashes this miserable frame" (Shelley, 190). Because of the way humans have treated him, the emotions driving him have led him toward disintegration.

Shelley represents the creature's anguish in its most extreme form through metaphors of dissolution. Bowlby called the anger of despair dysfunctional because it fails to reinforce bonds; it is destructive rather than instructive (Bowlby, 246–49). In Shelley's metaphors, the creature's strongest rage and hate rob objects of their forms and reduce them to insignificant components. The aim of such anger brings to mind Mephistopheles's self-description in Goethe's *Faust*, a play the German poet was still perfecting in 1818:

[I am] the spirit that eternally denies!
And justly so; for all that which is wrought
Deserves that it should come to naught. (Goethe, 33)

Unwanted beings do not treat the world kindly, and Shelley depicts the worst emotions of the rejected as a will to blast a world that seems to want to annihilate these beings. "I could have torn [Felix De Lacey] limb from limb, as the lion rends the antelope," says the creature (Shelley, 110). His urge to rip the man who has torn him emotionally would let him act out what others have done to him. Goethe represented the force of evil as a generalized destructive wish, and it is significant that the creature *learns* to rend. Based on his ugly appearance, people expect him to mutilate them: "You wish to eat me, and tear me to pieces," cries little William (Shelley, 117). With the creature watching Frankenstein build a mate, the creator "tore to pieces the thing on which [he] was engaged" (Shelley, 139). The creature adopts the phrases of people he encounters, and his wish to tear up bodies—which would reverse his creation—echoes through Shelley's novel. After the De Laceys reject the creature, his fury seems directed toward every atom of the world's matter. He "wished to tear up the trees, spread havoc and destruction around [him], and then to have sat down and enjoyed the ruin" (Shelley, 111). The thought that there is "none to lament his annihilation" makes him want to annihilate the world (Shelley, 104).

In *Frankenstein*'s two outer narrative layers, images of disintegration work almost as a refrain. Repeatedly, Walton and Frankenstein close scenes by describing the creature dissolving into the landscape. Walton watches the creature pass until "he was lost among the distant inequalities of the ice" (Shelley, 12). After the creature has told Frankenstein his tale, the creator "quickly lost him among the undulations of the sea of ice" (Shelley, 122). The creature threatens Frankenstein when he destroys his mate, then is "soon lost amidst the waves" (Shelley, 141). Walton closes the novel with the same refrain: "he was soon borne away by the waves, and lost in darkness and distance" (Shelley, 191). The creator's and the surviving storyteller's repetition of "lost" indicates that the creature isn't paranoid. Frankenstein would love nothing more than to lose his creature, to see him dissolve back into the earth. The creature's emotional urge to annihilate replicates his creator's wish to unmake him.

When Frankenstein was building his creature, he envisioned himself as fighting death. Having lost his mother to scarlet fever, Frankenstein tells readers, "I saw how the fine form of man was degraded and wasted; I beheld the corruption of death succeed to the blooming cheek of life" (Shelley, 34). In animating his creature, he learns little, for he continues to see himself as a knight battling death. He changes only when he projects his concept of death onto his creature. To describe his emotions, Frankenstein uses a metaphor that the creature does not. The scientist speaks of a "blight," a plant disease that cripples growth. In a moment of compassion, he considers "the subsequent blight of all kindly feeling [in his creature] by the loathing and scorn which his protectors had manifested toward him" (Shelley, 121). Frankenstein cares more about his own emotions, however, and soon afterward remarks that "a blight had come over my existence" (Shelley, 131). For Frankenstein, the creature becomes the blight, a threatening destroyer of life.

Shelley describes the emotions of rejection as visceral, but she also represents them as learned. Her inclusion of the creature's narrative lets her show that he doesn't conceive of himself as evil until human beings treat him as such. Shelley links this painful learning to language, since the creature's first vision of himself in a pool immediately follows his realization that signs and sounds carry meanings. "When I became fully convinced that I was in reality the monster that I am," he describes, "I was willed with the bitterest sensations of despondence and mortification" (Shelley, 90). While hovering near the De Laceys, he learns to speak and read and to think of himself in the terms that language provides. He reads Milton's *Paradise Lost* as a "true history," and Shelley emphasizes this epic's importance for *Frankenstein* in the novel's epigraph:

> Did I request thee, Maker, from my clay
> To mold Me man? Did I solicit thee
> From darkness to promote me? (Milton, 232)

In Milton's poem, Adam speaks these words, but the creature identifies with the rejected angel, Satan. The unhappy creature reminds Frankenstein, "Remember, that I am thy creature: I ought to be thy Adam; but I am rather the fallen angel, whom thou drivest from joy for no misdeed" (Shelley, 77). The creature describes his sensations and emotions in Milton's language, such as when he finds a shepherd's hut "as exquisite and divine a retreat as Pandemonium appeared to the demons of hell after their sufferings in the lake of fire" (Shelley, 83). At the time he found the hut, the creature had not learned language, so there is no knowing how he experienced his sensations. Since discovering the hut and telling his tale to Frankenstein, he has learned how his culture represents good and evil and has realized that Satan is the "bitter emblem of [his] condition" (Shelley 105). The creature tells Walton, "Evil thenceforth became my good . . . the fallen angel becomes a malignant devil" (Shelley, 188–89). One is reminded of the sad line of Dostoevsky's Underground Man: "They won't let me . . . I can't be . . . good!" (Dostoevsky, 84). Shelley makes it clear that metaphors identifying the rage of rejection with evil are learned.

In *Frankenstein*, Shelley drops hints that the creature is not the only angry, rejected character. In giving the creature a voice, she indicates that he doesn't speak only for himself. As Victor Frankenstein prepares for a two-year tour of Europe with Henry Clerval, Victor's fiancée Elizabeth "only regretted that she had not the same opportunities of enlarging her experience, and cultivating her understanding" (Shelley, 127). Felix De Lacey's beloved Safie (the daughter of the disloyal merchant) fears "being immured within the walls of a haram, allowed only to occupy herself with puerile amusements" (Shelley, 99). In quiet, subtle terms, these female characters protest their lack of access to learning and lack of freedom to explore the world. In a classic work of feminist criticism, *The Madwoman in the Attic*, Sandra Gilbert and Susan Gubar argued that 19th-century female novelists recognized themselves in Milton's rebellious, banished angel and created characters like the creature who identified with Satan (Gilbert and Gubar). In the culture Shelley depicts, Elizabeth cannot express her rage at being rejected, but the creature can do it for her.

In describing a creature whose life is unwanted, Shelley crafts revealing metaphors for rage. The anguish of the rejected creature emerges through figures of pain, ice, and fire, and urges to smash the world to atoms. Shelley grounds most of these metaphors in bodily sensations or in violent natural forces. The metaphors that tie rage and hate to evil work differently, because Shelley indicates that these are learned. In the experience of emotion, one can't separate what is learned from what is physiological. Shelley points to a relative difference, however, first by giving the creature a voice at all, and second, by showing that he is taught to think of himself as evil. When he does speak, he asks, "Am I to be thought the only criminal, when all human kind sinned against me?" (Shelley, 189). His emotions may arise from his body, but he sees their causes in the treatment he has received, in people's determination to see him as evil.

Shelley's decision to let the creature speak has proved crucial for *Frankenstein*'s legacy. As Frankenstein warns Walton, the creature is eloquent, and any reader—female, disabled, proletarian, colonialized—whose humanity has been rejected may hear his or her thoughts in the creature's words. Social structures rarely benefit everyone, and those who are denied privileges granted to others will get angry. Metaphoric representations of deprived people's anger tend to depict it as a social threat, a volcano waiting to erupt; or as a character flaw, a tendency to wallow in self-pity. Such metaphoric patterns divert attention from social causes to supposed defects in the people suffering their consequences. In the words of Amy Li:

> What if we treat rage as a legitimate response from marginalized persons and groups? . . . Those labeled as monsters signal that something is wrong, and their rage functions as a call for attention, not in the negative sense, but rather, as an ethical demand. . . . We must affirm rage as a viable response, and then think of what we might do to change the social conditions which elicited that rage. (Li, 1, 2, 16)

Shelley does exactly this in portraying a rejected creature who learns to hate. His emotions emerge from his suffering body but also from his monstrous education. Through descriptions of fire, ice, pain, and disintegration, Shelley illustrates how physical and cultural factors can blend to shape emotional experience.

4

WHO IS A MONSTER, WHEN?

Steven J. Kraftchick

I. INTRODUCTION

The two questions that make up this essay arose during a four-week Great Works reading seminar I participated in recently.[1] At the start of our conversations, all of us knew the story of *Frankenstein*, or thought we did. We knew that it was a classic story, we knew its main characters, especially "The Monster." While we were less sure about some details, everyone knew the specifics of the monster: his name was "Frankenstein" and he was created by a manic scientist with the help of his assistant, Fritz or Igor, depending on the movie that was playing in our heads. Just about everyone knows the plotline: how the scientist, having placed the brain of a degenerate murderer into a cadaverous body, electrifies it using a Van de Graff generator and lightning, only to lose control of the lumbering, inarticulate monster, who proceeds to wreak havoc on the local village. Except, of course, none of this occurs in Shelley's novel, something we discovered as soon as we began to read it.[2]

No named monster, no lab, no assistant, no village mayhem, just a terse description of a "spark of being" infused into a creature. With discovery our "knowing" changed, and soon our discussions changed. Instead of knowing, we were asking and wondering what this story was about: just who is a monster, what is a monster, who is responsible for these monstrous things, and what does Shelley want us to discover by asking these questions of her book and of ourselves. Like almost every other question Shelley's book raises, the answers to these questions proved more complex than we had first imagined.

There were any number of reasons for this, but several stand out. First, Shelley's novel is a classic, and it suffers from the "classic curse." When a work attains the cultural status of "classic," this means that everyone "knows" it, or thinks that they do. In truth, what we know is *"almost"* the classic: we *almost* know the national anthem, or *almost* know *Hamlet*, or *almost* know *Frankenstein*. Our *almost* knowledge of *Frankenstein* is shaped by both the novel's classic status and the cinematic versions of the story, from James Whale's *Frankenstein* (1931) to Mel Brooks's *Young Frankenstein* (1974). So, while everyone knows Frankenstein is the name of the monster in Shelley's book (except of course it isn't; Victor Frankenstein is the name of the scientist who creates the monster), few people know much about Shelley's unnamed Creature. As a result, "Frankenstein's Monster" has become iconic, and his name is used to describe everything from genetically modified "frankenfoods" to kids' breakfast cereal (Franken Berry), while Frankenstein the science student has been transmogrified into a mad scientist and his creation has been lost in darkness.

However, when we begin to read *Frankenstein* and our "knowledge" of the story is contradicted by the contents of the novel, the reasons it became a classic in the first place reappear. The questions it raises about boundaries, relationships, and human longing, by asking who, what, and how a monster comes into being, are raised anew.

Secondly, defining the term "monster" is much more difficult than it appears, for the question, What is a monster? is intrinsically thorny. Statements about time by the 5th-century theologian and philosopher Augustine help make this point clear: "What then is time? If no one asks me, I know what it is. If I wish to explain it to him who asks, I do not know" (*Confessions* 11.14.17). The difficulty for Augustine and for us arises from the particular form of the question, in which the "is" appears straightforward but actually conceals the fact that the sentence is circular. Every definition of time is predicated on a notion that involves time. The same problem applies to the monstrous. We cannot define the terms "time" or "monster" without using their synonyms or incorporating their antonyms, thus making our definitions functional substitutions rather than substantive foundations for understanding.

The English term "monster" (by way of French) likely derives from the Latin words *montrare* 'to demonstrate' and *monere* 'to warn.' In effect, "monsters" demonstrate or warn; their presence attempts to make "something" evident. But of course, this raises the question of what, exactly, that "something" is. And, once we are here, we see that "monsters" demonstrate only that they are phenomena that press the limits of the ordinary, expanding or contracting the usual and normal to a point of individual and social discomfort or rupture. "Monsters" reveal not themselves but the limits of the ordinary and acceptable, as well as our inability to comprehend things that seem strange, unfamiliar, and discordant. We freely use the term "monster" in all sorts of settings: a monster deal at a store, a monstrous child, a monster truck, a monstrous ego, etc., thinking that we have identified an object or event, when, in actuality, we have simply pointed to its resistance to identification. Barbara Freeman suggests that this is what the monstrous does to all our attempts to define such terms, because by its very nature monstrosity defies definition, and the very attempt to do so demonstrates the limits of our language and our capacities to know and categorize ourselves and our surroundings.

In reality, if it is even correct to use the word "monster," it is only a placeholder, defined not intrinsically but in relationship to those things we do not consider monstrous. It is shorthand for those things, people, conditions, beings, that we consider outsized, outrageous, and out of our "ordinary" comprehension. We do not start with a given definition and discover the monster that embodies those traits; we see the phenomenon and call it monstrous in comparison to other phenomena with which we are already familiar. In other words, defining "monster" is not so much a matter of the physical but the existential. "Monster" and "monstrous" are themselves therefore monstrous terms, constantly escaping the bounds of our definitions and attempts to confine them. And they are fluid terms, not so much defining their referents as reflecting the limits of the definitions of other terms like "ordinary," "acceptable," "normal," and "human," the meaning of which we assume to be settled and stable.

Furthermore, in Shelley's preface to the 1831 edition of her novel, she refers not to the Creature but to the "idea" of her novel as "hideous." She recounts seeing "with shut eyes, but acute mental vision . . . the pale student of unhallowed arts kneeling beside the thing he had put together," a "hideous phantasm" of a man that through some infused power would stir with "half vital motion." Shelley does admit that the Creature is hideous, but points her readers more to the horrendous "effect of the human endeavor to mock the stupendous mechanism of the Creator of the world." The monster is not so much the thing created (though he is horrid in appearance) but the transgression of human boundaries in creating him, the usurpation of divine power.

We should also recall that Shelley entitles her novel *Frankenstein, or The Modern Prometheus*, and introduces it with an epigraph from Milton's *Paradise Lost*: "Did I request thee, Maker, from my clay to mould me man? Did I solicit thee from darkness to promote me?" Milton's lines do not simply introduce the novel; they hover over it like a specter, posing a question less about the identity of the created than the responsibility of the Creator. Who, ultimately, is responsible for the horrific destruction and death that the story details? No doubt the Creature looks hideous and was monstrous in appearance, but is he the only monster we should consider? The title and epigraph suggest that perhaps the answer is no.

Finally, as Fred Botting makes clear in his acute and insightful analysis of the novel, Shelley's story is itself a "monster," raising, but never answering, all types of social, philosophical, and ethical questions. Botting argues that Shelley's story:

> . . . incorporates its (critical readers) into its monstrous textual body and confronts them with shifting relationships, disperses them among its textual positions and along its narrative chains which pull in two directions: they are drawn toward an illusory centre that disintegrates into infinite untold stories, and towards the edges of the text where the unknown reader, constitutive and beyond the narrative frames of the text's stories and letters, is addressed, an augur of the frames and readers the text has always still to reach. This double momentum, endlessly inwards into absent and unknown stories, and ever outwards to transgress the framing limits of unpresentable readers, destroys any hope of narrative teleology, whereby a definitive authoritative voice will be heard enunciating a unifying conclusion, a final presentation of *the* meaning of the text. (Botting 1991, 4)

I wish to call attention to Botting's language, because with it, he has casually yet deliberately shown us that Shelley's novel presents its readers with a form that will not stay within the accepted limits for a novel. It is constantly straining the center and the edges, constantly confronting us with shifting relationships between its characters and our evaluations of them. The "monstrous textual body" pulsates in and out, transgressing its limits and destroying hope of finding any definitive meaning for terms like "monster," "justice," and "morality." The novel demonstrates the limits of *certain* knowledge, the limits of *true* humanity, and the limits of *accurate* reasoning. The monstrous (and this monstrous novel) shows us that we do not have, cannot have, a "God's eye" view of ourselves or our worlds—when we presume to have attained such a view and act on it, all hell quite literally breaks loose. This may not be *the* meaning of *Frankenstein,* but it is surely one of its lessons.

A few paragraphs later Botting underscores this when he points to the elusive nature of Shelley's text, "whose allusions subvert notions of originality and source, whose meaning eludes those pursuers who would control its plays, and whose illusions, like those of Frankenstein and Walton, invite identifications with the quest for exclusive singularity" (Botting, 5). Instead, with this text, "issues of justice, society, gender and identity are raised and rendered unstable: the limits that guarantee the respective identities of man against woman, self against other, nature against culture, and truth against falsity are transgressed" (Botting, 5). We *critical* readers are forced to reconsider our understandings of these binaries and their insufficiencies, and this is why we understand *Frankenstein* to be a classic.

Because we are lured into comfortable, *almost* knowledge of the classic, because defining the monstrous is, at best, elusive, and because Shelley's novel is fluid, atypical, and confounding and therefore is itself monstrous, we need to reread her tale, taking time to explore her depictions of monstrosity to understand her text more fully, even while allowing that our understanding of the novel will never exhaust its potential for meaning. For intentionally or inadvertently Shelley has complicated our understandings of monstrosity, of who deserves such a designation, and of when we judge the monstrous beings in this story. In doing so, she forces us to ask how much we are responsible for passing these verdicts.

II. REPHRASING OUR QUESTIONS FROM, WHAT AND WHY? TO, WHO AND WHEN?

Among the many questions Shelley's story poses for its readers, the question of "The Monster" stands out. In one sense, there are two questions here. Was the Creature a monster from the moment of his creation, or did he become a monster later in his existence? If the first, what caused this essential monstrosity to occur? If the second, then who or what turned the Creature into a monster? As with so many of the questions Shelley poses, she is coy in answering these. She does not provide an answer to the first question, telling us nothing of the Creature's brain or the origin of his component parts except that they were taken from the "dissecting room and the slaughterhouse." When we attempt to answer the second question, her evidence is even less clear: shall we choose Frankenstein, or the De Laceys (the destitute family the Creature aids and emulates, but that later rejects him) as the cause of the monstrosity? Or is the monstrosity the result of the physical hardships and loneliness the Creature experiences, or his own vengeful actions? Again, Shelley does not offer unambiguous evidence, and perhaps we should rephrase our question from, Who or what is a monster? to, *When* does monstrosity appear? if we hope to understand the author's perspective on this state of being.

I suggest this reframing because to speak of how or when the Creature *became* a monster is to suggest that monstrosity is a static state or a definite ontological category, that is, a category of being. If, however, we ask instead, When is the Creature a monster? and so consider monstrosity as a dynamic state, our perspective changes. In this case, it might be possible to identify more than one monster in Shelley's novel and explain our alternating evaluations of the Creature. In this light, we may discover a clue to another of Shelley's motifs: the description of her character's physical appearances. She is meticulous about doing this for almost every character in the novel, especially Frankenstein's betrothed, Elizabeth; his brother, William; his boyhood friend Henry Clerval; and the Frankenstein family's servant/foster daughter Justine. Precise descriptions are also given of the De Laceys and of the Creature. The effect of these descriptions is to imply that the outward beauty of a person is a trustworthy indicator of his or her inward spirit, an implication that the novel's plot will eventually confound. The result is that Shelley's novel challenges its readers' presumed criteria for judging the relationship of appearance to character.

To rephrase the question of the monster, I wish to proceed in the following manner: (1) to see how Shelley employs the term "monster"; (2) to consider who uses this term and why; and (3) to briefly reflect on the doppelgänger relationship between Frankenstein as the Creator, and "Frankenstein's monster," his creation. The result will be to suggest that: (1) it is more helpful to perceive the status of monster as dynamic rather than static. That is, to be monstrous is a dynamic condition rather than a fixed existential state; (2) that the presumption that there is a continuum between external appearance and internal identity blinds us to their actual relationships so that physical monstrosity is not an accurate gauge of ethical monstrosity; and (3) that identifying a monster is less a matter of depicting an Other than it is a revelation of our Selves in relationship to an(other).

III. "MONSTER" IN SHELLEY'S *FRANKENSTEIN*

Shelley uses various nouns and adjectives to identify Frankenstein's Creature: "fiend," "wretch," "devil," "insect," "enemy," "creature," and "monster." Often these occur in the same passage, suggesting that she does not use them as technical terms but to construct an image, or better, a collage. Except for the description of the Creature just before and after his animation, and in the final scene with the Arctic explorer Robert Walton, Shelley rarely refers explicitly to his appearance in detail. Instead we read of the responses to his appearance, which she details with great care. The most frequently used terms are "creature" (approximately thirty uses) and "monster" (approximately fifty uses). "Creature" is a neutral term, describing birds, animals, humans, and particularly, Frankenstein's creation. It is the narrator's preferred manner of reference, and this connects the animated body of the Creature with the rest of the natural order. However, when "monster" is used, it is almost always by Victor Frankenstein, who determines initially that the Creature is a monster solely by his shocking physical appearance.

The initial scene describing the Creature's animation contains elements of visceral reaction to the sight of its unusual body, though the term "monster" is not used there. Recalling this moment, Frankenstein refers to the Creature as a wretch. Moments before animating him Frankenstein beholds his beautiful proportions, his hair, teeth, and musculature. Moments after the Creature stirs, however, Frankenstein experiences his successful experiment as a catastrophe. No words are exchanged, the Creature is almost sedated, making no other movements than to breathe and to struggle with its limbs like a newborn calf. Evidently, seeing an *object* is different from perceiving a *being*. Frankenstein, "unable to endure the aspect of the being [he] had created," flees from the room, hiding in his bedchamber. Troubled, disgusted by the sight of his own "child," he seeks refuge in sleep, which eventually comes, but only fitfully.

Then, awakened by a nightmare, in which Elizabeth is transformed into his mother's worm-infested corpse, Frankenstein sees the Creature: "I beheld the wretch—the miserable monster whom I had created" (Shelley, 84). The Creature reaches for him, gurgling and grinning as an infant might upon seeing its parent, but Frankenstein, unlike even the basest of animals, does not return the gesture but rather panics, rushing downstairs and fleeing his apartments to remain away for hours. Left alone, the Creature, destitute, bewildered, unable to comprehend itself or its surroundings, leaves, carrying its only provisions, a cloak and a satchel. This initial reference to the Creature as a "miserable monster" is evoked solely from its appearance, and from this point in the narrative Frankenstein continually refers to his creation as a monster. However, at some point, the reference is not only to the Creature's outward appearance but also to Frankenstein's evaluation of him as a being, based on his indictment of the Creature as the murderer of his friends and family. Thus, despite the repetition of the term "monster," we should remember that all of these are predicated upon Frankenstein's own initial response to, and designation of, his creation.

There are relatively few occasions when someone other than Frankenstein uses the term "monster": when Justine explains to Elizabeth why she confessed to a crime that she did not commit, when Frankenstein implores a magistrate to find the criminal who murdered his friend Clerval, when William meets the Creature, and finally when the Creature tries to comprehend his existence.

Justine refers to herself as a monster when she admits that, in order to obtain absolution, she lied to her priest/confessor. She rues this and avers,

> . . . now that falsehood lies heavier at my heart than all my other sins. The God of heaven forgive me! Ever since I was condemned, my confessor besieged me; he threatened and menaced, until I almost began to think that I was the monster that he said I was. He threatened excommunication and hell fire in my last moments, if I continued obdurate. Dear lady, I had none to support me; all looked on me as a wretch doomed to ignominy and perdition. What could I do? In an evil hour I subscribed to a lie; and now only am I truly miserable. (Shelley, 107)

Justine's words echo those of the Creature. Abandoned, a wretch doomed to ignominy, she is miserable, as he was. Isolated from all humanity, made singular by "all who looked at her/him" one becomes monstrous. In such a state, believing one is a monster is a natural response to the claims and evaluations of one's peers and superiors.

Along this line, Walton and his ship's crew also refer to the Creature as a monster, but only after Frankenstein tells them he is a monster. When Walton first reports seeing the creature, he refers to him as "a being which had the shape of a man, but apparently of gigantic stature"—but he and his crew still perceive this being as a fellow human. As Walton says, "We were, as we believed, many hundred miles from any land; but this apparition seemed to denote that it was not, in reality, so distant as we had supposed" (Shelley, 58). Seeing the creature, they draw the conclusion that his appearance is evidence of civilization nearby.

However, following the death of Frankenstein aboard his ship, Walton encounters the Creature face-to-face. Walton enters the cabin that contains Frankenstein's remains and sees a "form which I cannot find the words to describe: gigantic in stature, yet uncouth and distorted in its proportions. As he hung over [Frankenstein's] coffin, his face was concealed by long locks of ragged hair; but one vast hand was extended, in colour and apparent texture like that of a mummy . . . Never did I behold a vision so horrible as his face, of such loathsome, yet appalling hideousness. I shut my eyes involuntarily, and endeavored to recollect what were my duties with regard to this destroyer. I called him to stay" (Shelley, 217).

Here we have the only sighted person to encounter the Creature without exclaiming that he is a monster, as every other human who has seen him has immediately done. And unlike Frankenstein, Walton does not flee, he does not abandon or expel the Creature, but invites him to stay. In response, the Creature pauses, and looks at Walton "in wonder," no doubt because, for the first and only time in his existence, he has experienced a human being engaging him as another being. Indeed Walton chooses not to obey Frankenstein's dying wish that the Creature be destroyed. Instead Walton hears his confession, but he does hear him as a monster. He cannot give absolution, stating, "If you had listened to the voice of conscience, and heeded the stings of remorse, before you had urged your diabolical vengeance to this extremity, Frankenstein would yet have lived."

The Creature responds, "Do you think that I was then dead to agony and remorse?" and pointing to the corpse, continues, "he suffered not more in the consummation of the deed—oh! Not the ten-thousandth portion of the anguish that was mine during the lingering detail of its execution" (Shelley, 218). And the Creature, while not eschewing responsibility for his crimes, reminds Walton, "You, who call Frankenstein your friend, seem to have a knowledge of my crimes and his misfortunes. But, in the detail which he gave you of them, he could not sum up the hours and months of misery which I endured, wasting in impotent passions. For whilst I destroyed his hopes, I did not satisfy my own desires. . . . I desired love and fellowship, and I was still spurned. Was there no injustice in this?" (Shelley, 219). The speech continues until this final and sad farewell, "I leave you, and in you the last of human kind these eyes will ever behold! . . ."

This exchange, a person-to-person exchange, is the last we hear from the Creature. With that he springs overboard and as Walton notes, was no longer seen, lost in the waves of darkness and distance.

IV. KEEPING THE "MONSTER" IN SIGHT

Taking a cue from Melissa Bloom Bissonette, we turn finally to "seeing the monster," employing Bissonette's "pedagogy of alienation" to see how the monster is depicted by "emphasizing the monster, returning to the monster *as* monster, refusing to allow him to melt into a symbol in the classroom" (Bissonette, 108). In general, the Creature as monster has been understood in one of two ways: either as a child made defective by its willfully negligent parent, or as deeply, intrinsically and organically, an evil being. A closer reading of Shelley's portrayal shows that this binary opposition collapses almost as soon as it is constructed. The character she has created is more complex than this either/or suggests. Certainly, the monster exhibits hideous physical traits. What Frankenstein and the De Laceys see on beholding the Creature would surely frighten anyone, given his size, appearance, and sinister visage—doubtless the Creature appears monstrous. He is also monstrously more powerful and athletic than his human cousins. As the Creature says of himself when, finally, he is able to confront his creator,

> And what was I? Of my creation and creator I was absolutely ignorant; but I knew that I possessed no money, no friends, no kind of property. I was, besides, endowed with a figure hideously deformed and loathsome; I was not even of the same nature as man. I was more agile than they, and could subsist on a coarser diet; I bore the extremes of heat and cold with less injury to my frame; my stature far exceeded theirs. When I looked around, I saw and heard none like me. Was I then a monster, a blot on the

earth, from which all men fled, and whom all men disowned?" (Shelley, 136)

But in that same moment the Creature is also able to reflect on his monstrous status, causing him (and us) to doubt whether the answer to his question must be yes. He tells Frankenstein, "I cannot describe to you the agony that these reflections inflicted upon me; I tried to dispel them, but sorrow only increased with knowledge. Oh, that I had forever remained in my native world, nor known or felt the sensations of hunger, thirst, and heat." Conscious of his almost human condition, he realizes that the only release from these sensations is death, a state he "feared but did not understand." He "admired virtue and good feelings," but was "shut out from intercourse with them," except when he was "unseen and unknown . . . which rather increased than satisfied the desires I had of becoming one among my fellows" (Shelley, 136).

The Creature also reflects even more deeply on the lessons he had learned from his reading and from listening to Felix De Lacey: the difference between the sexes, the birth and growth of children, the loving care of parents for their infants, "of brother, sister, and all the various relationships which bind one human being to another in mutual bonds." Eventually, as an educated human might, he asks, "Where were my friends and relations? No father had watched my infant days, no mother had blessed me with smiles and caresses; or if they had, all my past life was a blot, a blind vacancy in which I had distinguished nothing. From my earliest remembrance I had been as I then was in height and proportion. I had never yet seen a being resembling me, or who claimed any intercourse with me. What was I? The question again recurred, to be answered only with groans" (Shelley, 136–137). Is this not the most human of moments, to ask about the consciousness of our conscience, to reflect on our own subjectivity?

These desires and hopes for family are also fully expressed and experienced by Victor Frankenstein, but less to ask himself what he might be and more to justify his deserting his responsibilities toward those very people. He deliberately describes them to Walton in the first chapters of the novel, recounting his Genovese heritage, his father's reputation and that he "devoted himself to the education of his children," concluding, "No creature could have more tender parents than mine. My improvement and health were their constant care, especially as I remained for several years their only child" (Shelley, 65).

In these reflections both the creator and his Creature express the importance of these essential human experiences: the Creature, who wonders if he is a monster for his lack of them, and Frankenstein the creator, who revels in his good fortune to have had them. Yet, knowing this, he did not, would not provide them for his "only child." One cannot help but think that, upon hearing the Creature's tale, Frankenstein should have asked himself: Am I then a monster?

There is a mixture here; for all his "monstrosity," the Creature is filled with wonder, reflection, compassion, and care. Indeed, hearing his story, the elderly De Lacey tells the Creature, "I am blind, and cannot judge your countenance, but there is something in your words which persuades me that you are sincere. I am poor, and an exile but it will afford me true pleasure to be in any way serviceable to a fellow human creature" (Shelley, 147–148). Yet, combined with his goodness, the Creature willfully kills, seeks to deceive and destroy, and murders the innocent.

Conversely, for all his appearance of innocence and his claims of virtue, Frankenstein never publicly admits his own culpability in these deaths. Faced with the opportunity to exonerate Justine by revealing his role in creating the monstrous being, he will not do so, caring more for his own well-being than Justine's life. Repeatedly assuring his family that Justine was innocent, he remains silent, protecting himself from blame. Even worse, watching the trial, watching Justine's psychological terror mount until it ceases only at her death, Frankenstein thinks only of himself. "My own agitation and anguish were extreme during the whole trial, I believed in her innocence, I knew it." Blaming the creature for betraying the innocent Justine, Frankenstein does nothing to remit her either. Instead he remarks, "When I had perceived that the popular voice, and the countenances of the judges, had already condemned my unhappy victim, I rushed out of the court in agony. The tortures of the accused did not equal mine; she was sustained by innocence, but the fangs of remorse tore my bosom, and would not forego their hold" (Shelley, 106). Can we not admit that it is monstrous for Frankenstein to consider his feelings of guilt and despair as equal to those of an innocent child about to be executed?

There is only one fleeting moment when Frankenstein explicitly admits his culpability for the death of his loved ones, when he sees the body of Clerval, and admits that "Clerval, my friend and dearest companion, had fallen victim to me and the monster of my creation." He feverishly asks himself the same questions the Creature had asked himself. "Why did I not die? More miserable than man ever was before, why did I not sink into forgetfulness and rest?" (Shelley, 183, 188). These are private thoughts, but they show us that the outwardly human Frankenstein is inwardly monstrous. Moreover, at the point of actual self-awareness, when he remembers his whole life including his "mad enthusiasm" for the creation of the "hideous enemy," he cannot bring himself to an honest appraisal but is "unable to pursue the train of thought . . ." (Shelley, 188). Had we not been shown that these were Frankenstein's words, we would have taken them for the Creature's, except that the Creature may well have been more honest.

The Creature's behavior while connected to the De Lacey family offers another instance of the contrast between appearance and ethical makeup. When Frankenstein abandons him, the Creature must find shelter, sustenance, and safety. Initially he forages for food, drinks from streams, and covers himself from cold. Eventually coming to a village with its neat huts and carefully tended gardens, he cautiously enters one of the homes. But as he relates, "hardly had I placed my foot within the door, before the children shrieked, and one of the women fainted. The whole village was roused; some fled, some attacked me until, grievously bruised by stones and many other kinds of missile weapons, I escaped . . ." (Shelley, 124).

This leads him to a hovel near the De Lacey cottage, a place the Creature refers to as a paradise. There, looking through a chink in the wall, he watches the De Lacey family struggle to survive in poverty. He secretly provides them with food, collects kindling for their fires, clears their farmland, and gradually comes to love them, saying, "The gentle manners and beauty of the cottagers greatly endeared them to me; when they were unhappy, I felt depressed; when they rejoiced, I sympathized in their joys" (Shelley, 129). Experiencing his secret kindnesses, the De Laceys utter the words "good spirit, wonderful" when thanking their anonymous helper. He finally determines to meet them in person, to risk being seen by them. But he hesitates after seeing his own reflection in a pond. This is the one instance when the Creature uses the term "monster" in relationship to himself in a declarative sentence.

The Creature realizes that without the ability to converse, he would never be accepted by the De Laceys because of his appearance, which terrifies even him. Relating this instance of self-loathing to Frankenstein, he admits, "At first I started back, unable to believe that it was indeed I who was reflected in this mirror; and when I became fully convinced that I was in reality the monster that I am, I was filled with the bitterest sensations of despondence and mortification" (Shelley, 130). As we have seen, the Creature has wondered before if he might be a monster, but when he actually sees himself in the pond, he succumbs to the calculus that appearance equals evidence—an equation, ironically, he has learned from his experiences with humans.

During this time, the Creature learns to speak, to read, and educate himself by reading Goethe, Milton, and the French philosopher Constantin Francois Volney. Eventually he decides to reveal to the blind old De Lacey father that he is the family's unknown benefactor. He thinks, "I had the sagacity enough to discover that the unnatural hideousness of my person was the chief object of horror to those who had formerly beheld me . . . I thought, therefore, that if, in the absence of his children, I could gain the good-will and mediation of the old De Lacey, I might, by this means, be tolerated by my young protectors" (Shelley, 146).

Entering the cottage, he entrusts himself to the old man, recounting the past months and hoping for acceptance, but ruing that "I am full of fears; for if I fail here, I am an outcast in the world forever" (Shelley, 147). The old man encourages him, assuring him that the hearts of men can be "full of brotherly love and charity." The Creature agrees, but still is reluctant. "They are kind—they are the most excellent creatures in the world; but, unfortunately they are prejudiced against me. I have good dispositions; my life has been hitherto harmless, and, in some degree, beneficial, but a fatal prejudice clouds their eyes, and where they ought to see a feeling and kind friend, they behold a detestable monster" (Shelley, 147). It is his hope that the appearance versus reality formula he has experienced in every other encounter with humans will at last be proved false. If he is monstrous in appearance, he is not so in thought or spirit. He has made himself into a rational, caring, reflective being—hardly a monster in the rude sense of that word.

While the Creature speaks to the old man, he (and we the readers) see not a monster but a fellow human being, a person. Physical sight has not clouded the old man's vision of the Creature's ethical being. However, when the younger De Lacey returns, and sees only the Creature's externality, he perceives a threat to his family's safety, not the being who has sustained their existence. The Creature describes the fear this evokes. "Who can recount their horror and consternation on beholding me? Agatha fainted; and Safie . . . rushed out of the cottage. Felix darted forward, and with supernatural force tore me from his father . . . in a transport of fury, he dashed me to the ground, and struck me violently with a stick" (Shelley, 148). The Creature could have retaliated, could have "torn him limb from limb, as the lion rends the antelope. But my heart sunk within me as with bitter sickness, and I refrained" (Shelley, 148). Ironically, roles are reversed; the human acts with superhuman, monstrous fury, whereas the monster shows mercy and restrains its superhuman powers. Only alone in the woods that night does he vent his anguish like a howling beast. Fearing for their lives, the De Laceys flee, and the Creature, once again abandoned, is devastated. The result, he says, is "a kind of insanity in my spirits, that burst all bounds of reason and reflection" (Shelley, 151), and he sets the abandoned cottage on fire. Here, bereft of his one hope at companionship, his actions become truly monstrous.

He determines then to travel to Geneva to confront his creator, but on the way, he encounters a young girl running near a river. She slips into the water, and after he rescues her he relates that "I endeavoured, by every means in my power, to restore animation" to her unconscious body (Shelley, 153). Here the Creature does not act like a monster but quite the opposite, attempting to restore life to an inanimate body as his creator did. But his reward for this heroic act is to be shot and left for dead by the girl's "human protectors." "This was then the reward for my benevolence!" he says; "I had saved a human being from destruction, and, as a recompense, I now writhed under the miserable pain of a wound . . . The feelings of kindness and gentleness, which I had entertained but a few moments before, gave place to hellish rage and gnashing teeth. Inflamed by pain, I vowed eternal hatred and vengeance to all mankind" (Shelley, 153). For a second time, the Creature becomes a monster, again as a reaction to human actions prompted by his appearance. In every instance, outward appearance does not cohere with inward spirit.

This brings us to one more poignant scene when the Creature's appearance provokes his identification as a monster. When he comes upon Victor Frankenstein's younger brother, William, his vows of vengeance are forgotten. He sees a "beautiful child," and later recalls, "Suddenly, as I gazed upon him, an idea seized me, that this little creature was unprejudiced, and had lived too short a time to have imbibed a horror of deformity. If therefore, I could seize him, and educate him as my companion and friend, I should not be so desolate . . ." (Shelley, 154). Once more, the Creature acts in the belief that outside appearance equates with inner virtue. But when the Creature seizes the child, with no intent to harm him, William cries, "Let me go monster! ugly wretch! you wish to eat me, and tear me to pieces—You are an ogre." Even after the Creature attempts to quiet him, the child shrieks, "Hideous monster!

let me go!" William Frankenstein, like all the human characters (with the exception of the elderly De Lacey), responds not to the person of the Creature but to his appearance.

There are linguistic cues in this passage that show us one aspect of the Creature which he shares with all the other characters: he too is compelled by what he sees. Three times in this episode the Creature is said to "have gazed" upon William: the moment he first saw him; immediately after having inadvertently killed him; and when he sees the portrait of a woman the child had pinned to his breast. Shelley insists that we attend to the power of seeing and the assumption that what we see with the eyes is an indicator of the inner being we cannot see. Like the other characters, the Creature believes that physical appearance reflects spiritual well-being, and, like them (and us), discovers that this association is wrong.

The Creature's gazes remind us of Victor's own obsession with countenances: his mother's, Elizabeth's, Justine's, and that of his creation, when Victor assumes an isomorphism between outward beauty and inner character. Thus, when he relates his construction of the Creature, he notes that "his limbs were in proportion, and I had selected his features as beautiful" (Shelley, 83). Clearly, Victor expected that his arduous work, his finely crafted work of human art(ifact) would, when infused with energy, be beautiful. However, once the spark entered the body, his dream was shattered. He recalls, "Now that I had finished, the beauty of the dream vanished, and breathless horror and disgust filled my heart." This was the result of no more than the Creature's opening one eye, its labored breathing, and its spastic motions. The beautiful body parts, which moments before Victor exulted in, now "only formed a more horrid contrast with his watery eyes, that seemed almost of the same colour as the dun white sockets in which they were set, his shriveled complexion, and straight black lips" (Shelley, 83). His reaction is to flee, not to engage the live being that lies before him. He does not attempt to "see" this being but only reacts to its new ugliness and perceives only an animated corpse, saying, "Oh! No mortal could suppose the horror of that countenance. A mummy again endued with animation could not be so hideous as that wretch. I had gazed on him while unfinished; he was ugly then; but when those muscles and joints were rendered capable of motion, it became a thing such as even Dante could not have conceived" (Shelly, 84). Victor makes no attempt to educate the being, to create not simply a being but a companion. Unlike the Creature, who, gazing upon William, saw beauty and hoped to create a relationship with him, Victor sees the essence of ugliness and hopes that his own "child" will die in the night.

We should mention one other lexical cue from Shelley's description of the Creature's fatal encounter with William. The child exclaims to the Creature "monster! ugly wretch! you wish to eat me, and tear me to pieces" but that does not occur. Instead the Creature seeks to keep William whole and safe, and to establish a bond of companionship, based not on appearance but on shared care. When William exclaims "you wish to . . . tear me to pieces," we are first reminded that the Creature is himself made of pieces and abandoned at his birth, and that he is never provided a chance to become whole. The phrase also foreshadows what Victor will do to the mate he promised to the Creature.

The possibility of a mate arises when Frankenstein, hearing the Creature's account, is eventually moved to compassion for his loneliness. Appearing to make reparations for his initial rebuff of his creation, Victor promises to make the Creature a companion (Shelley, 158–159). Hearing this, the Creature swears that he will go into exile, telling Frankenstein, "You will never behold me again." However, when Frankenstein finally completes and is preparing to animate this new female Creature, he recants, fearing that he might be abetting a race of demonic beings. While Frankenstein prepares her, the Creature appears at his window. Victor, seeing this, "thought with a sensation of madness on my promise of creating another like him, and, trembling with passion, tore to pieces the thing on which I was engaged" (Shelley, 174–175). Victor then relates, the "wretch saw me destroy the creature on whose future existence he depended for happiness, and, with a howl of devilish despair and revenge, withdrew" (Shelley, 175). This is the final turning point for the Creature; from this point on, his inner being matches his external appearance as he finally becomes a monster both inside and out.

As Bissonette rightly suggests, to return to the "monster" is to keep him in sight, and in doing so we replicate the actions of the novel's characters. Almost without exception, Shelley's characters "see" the Creature as a monster. This is not an evaluation but a response to the Creature's physical appearance. They quite literally "see a monster," whether one actually exists or not. In fact, beyond Shelley's description of the Creature at its creation, we are told only of responses to its appearance by the other characters, inevitably responses of revulsion and fright. In doing so, Shelley inverts the logic of direct proportionality between external "evidence" of an internal being. The physically attractive creatures cannot see a fellow creature because their sight is occluded by its ugly appearance. As a result, our sense of "monster" is confounded: we can no longer simply characterize someone in response to hideous form but must look beyond or through such forms to the being itself. In effect, Shelley is requiring her readers to adopt a different understanding of "re-cognition."

It is this blending and bending of the monstrous identities of both Victor Frankenstein and his creation that make Shelley's portraits so compelling. We simultaneously wish for the Creature what he most desperately seeks, companionship, while also gasping at his callous destruction of humans who have the same needs. We are appalled at the actions of his creator, while continuously hoping that he will regain some semblance of redeeming, humane behavior.

The interior and exterior do not equate. The creature is hideous but often acts virtuously. His creator, to all appearances an upright member of society, acts in a cowardly and callous manner and without regard to anyone's safety except his own. Despite his protestations to the contrary, he never risks himself on behalf of anyone else. Shelley's depictions of these "twinned beings" makes it difficult to suggest which one is more monstrous. This doubt about monstrosity as a static reality suggests to us that "monster" is less a state than an attitude. It is volitional, and one seems to become a monster when acceptable responses to failure or rejection feel impossible and the solitary conditions of our lives seem indomitable. Then, there appears to us no other alternative but to act monstrously, to assert an identity that refuses to be constrained by the identifications of others. The creature is surely a monster on these grounds, but then so too are Frankenstein, Felix De Lacey, and the village people who react to the creature's appearance rather than his being. It would appear (at this point, I use the word advisedly) that "monster" pertains to all sorts of creatures, those born naturally and those born elsewise.

Just prior to stating his quandary about time, Augustine asks his question in another way: "For what is time? Who can easily and briefly explain it? Who can even comprehend it in thought or put the answer into words? Yet is it not true that in conversation we refer to nothing more familiarly or knowingly than time? And surely we understand it when we speak of it; we understand it also when we hear another speak of it." Augustine, baffled by "time," trusts that God will make such things known. Shelley is not so sanguine about the monstrous. If we recast Augustine's question about time and make it our own, we can then ask, For what is a monster? Who can easily and briefly explain it? Who can even comprehend it in thought or put the answer into words? Yet is it not true that in conversation we refer to nothing more familiarly or knowingly than a monster? And surely we understand it when we speak of it; we understand it also when we hear another speak of it. Or, perhaps, we do not.

PART TWO

THE MONSTER, THE MEDIA, AND THE MARKETPLACE

I was now about to form another being of whose dispositions I was alike ignorant . . . Even if they were to leave Europe and inhabit the deserts of the new world, yet one of the first results of those sympathies for which the daemon thirsted would be children, and a race of devils would be propagated upon the earth who might make the very existence of the species of man a condition precarious and full of terror.

> —Victor Frankenstein, considering the possible future consequences of his next experiment.
> Mary Shelley, *Frankenstein*

One of the most striking things about the Frankenstein phenomenon is how many people become familiar, often intimately so, with elements of Mary Shelley's remarkable story long before they ever get around to actually reading it, if indeed they ever do. This is of course because within a scant few years of its first, anonymous printing, *Frankenstein*, a tale peculiarly compelling to a rapidly changing, increasingly technological and industrialized age, found its way through adaptation, imitation, and parody into many modes of mass and popular culture.

From music hall comedies in the 19th century to video games in the 20th, versions, revisions, and knockoffs of "mad" Doctor Frankenstein and his homemade Monster have appeared in virtually every form and format imaginable. Some of these iterations have run with the themes and expanded on the arguments presented in the novel. Some have only a most limited relationship to the book that ostensibly inspired their creation. All, though, serve to impress ever deeper on the popular imagination at least the gross anatomy, if not the finer features, of Shelley's masterpiece. The spawn of Frankenstein's experiment have indeed traveled far.

The essays in the following section address *Frankenstein*'s prominence within, and its impact on, popular culture, entertainment media, and the performing arts, bringing together the voices of scholars and practitioners alike. Film historian and analyst Evan Lieberman surveys the impressive temporal and territorial range of *Frankenstein* on film, from the silent era onward, and across the globe. His essay addresses as well the question of why so many filmmakers have been drawn to the subject, looking at the uncanny connections between Victor's taboo obsession and the mechanics of movies, both of which defy death through technology.

For a firsthand view from the front lines of that century-long love affair between cinema and Shelley, Kevin LaGrandeur talks with Mel Brooks, himself an iconic figure, about his cherished, reverent, irreverent 1974 send-up, *Young Frankenstein.* Brooks's trademark wit sheds new light on this milestone of American film comedy, and reveals the many ways in which he and his collaborators were sensitive and stayed true to the spirit of not only *Frankenstein, or the Modern Prometheus* but also to the cinematic tradition the novel sparked in Hollywood.

Alexis Gambis, filmmaker and founder of Imagine Science Films, which creates, promotes, and screens science-related media, thinks about another kind of Frankensteinian legacy in film. Regarding the resurrected being in the story as a kind of hybrid or chimera, a synthesis of disparate elements, and embracing the liberating potential of crossing lines and transgressing boundaries, he considers the ways in which a like impulse to Victor Frankenstein's is driving contemporary scientists, artists, and filmmakers to create innovative works that merge and blur the distinctions between the worlds of research and creative expression, the human and the animal, the technological and the aesthetic.

Another creative professional deeply stirred by Shelley's story, screenwriter and director Jaime Paglia, cocreator and showrunner of the science fiction television series *Eureka*, shares his perspective on his incorporation of the themes of *Frankenstein* into a modern media text. A multi-episode arc in Paglia's endlessly inventive series explored the myriad ramifications of using the awesome potential of science to counteract the dreaded finality of death—with results more bittersweet than horrific in this case.

Underscoring the complexity and diversity seen in this ever-growing family of texts, filmmaker and entertainment industry historian Eddy Von Mueller talks with John Logan, creator and writer of Showtime's recent horror series *Penny Dreadful*, and Stuart Beattie, the writer and director of the 2014 film *I, Frankenstein*, based on Kevin Gevioux's graphic novel. While their Shelley-inspired works are very different, both offer insights into the continuing appeal of the *Frankenstein* story for contemporary artists and audiences, and discuss the opportunities and challenges that 21st-century media forms present those seeking to build onto this enduring legacy. Logan and Beattie also both offer perspectives on the Monster—a figure seen far more sympathetically in more current screen versions.

In light of so many and such varied versions of the Frankenstein myth making their way onto our screens, in another chapter Von Mueller traces the evolution of the Monster across a century of screen entertainment, and explores the creation of what has become the definitive image of the Monster, an image that owes as much to the now-classic 1931 film adaptation of *Frankenstein* as it does to the potency of Mary Shelley's prose. Once established, this single iteration of the Monster becomes a kind of brand or trademark that competes with, and often overshadows, the novel to which it owes its genesis.

Carol Colatrella, a scholar of literature, media, and material culture, looks at the permanent place the Frankenstein mythos has attained off-screen in our cultural landscape as well. Grounded in an appreciation of the pivotal place of play and the immense importance of childhood experience in shaping individual and social identities, her essay examines the myriad ways in which the narrative and underlying themes and issues associated with *Frankenstein* have informed a range of diversions and educational and entertainment media for young people and adults—an exercise that raises intriguing questions about what this steady stream of experiences might teach consumers about nature, science, and the immense creative potential of assembly, so central to the fictional Frankenstein's method.

Taken together, our contributors demonstrate *Frankenstein*'s pervasive presence in our cultural landscape. From 1910 to 2017, from Hollywood to Tokyo, from *Sesame Street* to Showtime and from cradle to grave, the overreaching scientist and his misbegotten semi-human experiment are seemingly always with us. Since the march of exploration, innovation, and scientific progress that helped inspire the writing of the story in the first place has only continued and even dramatically accelerated, we now face a world in which the kinds of power and the kinds of problems Mary Shelley imagined are rapidly becoming realities. Given the prominence of her story, it comes as no surprise that *Frankenstein* often serves as map, metaphor, and manual for understanding both the new frontiers of science and the moral, ethical, and legal dilemmas they may raise.

5

FRANKENSTEIN AT THE BOUNDARIES
OF LIFE, DEATH, AND FILM

Evan Lieberman

In the penultimate moment of the 1931 Universal Studios film *Fran-kenstein*, arguably the most iconic cinematic adaptation of the Mary Shelley novel, Dr. Henry (not the usual Victor) Frankenstein (Colin Clive), having been interrupted by several unwanted observers at his laboratory, sees movement in the hand of his creation and begins repeatedly, indeed maniacally, chanting, "It's alive!" before proclaiming, "In the name of God, now I know what it feels like to be God!"

One can imagine a similar, if perhaps less melodramatic, expression of wonder and Promethean achievement from Étienne-Jules Marey, Augustin Le Prince, or the employees of Thomas Edison's laboratory led by W. K. L. Dickson when, during the 1880s, these forefathers of the cinema first saw, respectively, birds in flight, the upper crust strolling through Roundhay Garden, and lab employees engaging in hijinks they called "Monkeyshines." Each of these tiny slivers of lived reality was captured and reproduced by machinery these visionary pioneers had spent years designing, refining, and perfecting, until finally it produced something approaching lifelike motion. In this sense the founding scientists of cinema can be seen as parallel in some degree to Shelley's Dr. Frankenstein. Like their literary predecessor, these inventors had used technology to create life, or at least the appearance thereof as the flickering black-and-white images from the very beginning existed in a strange mummified realm somewhere between life and death.

One of the best and earliest accounts of film spectatorship comes from the Russian and Soviet author Maxim Gorky, who was present at one of the first showings of the Lumière brothers' Cinématographe camera and film projector in 1896 at the Nizhny Novgorod Fair. He wrote, "Last night I was in the Kingdom of Shadows. If you only knew how strange it is to be there. It is a world without sound, without colour . . . It is not life but its shadow." Gorky further recognized that inherent in this cinematic confrontation with a world suspended between life and death was the emotion of fear. "Before you a life is surging, a life deprived of words and shorn of the living spectrum of colours—the grey, the soundless, the bleak and dismal life. It is terrifying to see, but it is the movement of shadows, only of shadows . . ."

The concept that fear was one of the most powerful reactions to the initial experience of moving images has been broadly described in the theoretical literature on cinema. In an essay by Martin Loiperdinger entitled "Lumière's Arrival of the Train: Cinema's Founding Myth," the author discusses how the mythology of terror accompanying the screening of the Lumière brothers' film *Arrival of a Train at La Ciotat Station* (1896) has become for film historians a model for understanding the dynamics of early cinematic spectatorship. This fifty-second-long film of a train pulling into a station, coming towards the viewer on a diagonal trajectory, allegedly caused the first film audiences to recoil or even flee the theater in fear.

Indeed some of the first commentary on cinema espouses this view, mirroring Gorky's observations. The film scholar Hellmuth Karasek wrote in the German magazine *Der Spiegel* in 1994 (in translation): "A short film had a particularly sustained effect, indeed it produced fear, terror, even panic . . . It was the film *The arrival of a railway train at the La Ciotat station*." Despite the fact that the historical accuracy of these accounts has been credibly challenged, most persuasively by Loiperdinger but also by Karin Littau in her chapter in *Film Analysis* about the Lumières' most famous film, this mythic terror remains deeply connected to our understanding of the relationship between the motion picture and its audience.

This intriguing double parallel between the creators of cinema and Dr. Frankenstein, and between their flickering, gray on-screen creations and Frankenstein's monster, points to a uniquely close relationship between Mary Shelley's romantic-era narrative and the emergence of the movies. Though a complete listing of films based on the Frankenstein myth would be nearly impossible to compile, *Romantic Circles*, a refereed scholarly website devoted to the study of romantic-period literature and culture, lists seventy-nine such films made between 1910 and 2005, while allowing that "a complete list of films based directly or indirectly on *Frankenstein* would run into the thousands." This staggering number of films featuring some variant of Dr. Frankenstein and his Monster makes the Monster (along with Dracula) without question the most popular single character in the history of the motion picture.

This allows us to use this figure as a lens through which to view not only the relation between film and its audience in any given time and place but also the progressive movement of the medium towards its ultimate fulfillment of a conceit central to the enduring Frankenstein myth: the use of technology to traverse the barrier between reality and its representation, or in more metaphorical terms, the line between life and death. The meanings generated by the extraordinary number and variety of *Frankenstein*-based films are not fixed. As Judith Halberstam argues in *Skin Shows: Gothic Horror and the Technology of Monsters*, *Frankenstein* works as a "machine that, in its Gothic mode, produces meaning and can represent any horrible trait that the reader feeds into the narrative" (Halberstam, 21). To explore this phenomenon, this chapter undertakes a limited historical survey of the *Frankenstein* films between 1910 and the 1970s in order to chart these developments over a half century of cinema.

The first cinematic adaptation of Shelley's novel was produced appropriately enough by the Edison Company in 1910, and though it was thought for decades to be a "lost film," a single surviving print reappeared in the mid-1970s in the private collection of Alois Dettlaff. Excerpts of Dettlaff's print were seen in a BBC documentary in the late 1970s, but the film was not shown publicly until 1993, and since then it has become widely available. Running a mere thirteen minutes, the opening title card refers to the film as "a liberal adaptation from Mary Shelley's famous novel," recognizing that any fidelity to the literary source material was clearly impossible, given the abbreviated running time of the single-reel film and the limitations of motion picture technology before World War I.

Directed by James Searle Dawley, Edison's *Frankenstein* was a prestige production, requiring a week to shoot, rather than the typical one or two days, and costing much more than the average Edison budget of five hundred dollars as a result of a particularly elaborate (for the time) special effects sequence in which the monster emerges from a cauldron. Upon the release of the film, Edison himself claimed the variations from the novel derived from the intention of the company "to eliminate all actual repulsive situations . . . Wherever, therefore, the film differs from the original story it is purely with the idea of eliminating what would be repulsive to a moving picture audience" (Edison Kinetogram, March 15, 1910). Edison's statement reflects the negative attention moving pictures were just beginning to attract from moral and religious groups who recognized the power of the new medium and very quickly turned a critical eye in its direction.

The strategy of adapting well-known and highly regarded literary material would become one way in which the film industry would seek to combat the forces of censorship even as they played to the more prurient interests of their audiences. In this regard Edison's *Frankenstein* can be seen as a pioneering work. At the very least the appearance of the Monster (Charles Ogle) can be seen as repulsive and shocking, but even more clearly and contrary to Edison's contention, the scene where the Monster arises is without question designed to produce a strong horror effect upon the audience.

In this sequence, which has no corollary in the original novel, a bizarre ephemeral skeleton gradually begins to constitute itself within a smoking cauldron, as a torso is formed, then one strangely angled and moving arm and then a head and shoulders, seemingly born of magical flames. Grotesque material pours from the eyes and eventually the twisted shape of the Monster can be seen. Dr. Frankenstein (Augustus Phillips) is so repulsed by the horrifying visage of the creature he has created that he faints dead away. There is a very visually clever mirror shot while the Monster is stalking Dr. Frankenstein during his reunion with his beloved Elizabeth (Mary Fuller) that sets up the terrible moment when the Monster first sees himself and runs in horror from his own reflection, but otherwise the film is not particularly advanced in the formal sense.

In fact at a time when D. W. Griffith and Billy Bitzer were revolutionizing film form in their work at Edison's competitor, Biograph Studios, Edison's *Frankenstein* still adheres closely to what Noël Burch has called the "primitive mode of representation" in his book *Life to Those Shadows*. It uses theater-like proscenium staging and long camera shots only, shows virtually no cutting within individual scenes, and displays a histrionic acting style. It also lacks narrative self-sufficiency, meaning that without knowing the novel or the half century of productions of the *Frankenstein* story onstage, it would be difficult indeed to follow the film's narrative. In many ways this early *Frankenstein* can be seen as a film on the border between what film scholar Tom Gunning calls "a cinema of attractions" and film as a fully narrative medium; between the movies as a sideshow act and a serious art form capable of translating important literature from page to screen; between the motion picture as a technological curiosity and an industry central and vital to American culture.

Two more *Frankenstein*-based films were produced during the silent era, the feature-length *Life Without Soul* directed by Joseph W. Smiley in 1915 for the Ocean Film Corporation, which is now lost, remaining only as a lobby card and a handful of still images, and *Il Mostro di Frankenstein* (1920) directed by Eugenio Testa for the Albertini Film Company, of which no prints exist either. The two German films based on the Jewish Golem myth, one from 1914 (lost) and the other from 1920 (fully preserved), both starring and codirected by Paul Wegener, are often mistakenly classified as *Frankenstein* films but are derived from distinctly different source material and are focused on mysticism and spirituality as opposed to science and technology.

Unquestionably the most historically important version of the Shelley novel was produced in 1931 by Universal Studios, based on the successful 1927 theatrical adaptation by Peggy Webling. Directed by James Whale, with Boris Karloff embodying the version of the Monster, it would be cemented into popular consciousness due to the extraordinary enduring popularity of the film. Almost all the visual and narrative metaphors associated with *Frankenstein* in contemporary culture derive from the 1931 film version rather than Mary Shelley's novel. The monster's squared-off head, strange, lumbering gait, bolts in the neck for electrical contact, and inarticulateness; the frighteningly isolated expressionistic castle and the elaborate devices used to channel the electric charge of lightning that reanimates the corpse that will become the monster; even the appearance of Igor (called Fritz in the 1931 film), Dr. Frankenstein's frequently hunchbacked assistant who does not appear in the original book—all these are found first in this film and go on to become foundational elements of cinematic and post-cinematic images of *Frankenstein*.

When Universal produced *Frankenstein*, the studio was coming off a financially devastating year, having lost $2.2 million in 1930 and teetering at the edge of solvency. As a strategy for expanding its markets and indeed for its very survival, the studio took the risky move into the production of horror films, a genre that until then had been significant only in Germany during the late 1910s and early '20s. Its first entry in the series was *Dracula*, a surprising and solid hit that earned $700,000 in 1931, its first year of release (Vieira, 35). *Frankenstein* was an even greater box office success, earning $1.4 million in movie theater rentals in its first year of release and going on to become an extremely profitable franchise, generating $13 million by 1953 (Jacobs, 107). Again we find a cinematic Frankenstein emerging at a transitional moment in film history, poised between silent and talking pictures, between the freedom of early Hollywood and the stringent restrictions of the Production Code, and between the international style of the early American cinema and what would become the Classical Hollywood style that would come to dominate the next several decades.

Although experimentation with sound in motion pictures goes back to the Experimental Sound Film produced by W. K. L. Dickson for the Edison Company in 1894, "talking pictures" did not become commercially viable until 1927 with the release of *The Jazz Singer* from Warner Brothers Pictures. The years 1928 through 1931 saw film industries across the globe moving rapidly away from silent films, which depended on pantomime and title cards, toward films with synchronized sound tracks. It is perhaps not too far a leap to see the Monster, so brilliantly embodied by Boris Karloff, struggling towards speech and communicating primarily in grunts and cries, reflecting a cinema trying to find its voice. The monster in Shelley's original novel speaks with great insight and elegance, learning multiple languages soon after his "birth" and reflecting philosophically on his tragic state.

The basis of the inarticulate *Frankenstein* monster can be found in the first successful stage adaptation of the novel, titled *Presumption: Or, The Fate of Frankenstein*, written by Richard Brinsley Peake and initially performed in 1823. Peake refers to the Monster as Demon, and his muteness can be traced in part to the peculiar legalities of the British theater in the early 1800s that limited "legitimate performances" to the small number of approved theaters of Covent Garden and Drury Lane, while melodrama, musicals, and pantomime (to which the mute monster is reduced) could be staged at a much wider variety of venues. The inarticulate Monster in the 1931 film can be seen as something of a remnant of the silent motion picture, a frightening reminder of the cinematic landscape so recently abandoned, a superimposition of the wordless onto the speaking.

In addition to the Monster's silence, the 1931 film extends its connection to silent cinema by employing a visual iconography drawn from an earlier film movement, German Expressionism. This flourished between 1919 and the late 1920s and gave the world the first body of works that might legitimately be called horror films. The stylistic characteristics of Expressionism include chiaroscuro lighting with large portions of the image left dark, oblique camera angles that create a distorted sense of space, an experimental approach to set design that veers between abstract minimalism and a foreboding complexity but always works to externalize the psychological and emotional qualities of the characters and the drama, and imagery that can be grotesque, bizarre, and frightening. The opening action of the film as Dr. Frankenstein and Fritz cut down the body of a hanged man from a scaffold in a bleak, stark landscape; the beautifully designed and photographed scene of Fritz breaking into the college laboratory and stealing the criminal brain; and the best-known sequence in the film as Henry brings the Monster to life while his uninvited guests look on in stunned horror—all could have been taken directly from a German film of the previous decade.

In a particularly notable shot from the end of the film, the torch-carrying villagers who hunt the Monster are framed within the archway of a tunnel. This image is reminiscent of the work of Expressionist director F. W. Murnau and his frequent collaborator, cinematographer Karl Freund, who was working for Universal at this time and had both provided extraordinary camera work for *Dracula* just a few months earlier and contributed to Universal's adoption of the Expressionist style he had helped to pioneer. The cinematographer for *Frankenstein*, Arthur

Edeson, would move to Warner Brothers later in the decade, where he employed a visual style rooted in Expressionism and the work he had done at Universal on such landmark films as *The Maltese Falcon* (1941) and *Casablanca* (1942). In this way Edeson's work, as well as that of fellow Universal cameraman Karl Freund and his colleague/protégé Gregg Toland (best known for shooting *Citizen Kane* in 1941), bridged the representational approaches of the silent and the sound cinemas, as well as the international style of German Expressionism and what developed during the 1930s and 40s as the Classical Hollywood style.

The American cinema of the late 1920s and early '30s was quite adventurous in terms of its subject matter and its depictions of sexuality, even while states and cities had their own censorship boards and the Hays commission began attempting to establish moral standards for Hollywood films beginning in 1922. While the Motion Picture Production Code was not formally put into place until 1934, it was initially proposed in 1927, and the years in between saw the gradual imposition of strict censorship standards for Hollywood films. Again, *Frankenstein* stands on the cusp of a major shift in film culture. *Dracula* passed local censorship boards without much problem, since all its sexual undertones were subtle and there is very little on-screen violence, but *Frankenstein* was quite a different story.

There were significant objections in particular to the scene in which the Monster, having befriended a young girl who is throwing flower petals into a pond, picks her up and throws her in when they run out of flower petals, unaware that he is murdering her and believing it is part of their game. Several state censorship boards ordered the drowning of the young girl to be cut from the film. Many others demanded the excising of Henry's dialogue, cited at the beginning of this essay, in which he compares himself to God. In fact, Thomas Doherty, one of the leading scholars of pre-Code cinema, writes that the state of Kansas demanded the complete or partial removal of thirty-two scenes in *Frankenstein*, which would have cut the film's running length in half (Doherty, 297). In 1931 *Frankenstein* was clearly a film that tested the limits and pushed the boundaries of both the audience and the industry, taking the

American cinema in a new direction even as it helped establish the lines of acceptable content and representation.

Only the first 1931 *Frankenstein* from Universal drew such intense scrutiny from the censors, and the studio continued quite successfully producing *Frankenstein* films throughout the 1930s and early '40s. James Whale directed the sequel, *Bride of Frankenstein* (1934), which is often considered the pinnacle achievement of the series due to its visual inventiveness, richer characterizations of both Dr. Frankenstein and his Monster, and its playful if sometimes mordant sense of humor. Following *The Bride of Frankenstein* was the intelligent and stylish *Son of Frankenstein* (Roland Lee, director) in 1939, the distinctly less appealing *Ghost of Frankenstein* (Erle C. Kenton, 1942), in which Lon Chaney, Jr. replaced Boris Karloff as the Monster, and *Frankenstein Meets the Wolf Man* (Roy Neill, 1943). This is oddly enough simultaneously both a sequel to *Ghost of Frankenstein* and *The Wolf Man* (George Waggner, 1941), as well as the first horror film mash-up featuring multiple monstrous characters from different sources, of the type that would become increasingly popular in subsequent years.

The Universal series ended with two more films, *House of Frankenstein* (Erle C. Kenton, 1944), which again included the Wolf Man but added Dracula and an evil hunchback to the mix, and finally the delightfully funny *Abbot and Costello Meet Frankenstein* (Charles Barton) in 1948, which includes all three major monsters (Frankenstein's monster, Dracula, and the Wolf Man) only now in a new generic form, the horror comedy. Interestingly, though these two final films in the Universal series feature multiple monsters, only Frankenstein's monster is in the title. In fact the Abbot and Costello film was originally titled *Brain of Frankenstein*, but that was changed during production to capitalize on the growing popularity of the comedy duo.

In terms of its transitional and boundary-crossing power then, the *Frankenstein* series introduced the concept of the cross-narrative combination of monsters and the idea of reversing the emotional polarity of horror. In his study *Laughing Screaming*, William Paul discusses the way in which comedy and horror as "body genres" are two sides of the same generic construct, and after the release of *Abbot and Costello Meet Frankenstein*, the great Universal monsters might just as easily be seen in films that elicit laughter as ones that evoke horror.

From early in its inception, Frankenstein was a transnational cinematic figure, with the Italian *Il Mostro di Frankenstein* predating the Universal series by over a decade, and a Mexican variation, *El Super Loco* (Juan Jose Segura), produced in 1937 with future directorial legend Emilio "El Indio" Fernandez in a minor role. This film anticipates a veritable deluge of *Frankenstein* films coming out of Mexico from the mid-1950s until the 1980s. The movement really begins with *El Castillo de los Monstruos* (Julián Soler, 1958), a horror-comedy featuring Mexican comic star Antonio Espino and a cast of monsters very similar to those in the 1948 Abbot and Costello film, adding a mummy and a gill-man from *The Creature From the Black Lagoon* (Jack Arnold, 1954); and the more traditional horror of the stylishly produced *Orlak, El Infierno di Frankenstein* (Rafael Baledón, 1960). The Mexican films then become increasingly bizarre, including *Santo y Blue Demon contra El Dr. Frankenstein* (Miguel Delgado, 1974), in which masked wrestler/superheroes have to battle brain-transplanted monsters created by Victor's grandson Irving Frankenstein, who are terrorizing Mexico City; and the almost unimaginably weird (and frankly terrible) *Frankenstein's Great-Aunt Tillie* (Myron Gold, 1984,) starring Aldo Ray and Zsa Zsa Gabor.

During this same period *Frankenstein* films were produced in Japan, Spain, Portugal, Italy, France, Turkey, Sweden, Canada, and Lichtenstein, virtually all of which were targeted at an international youth market that had only emerged during the 1950s as the spread of television began to keep older patrons at home while newly minted teenagers still needed a reason to get of the house. In the same year as *El Castillo de los Monstruos* was released, in the United States B-movie specialists American International Pictures produced *I Was a Teenage Frankenstein* (Herbert Strock), in which now Visiting Professor Frankenstein uses spare body parts he keeps in drawers in his lab and a face "harvested" from a local lover's lane to build a teenager. These films were never designed to deliver the same type of horror as the Universal cycle, but rather put the teenaged spectator in a dominant, knowing position that turned any potential fright into simple and silly fun, while utilizing the familiar iconography of *Frankenstein* as a marketing device.

Occasionally this movement in the *Frankenstein* film produced something of interest, such as the early Phillip Kauffman–directed comedy *Fearless Frank* (1967), the movie debut of actor Jon Voight, narrated by "word jazz" pioneer Ken Nordine, and the first feature film shot by Bill Butler, who would be the director of photography on *Jaws* (Steven Spielberg, 1975) and *Rocky* (John Avildsen, 1976) less than a decade later. Far more often, though, this explosion in B-grade *Frankenstein* cinema churned out films like *Frankenstein Meets the Space Monster* (Robert Gaffney, 1965), in which neither Dr. Frankenstein nor the Monster appears at all, and *Dr. Frankenstein on Campus* (Gilbert Taylor, 1970), an obscure example of Canadian psychedelic exploitation cinema. In these cases the very titles of the films say it all.

Without question the most aesthetically and historically important *Frankenstein* films during this peculiar but prolific period came perhaps unsurprisingly from Great Britain, where Hammer Films made a series of seven *Frankenstein* films between 1957 and 1974 that would rival the Universal cycle for popularity and influence. *The Curse of Frankenstein*, directed by Terence Fisher in 1957, was not the first horror film made by Hammer Films—those were the first two films in the more science fiction–oriented Quatermass series, *The Quatermass Xperiment* (Val Guest, 1954) and *Quatermass 2* (Val Guest, 1957)—but it was without question the movie that put the studio at the forefront of authentic horror production.

Hammer horror represented a return to the Gothic style of Universal. Unlike so many of the other *Frankenstein* films aimed at the youth market during this period, Hammer's films were far more serious endeavors, with truly memorable acting performances from Christopher Lee as Baron Victor Frankenstein (also using the alias Dr. Victor Stein) and

Peter Cushing as the Monster, elegant sets and costuming that belied the film's rather modest budget, and a literate yet gruesomely shocking script by Jimmy Sangster, which provided a model for balancing intelligent writing with cutting-edge gore.

The single most important element that the Hammer *Frankenstein* films brought to the horror genre, though, is that they were the first horror films to be shot in color, and in doing so brought to the cinema its first look at realistic red blood. To be sure, *The Curse of Frankenstein* is not the kind of onscreen gore fest that would soon follow, but there are two scenes worth noting for their innovative use of brightly colored blood.

In the best-known moment of violence in the film, the Monster is shot in the eye, and more blood than had ever been previously seen on-screen pours from the wound. It is indeed a stirring scene, but not as psychologically affecting as an earlier scene in which Frankenstein in his lab works on the cadaver from which he is going to make the monster. He picks up a scalpel in order to remove the corpse's head, and the camera holds on the razor-sharp instrument for an extra beat, allowing the audience to contemplate the gruesome action about to occur. Though the actual sawing off of the head happens just out of frame, there is a moment that still elicits shock when the audience sees Frankenstein's bloody hands, which he wipes on his jacket, leaving a bright red smear that will remain there for the rest of the film and in some sense change the direction of the cinema towards a more realistic depiction of violence.

Another aspect that differentiates the Hammer *Frankenstein* films from their predecessors is that the Baron is a much more complex and generally sympathetic figure, constructed for audience identification, in contrast to the Dr. Frankenstein characters in the Universal films, who tend to be clearly drawn as twisted, psychotic villains. In those earlier films the audience's sympathy tends to be for the Monster, who is an innocent even as he wreaks havoc everywhere he goes. This change in psychological focus from the Monster to its maker does not necessarily render Victor as always heroic, yet Peter Cushing's performance as Baron Frankenstein and his complete dedication to his character's internal dynamics maintain the audience's connection to him even as he does the most terrible things. In *The Curse of Frankenstein*, a maid, with whom Frankenstein has been having a clandestine, clearly sexual relationship, finds out about the existence of the Monster. To quiet her, Frankenstein locks her in a room with the Monster. Though nothing is shown beyond the Monster reaching out for her, the maid's shrieks immediately provoke the audience's horrified wonder at whether she is being murdered or raped.

This intimation of the unimaginable continues to be a trademark of the Hammer *Frankenstein* films throughout the run of the series, as the sequel, the *Revenge of Frankenstein* (Terence Fisher, 1958), gives dark hints of vivisection and cannibalism. As the studio moved into the 1970s, the sexuality that had always been subtly present in the films became increasingly explicit as Hammer's films continued to push the boundaries of acceptable representation even as their quality tended to diminish. In this way the sex and violence that are inherent in the thematic structure of the horror genre were brought increasingly to the surface by Hammer, in many ways representing a transition from a cinema that repressed these forces to one that revealed them as the heart of the horror.

During the 1970s the Hammer series gradually waned, as did the youth-culture-oriented *Frankenstein* exploitation film, but the Baron and his Monster remained important cinematic figures, only now in various self-consciously artistic and more often parodic formulations. John Cawelti, in his essay "*Chinatown* and Generic Transformation in Recent American Films," has written about the notion of genre cycles, and *Frankenstein* presents an interesting case study in this regard. There is the classical period of genre, which in this case can be seen as the Universal cycle, but Cawelti suggests that subsequent stages of generic development include first a demythologization and then finally a re-mythologization as the thematic underpinnings of the genre are challenged and then renegotiated in order to maintain their currency. For the *Frankenstein* subgenre of the horror film, this de- and re-mythologization occurred simultaneously, with the teen-oriented exploitation films undermining the foundation of fear that is the basis of all horror. At the same time, the Hammer films were reinterpreting that mythology in a way that made the films legitimately frightening again, if only for the presence of full-colored blood; they also switched the focus from the pathos of the Monster to the aspirations of Frankenstein as a seeker—a desire that resonated with the cultural changes that were altering the world at this time of technological optimism and US President John Kennedy's New Frontier.

The final stage of genre development is parody, which traditionally happens between the de- and re-mythologization cycles but, in this case, follows both. After nearly a decade producing some of the least audience-friendly experimental films in all cinema history, including *Empire* (1964), an eight-hour-long static shot of the Empire State Building, and *Sleep* (1963), with a similarly static shot of poet John Giorno sleeping (though only five hours in length), Andy Warhol moved into a more narrative style of filmmaking eventually leading to *Andy Warhol's Frankenstein* (Paul Morrissey, 1973), more frequently appearing under the title *Flesh For Frankenstein*. If Hammer introduced more explicit sex and gore into the *Frankenstein* film, and in some sense into the mainstream cinema, then *Andy Warhol's Frankenstein* took this representation to its absolute limit.

Produced in Italy, the film has the look and feel of an Italian *giallo*, the graphic horror subgenre that grew to great popularity in Italy, but it exceeds even that style's devotion to free-flowing blood and realistically detailed open wounds. Now not only is Baron Frankenstein's (Udo Kier) beloved (called Katrin in this version and played by Monique van Vooren) his wife but she is also his sister, who meets her unsavory end during sex with the Monster as she tries to fulfill her insatiable carnal desires. There is also a scene in which the Baron seeks to gratify his sexual needs by copulating with a surgical wound in his female Monster. Given that the film was originally released in an X-rated version and that the makeup effects were done by the great Carlo Rambaldi, who would go on to create *E. T. the Extra-Terrestrial* for director Steven Spielberg, these scenes are shocking in their visual realism. However gruesome such moments may be, the film plays as comic parody, with purposely stilted acting, campy staging and direction, and a bizarre focus by Dr. Frankenstein on finding the "perfect Serbian nose" for his Monster, who further suffers from what the doctor considers an insufficient libido.

There are many similarities between *Andy Warhol's Frankenstein* and a film that would follow two years later, *The Rocky Horror Picture Show* (Jim Sharman, 1975). Filmed at the same Bray studios and Oakley Court castle location employed by Hammer for their *Frankenstein* films, this musical-comedy-horror parody turns the conventions of the *Frankenstein* story inside out, as now the doctor, here named Dr. Frank N. Furter, a flamboyantly omni-sexual transvestite played by Tim Curry, creates the monster named Rocky (Peter Hinwood) to be his ultimate boy toy, beautiful, muscled, and a sexual dynamo. However, when newlywed Janet (Susan Sarandon), who seeks refuge in the castle with her husband because their car has broken down, becomes the object of Rocky's amorous affections, both Frank N. Furter and her new husband, Brad (Barry Bostwick), are understandably dismayed to find them having sex in the lab.

In the end it turns out that the lab assistant (or handyman, as he is referred to in the film)—here called Riff Raff, rather than the traditional Igor, and played by Richard O'Brien, cowriter and creator of the original stage production on which the movie is based—has been in control all along. Both the assistant and the Monster are then stronger than the doctor, reversing the power dynamic that had been in place since Colin Clive's Dr. Henry Frankenstein abused his henchman, Fritz, who in turn tormented the Monster in Universal's 1931 production. *The Rocky Horror Picture Show* becomes a celebration of individuality, sexuality, the monstrous, and the films that had by that time been enthralling audiences for nearly fifty years.

The parody of *Andy Warhol's Frankenstein, Rocky Horror Picture Show,* and of course Mel Brooks's *Young Frankenstein* (1974) do not reveal the conventions of the genre to be lacking social currency but rather affectionately adapt those conventions in order to reinterpret them in a contemporary context: one in which the outsider, the freak, the monster is embraced rather than rejected, at the same time as society's marginalized—whether because of race, sex, or sexual orientation—were just beginning the long and still ongoing struggle for acceptance and inclusion. In considering *Frankenstein* as a transitional text, this is perhaps the most important boundary the films have traversed during their century of production.

The rate of production of films based on *Frankenstein* has not abated since the parodic period of the 1970s but, on the contrary, has increased significantly, with *Mary Shelley's Frankenstein* directed by Kenneth Branagh in 1994 standing as perhaps the most faithful adaptation of the original novel yet to appear on-screen but hardly the most interesting. Director Tim Burton has reimagined the Doctor as a young boy who reanimates his beloved dog in *Frankenweenie* (1984), while 1990 saw the release of *Frankenhooker* (Frank Henenlotter), *Frankenstein's Baby* (Robert Bierman), and *Frankenstein Unbound* (Roger Corman). *Frankenstein Goes to College* (Tom Shadyac) was released the following year, and at the same time audiences were promised the *Last Frankenstein* (Takeshi Kawamura), though of course this was hardly the case.

Frankenstein and the Monster continue to be significant figures and narrative models across all media throughout the world. The essential, seemingly eternal fascination that lies at the heart of Shelley's tale, the miraculous, dreamlike (or nightmarish) quest to use human ingenuity to restore life to the lifeless, to quicken the dead, lies too at the heart of cinema. As long as the story and its characters retain their ability to produce powerful meanings and metaphors and to transgress boundaries, *Frankenstein* will stand at the boundary of life and death, of science and magic, of the cinema and its audience.

6

FRANKENSTEIN, YOUNG AND OLD: AN INTERVIEW WITH MEL BROOKS

Kevin LaGrandeur

I t may seem odd to think that Mary Shelley's original *Frankenstein* stories (the original written in 1818 and her revision of 1831) could be converted to comedy, given their focus on the tragic downward spiral of the title character and his creature—and given the horror and fright that the story's early-20th-century cinematic descendants were meant to engender. But that is in fact what the film *Young Frankenstein* does. The writers of *Young Frankenstein*, Mel Brooks and Gene Wilder, pay homage to the *Frankenstein* movies of the 1930s and to Shelley's books by making us laugh at their familiar and frightening motifs. *Young Frankenstein*'s slapstick satire undermines the scary nature of the creature as it was portrayed in films and by Shelley. But it also bows to the serious themes in Shelley's books: Gene Wilder's character, Dr. Frederick Frankenstein, cannot resist accepting the inheritance of his grandfather Victor's secret knowledge and the discovery and glory that it might represent, even though he says at the beginning of the movie that he hates everything about its legacy. And the tortured humanity that resides in the ugly creature of Shelley's story, which nobody recognizes, is a constant theme in Brooks and Wilder's film—although Frederick, unlike Victor, realizes it and keeps trying to exhibit it to people by such ill-advised displays as the movie's comic song and dance number, "Putting on the Ritz."

Mostly though, Brooks and Wilder want us to laugh. And in that their creation succeeds: along with *Abbot and Costello Meet Frankenstein*, the film *Young Frankenstein* has made it onto the American Film Institute's list of the 100 Funniest American Movies. (It sits at number 13 and the Abbot and Costello film sits at number 56.) Another measure of its success is the amount of money it has made: after it was released in 1974, at a cost of $2.8 million, it made $86,273,333 at the box office. At today's ticket prices, that would be the equivalent of $393,023,000 (BoxOfficeMojo.com).[1] A more important measure is the critical acclaim it has garnered. In addition to its ranking near the top of the AFI's list of funniest movies, it has won a number of awards, including the 1976 Nebula Award for the best science fiction script, the 1975 Hugo Award for Best Dramatic Presentation, and two Saturn Awards (1974 and 1975) for set decoration.

Mel Brooks not only cowrote the screenplay with his friend Gene Wilder, who starred as Victor Frankenstein's grandson in the film, but he also directed the movie—which earned him an additional award: besides his share in those mentioned above, he won the 1976 Saturn Award for Best Director of a science fiction, fantasy, or horror film. These are part of an amazing record of awards Mr. Brooks has won over his lifetime as a director, actor, comedian, and songwriter. For his various endeavors he has won more than twenty-five awards; most impressively, he is one of only twelve people to have won all of the major American entertainment awards: the Oscar, the Grammy, the Emmy, and the Tony.[2]

In the interview below, I talk with him about how the film *Young Frankenstein* came to be—how it was conceived, funded, designed, and filmed—and also about how it relates to the various versions of the *Frankenstein* story that came before. In the process Mel Brooks talks about his life, his experiences with *Frankenstein*, old and new, and how growing up in Brooklyn affected how he saw it all.

NOTE: The interview has been edited for clarity.

LaGrandeur: You said in some previous interviews that when you first heard about the idea of making *Young Frankenstein*, you thought it was a bad idea. I was wondering why you initially thought that.

Mel Brooks: Originally I said, "Between James Whale and Hammer Films, there have already been too many Frankensteins on the screen." But Gene Wilder had this original idea. We were making *Blazing Saddles*. I took a ten-minute break during a fight scene, and there was Gene with his knees up and a legal pad and a pencil. He was scribbling away. I said, "What the hell are you writing?" He said, "Look."

At the top of the pad, it said, "Young Frankenstein." Then he said, in one sentence, something that got me excited. He said, "It's all about a guy that changes his name, a scientist who changes his name to 'Franken*steen*' because he wants nothing to do with his ancestors, and especially his great-grandfather, Victor Frankenstein, who talked about turning dead tissue into live matter." He said, "But of course it's in his blood. He doesn't know that. When he protests, we'll see what happens."

I said, "That's a good idea. That's new." To attack the idea of making a creature from dead parts, it's a great idea. To attack it, and then to be, of course, immersed and swayed by simply the genealogy that's in him, and the blood that's in his veins. So, I liked the idea. I said, "You want me to write it?" He said, "I want you to write it with me, and I want you to direct it." I said, "Well, okay. Let's see how the script turns out. And if we like it, then we'll talk about it."

LaGrandeur: It's a very brave thing for you to do, to take on such a huge and famous story like that. Did you ever have any doubts?

Mel Brooks: Well, I was a fan of the Mary Shelley book. I had read it when I was a kid, and I read it again when I was a little older, when I was in the army, actually. I was amazed at this eighteen-year-old girl coming up with this incredibly brilliant idea. And at how well-written it was. Amazed that she was with her husband, [Percy Bysshe] Shelley, and [Lord] Byron, somewhere in northern Italy, at a retreat somewhere on Lake Como, I think, when she wrote it. They had this contest about who could scare each other with it. She came up with the greatest story ever told.

LaGrandeur: Did you ever worry about making that story funny?

Mel Brooks: Never. I never worry about making anything funny. I just take the utter truth, the utter truth, and I just move an inch to the right or left of it, and I've got comedy.

LaGrandeur: An interesting point.

Mel Brooks: In *Blazing Saddles*, for instance, I took every cliché in every Western—scraping beans from a tin plate, drinking black coffee out of a tin cup—and had one of the funniest campfire scenes ever. I was a big fan of Westerns, and I knew what the clichés were, and I knew how to move them around.

LaGrandeur: Do you have a favorite scene of your own in *Young Frankenstein*?

Mel Brooks: I have so many. I have a couple of favorite scenes. One of my favorite scenes happened after a big fight with Gene Wilder. We were writing the thing, and we were talking about having the monster doing a "heel-to-toe" dance in a scene to prove that it was cognizant and understood, and could actually do things like walk properly and respond to commands. Gene took this idea to some far place by saying, "Why don't the monster and Victor do a number together? Like, 'Puttin' on the Ritz'?"

I laughed and said, "No, I think that tears it. I think that spoils it. When a thing goes too far, it becomes silly or foolish. And we're going to lose the James Whale aspect of it." I said, "No, I don't want to do that." We had a big fight about it. He kept insisting, and finally I said, "Okay. We'll film it, but I don't care about voting. If I don't like it, it's out." He said, "Okay. That's a deal." So we filmed it, and after I saw it, I liked it. After it played for an audience, I loved it. I think it became maybe my most favorite, or at least one of my favorite scenes. I was totally against it to begin with.

LaGrandeur: That's interesting. What changed your mind? Was it Mr. Wilder's arguments?

MEL BROOKS: No. The only thing that really changes my mind about anything after I make a movie is the audience. The audience laughs and grabs their belly and falls in the aisle and laughs. Then it's in the movie. I'm out to make a comedy. If there's coughing, and harrumphing, and silence in the audience, then no matter how much I love a scene, I just take it right out of the movie.

LAGRANDEUR: So that's how you decide to put stuff in or take it out?

MEL BROOKS: Well in the beginning there's a lot of work and cutting, before it even gets to an outside audience. Sometime at the end of November 1974, I showed the first rough cut for *Young Frankenstein* to some people. They were just people from the lot, all kinds of secretaries and people in various jobs: accounting, editing, shipping. I even got all the secretaries from the suits, from the big executives. It was at this little theater on the lot at Twentieth Century Fox, about a 200-seater. I showed them this rough cut of the film, and about two thirds of it was good and one third was terrible. So, I made this speech after it ran. I said, "Thank you for coming. You have just seen a 200-minute failure of a movie. But," I said, "In one month, just one month from today, I'm going to ask you all to come back. I have taken copious notes on what you liked and didn't like, and you're going to come back, and you are going to see a 90-minute, big-hit success. It seems impossible, but that's show business. I'm going to prove it to you."

In a month they came back, and stood up and cheered at the end of the movie. We had a lot of good stuff. We just didn't know exactly what should stay in and what should come out.

LaGrandeur: That's amazing, that you could do all that in one month.

Mel Brooks: Well, It wasn't just that one audience. I took the rough cut of the movie to Pasadena, too. I had been taking it to different places and making notes each time on what the audience really hated and what the audience really loved, and what was so-so. I had four or five different screenings in that month. Edit, screen. Edit, screen. Edit, screen. That's what I did, until finally, when those Fox employees came back to that little theater, they saw a very artfully edited film.

John Howard was our editor. This is the first time I worked with him. He had done *Butch Cassidy and the Sundance Kid*. That's the way he worked—I was very lucky to get him—everything but the kitchen sink: throw everything in, shoot everything, and then make your own cut, and then let the audience start helping to cut it.

LaGrandeur: That's interesting. I was going to ask whether, now that some time has passed since you made it, there was anything you would do differently.

Mel Brooks: As far as I'm concerned, it's perfect. I wouldn't touch a second of it.

LaGrandeur: I noticed that although the monster in your film is mute, as it is in James Whale's first *Frankenstein* film, at the end of *Young Frankenstein* the monster, who has been transformed by this sort of "mind-meld" with his maker, gives a speech that is so incredibly intelligent and beautiful, it's almost like one of Shakespeare's monologues. At that moment, your monster becomes similar to the creature in Shelley's book, who is a genius of sorts: the creature in the book picks up language and learning faster than most humans, and speaks very eloquently about the ethics of what it does. So what was behind that very eloquent speech by the monster in your movie?

MEL BROOKS: We were saluting the book. We were true to the book. What happens in our movie is that the monster actually receives, through brainwaves, the genius of Dr. Frankenstein. We got many good ideas from Mary Wollstonecraft Shelley; the foremost of them was the basic idea that such a thing as Frankenstein's creature could exist. I think we thanked her on the screen. I'm not sure. Anyway, we based it on her book.

LAGRANDEUR: About twenty years ago, there was an A&E documentary in which they interviewed you, and in that documentary Roger Moore, its narrator, says, "Many critics told us the best of the *Frankenstein* films, and perhaps the one most faithful to the novel, came from the brilliant minds of two of America's most premier filmmakers, Mel Brooks and Gene Wilder." I wonder: did you and Gene Wilder see yourselves as first and foremost trying to stay true to Shelley's book, or to James Whale's 1931 film interpretation of it?

MEL BROOKS: I think that Whale made the most beautiful movie rendering of *Frankenstein*. Boris Karloff's performance as the monster was incredible, and Colin Clive's as Victor Frankenstein was too. It was a great movie, but I think we were more faithful to Shelley's book itself and to her spirit. We wanted to do that.

LAGRANDEUR: So you and Mr. Wilder saw yourselves as trying to stay true to Shelley's book?

MEL BROOKS: Well, to a point. The book is crazy. The book is brilliant, but there are fits of rambling in it that are insane. But also, when it's spot on, it is the best, and a great gift, a great premise to work with. We tried to make a comedy that was faithful to both James Whale and Mary Shelley. It was difficult, but I think we succeeded.

LAGRANDEUR: Did you have discussions about trying to balance your references to Whale's movies and your fidelity to Shelley's story?

MEL BROOKS: Shelley's story provided the spirit of the thing, and the emotions, and the very genius of it. Whale's movies provided style. We tried to stay close to Whale's timing, and his pace, and his style, and his beautiful black and white, back-lit movie. That's how we balanced them: the basic story was Mary Shelley's. James Whale provided the model for telling the story through film.

LAGRANDEUR: Speaking of Whale's version of *Frankenstein*, I was curious about the laboratory setting you used in your film: I noticed you used Kenneth Strickfaden's wonderful electric gizmos from the early movies directed by Whale.

MEL BROOKS: Oh yes, Strickfaden was a sweet-as-sugar, nice guy, little old man, and he had everything [all of the props from the laboratory sets] in a garage in Santa Monica near the ocean; it was rusting a little bit. We were lucky too. He said, "Just give me a small fee." In the end I begged Fox, who finally did the picture, to give him a little more money than he asked for to rent his stuff. And we gave all of his equipment back to him. I don't know where it is now. He may have given it to his children or his grandchildren.

I didn't know what the entire set would cost, but when I met with Dale Hennesy, who was the production designer, he said, "I can give you a building that looks like sweating stone." I'll never forget that. Like a castle somewhere in Edinburgh, or in Transylvania. Big, heavy stone, wet with mist, wet with thunderstorms. I said, "Perfect. That's what I need on the outside. On the inside, I need vast space, both in the laboratory and the entrance chamber." We just thought alike.

He gave me some sketches, and he built me some models. I said, "Dale, it's just a little expensive. If you can cut it down by thirty-five, forty thousand, maybe we could do it." And he did, the great Dale Hennesy.

LaGrandeur: Do you think you could have done the movie without Kenneth Strickfaden's gizmos from the laboratory setting in the original *Frankenstein* movies? Would the special effects of the '70s have worked instead for your movie, made as it was in black and white?

Mel Brooks: I don't think so. We were very lucky to do it in black and white, not only because that worked perfectly with Strickfaden's fantastic laboratory props, but also because of the makeup we used on the monster's face. I don't know if you've ever heard of Bill Tuttle, William Tuttle. He was our makeup guy. He told me, "I'm so glad you're doing it in black and white, saluting the old James Whale films, because if we did it in color, he would just have a blue-green face. It would just be silly. There's just no way to give the monster that deep, rich, crazy dead-alive face [other than in black and white]." He said, "When I do it in white makeup, for black and white film, it's going to look whitish-grayish. It's going to be perfect." He was right. That was one of the reasons. And the castle was another reason. Everything worked better in black and white.

As far as using special effects available in the '70s, when *Young Frankenstein* was made, I don't think I would have used them. I think I would have mimicked Strick-faden's tinker toys. I would have gotten lightning, that spark between two wires going up and down. I would have done it mostly with various scary machine sounds, and thunder, and all kinds of stuff. I didn't want to do what they call "blue screen" or "green screen" effects. I don't think that would really have worked. Even the kids in the audience would have known there was something wrong. I would have scoured around to find somebody to do the laboratory toys, in imitation of Strickfaden's props.

LaGrandeur: Was it difficult to get a movie like this made?

Mel Brooks: Sort of. I had made a deal with Columbia. The only thing Columbia Pictures and I disagreed on was a couple hundred thousand dollars that I needed to make it. I had made *The Producers,* and *The Twelve Chairs*; I made *Blazing Saddles* for Warner's, so I knew how movies worked and what they cost. They offered me close to a million-eight . . . two hundred thousand short of two million. I said, "I think I need that two hundred thousand. I think it's going to cost two million with the laboratory scene."

We were fighting about that. Finally, Columbia said, "Okay. Let's split the difference. You need another two hundred thousand; we need to be careful with our money and our budget. We'll give you another hundred thousand." I was going to make this, for Columbia, for one million, nine hundred thousand. It was a pretty low budget, but the big thing about it that helped is that I didn't have one big star. Instead, I had all these people that I had sort of discovered: Gene Wilder, Peter Boyle, Marty Feldman, Madeline Kahn. I really had found these people kind of on their way up. I was very lucky that they didn't cost much. Therefore, I knew for two million I could do this picture.

Anyway, Columbia and I were going to make the deal. We met, Mike Gruskoff, the producer, and myself. We finished the meeting, we shook hands. Okay. We were going to make the picture.

But, as I closed the door, I shouted in, I said, "Thank you. This is going to be wonderful. It will be great working with you. By the way, I forgot to tell you. The picture is going to be in black and white." I closed the door and I walked down the hallway. Ten seconds later, a herd of thundering executives followed us, thundered down the hall, saying, "Wait! No! Come back! No! No black and white. Let's talk!"

So we talked for three hours, and finally they said, "South America just got color. This is crazy. We can't do black and white." And I said, "No." They said, "Okay. Here. You can open it in America and Canada, and a few territories like France. You can do that in black and white. We'll give you color film, and you'll diffuse it into gray, black, and white. But you've got to give us new territories, like South America and stuff like that, that we must have in color."

I said, "No. Absolutely not." I said, "The film has to be black and white." Finally, they said, "Let's talk tomorrow." That night, Mike Gruskoff called Laddie [Alan Ladd Jr.] and told them where we were on the deal, and what was happening. I think Laddie had just taken over Fox.

Laddie loved it and said, "It should be in black and white, and it should have another couple hundred . . . It should not be one-nine [$1.9 million]. It should be something like two-two, or two-four," and that he would get that money for us, and that he wanted it to be one of his first Fox pictures.

Gruskoff went back to Columbia the next day—I wasn't with him—and said, "Black and white film and we upped it to two million." They said, "Absolutely not. We're not going to do it in black and white. We want to save most of the world for color." So the next day I moved to Fox and we started working, Gene and I, on the script.

LaGrandeur: What about casting?

Mel Brooks: We were very lucky regarding casting. Why? I'll tell you why. There was a guy called Mike Medavoy, who eventually ran TriStar Films. Mike Medavoy at that time was an agent, like Laddie had been. He handled a couple of people, and he was Gene Wilder's agent. So of course Gene told him that we were working on this film together.

Gene said, "Mel wants Marty Feldman. And I want Marty Feldman." Medavoy said, "Well, through our company in England, we have Marty Feldman. So it's up to Marty Feldman. If he wants to do it, we can deliver him." Then he said, "What about the monster?" Medavoy said, "Let me show it to Peter

Boyle, who is the biggest guy and the most talented guy we've got." They showed it to Peter Boyle, and Gene found Teri Garr: I don't know where he found her. I loved Madeline Kahn for Elizabeth, the society fiancée.

LaGrandeur: I've always wondered why you chose Peter Boyle for the role of the monster. He was so handsome. His features were quite pleasing and almost delicate, especially compared to Boris Karloff's.

Mel Brooks: Because of his size. He was big, and we had seen Joe Medavoy, so we knew he was a fabulous actor. We didn't have to audition these people. We gave them the parts. I didn't have Marty Feldman read for me. I knew how talented he was. He worked for Larry Gelbart, who produced and was the head writer of the *Marty Feldman Comedy Machine* somewhere in London. I never had to ask Gene to read anything, ever, in my life. He was a friend of mine and I knew how talented he was.

There's another good story [about how Dustin Hoffman almost played the Inspector Kemp character in *Young Frankenstein*]. Ready?

LaGrandeur: Yep. I'm ready.

Mel Brooks: I lived on 11th Street at the time, in the Village. Further up on 11th Street, closer to 5th, Dustin Hoffman lived with his first wife. I had seen him in *Death of a Salesman*, on television. He was fantastic. I had also seen him somewhere off-Broadway one night, doing a crazy German accent. He was terrific.

[While casting for *The Producers*] I met with him, and I gave him the script and I said, "Dustin, read Franz

Liebkind." He's the playwright character in *The Producers* who comes up with "Springtime for Hitler." I always had Dustin in mind for the part. I figure if he had done that, I probably would have used Dustin as Inspector Kemp, in *Young Frankenstein*. He was a natural. He could be a crazy German.

But one night [before the play got going], there was Dustin throwing pebbles against my window, like he was Cyrano or something and I was Roxane. I opened the window. I said, "It's two in the morning. What are you, crazy?" He said, "You won't believe this. I have to fly to California to audition for the part of Benjamin opposite your wife in *The Graduate*." I said, "Go, go, go. You're a mutt. You'll never get it. You're the funniest-looking guy, and once they see you on film, I'll get you back for *The Producers*."

So he went to Hollywood, and he called me two days later, and he said, "I got the part." But I got lucky, because I found Kenny Mars, who came to audition for the part of Franz Liebkind.

So, because of Dustin's "betraying" me [laughter], I got Kenny Mars, and once I got him, I never let him go. I immediately gave him the wooden arm that Lionel Atwell had in James Whale's *Frankenstein*. Kenny Mars went from *The Producers* right into *Young Frankenstein*. I didn't have to audition him. I knew how good he was. That's the Kenny Mars story for Inspector Kemp. It's a convoluted, crazy story, but that's one of the miracles of casting.

LAGRANDEUR: Regarding *Young Frankenstein*, I've heard you mention before, elsewhere, this fascinating idea you have that *Frankenstein*, at bottom, is a story about womb envy.

MEL BROOKS: I said, "This great scientist probably envied women who made life, and men couldn't make life. So he decided to make life." But that's my own theory. It may be all wet. Instead of penis envy, it's womb envy. From the womb comes life.

LAGRANDEUR: What was your first encounter with the story of *Frankenstein*?

MEL BROOKS: Okay. It's 1931. James Whale makes a movie, and Universal releases it. It plays at the RKO Republic [Theater]. It's called *Frankenstein*. There were no restrictions on kids in Brooklyn . . . you can't see this; you can't see that. We had no ratings. My brother Lenny took me to the movie. He is about six years older than I am. I'm five; he's about twelve. We go in and watch it, and I'm clutching Lenny. I'm ruining his jacket. I'm just, "Yikes! Holy s**t I hope this guy doesn't look at me again." You know, the Boris Karloff look with the slit eyes and the slow turn of his head . . . I was scared s*****ss. I really . . . it was terrifying. But I loved it. Somehow, I was only five, but I knew this was a beautiful, strange epiphany of some kind for me.

     I got home. We saw it in July, so it was hot in Brooklyn. We lived on the fifth floor, and the tar roof was melting; it was a really hot night. My brother Bernie was across the room, and my cot was right next to the fire escape. That was pretty good most of the time, because it was by the open window, and I got some breezes at night.

     Well, I told my mother, Kitty Kaminski . . . after seeing *Frankenstein* that night, "Mom, close the window." She said, "What are you, crazy? It's a hundred degrees out there. What do you mean, close the window? You'll die. You and Bernie, you will die." I said, "No, you have to close the window, because Frankenstein (we called the monster Frankenstein. Everybody called the monster Frankenstein), Frankenstein is going to come up the fire escape. He's going to come in the window. He's going to bite me and eat me. He's going to kill me." My mother was very smart, really smart. She took her time. She said, "Look, I'll come up and sit by the window. I'll watch through the sashes by the window. Don't worry. You can sleep with the window open." She said, "But let's examine this. Where is Frankenstein? Where does he live?" I said, "I don't know." She said, "Well, I know. He lives in Transylvania, which is very far away. So he would have to get money to buy a railway ticket to a seaport. He has to go to Hamburg. He has to go to Bremen. It's a long ride and a lot of money, just to get to the seaport, to get a boat. We're in America, and we're very far from there."

"Okay," she said, "so let's say he gets the money and he buys a ticket. He gets on a boat, and it takes him a long time to get here. When he gets to America, he doesn't know which subway to take. There's the BMT, there's the IRT, the Independent . . . He doesn't know his way around New York. Let's say he gets lucky, and he finds Brooklyn, and he finds Williamsburg, and he finds 365 South 3rd Street. When he goes up our fire escape to the first window below us that window is open, too. He's going to eat everybody *there*. He's going to be happy. He isn't going to climb up to the fifth floor. He's going to eat everybody on the first floor." So I said, "Okay, mom. Open the window." She won. Her logic won me over.

My mother: her husband, my father, died when I was only two. She raised four boys. My brother Irving was twelve, and Lenny was seven or eight, and Bernie was six, and I was two. She was left with these four boys. We had a great-aunt Sadie who gave half her salary to my mother. My grandmother lived across the hall, and she helped us. Everybody helped us.

We lived in this fourteen- or sixteen-dollar-a-month apartment . . . Happy to be there, happy to have family. I was five. I had no idea we were poor. I don't think my brothers knew we were poor either. We had enough to eat, and we played ball, and went to school, and had friends. We were never, "Woe is me, we live in poverty." We liked franks and beans.

LaGrandeur: That's a great story about your first encounter with *Frankenstein*.

Mel Brooks: It's a great story, isn't it? It's true.

LaGrandeur: I think that's my favorite story so far.

Mel Brooks: Yeah. I never forgot . . . From five years old to, I don't know, my thirties. A long time, it stuck with me.

LaGrandeur: I think you did the voice of a cat in *Young Franken-stein*, right: a screeching cat in the background of one scene?

Mel Brooks: I did the cat, who got hit with one of the darts [thrown by one of the characters during a dialogue]. Nobody could do the cat like me [Brooks screeches very convincingly like an angry cat].

LaGrandeur: I was wondering, if Mary Shelley were here right now, and you could say anything you wanted to about your movie or her book, what would you say to her?

Mel Brooks: I'd probably say, "Miss Wollstonecraft, you're a genius, and whatever money Fox gives me, you're in for a third. It's a third for Gene [Wilder], a third for me, and a third for you." I would hug her, and kiss her, and tell her what an inspired story she wrote and what a genius she was, to write something so imaginative and creative and profound, at such an early age. I would tell her how grateful we all are for her genius, her gift. That's what I would have said. But I would have let her in for a third of the money, too.

LaGrandeur: You yourself, I know, are a musician. You played the drums, and the piano, up in the Borscht Belt. So is that why you played a pretty big part in doing the score for *Young Frankenstein*?

Mel Brooks: Oh, yeah. I wrote every song, music and lyrics. About sixteen, seventeen songs in *Young Frankenstein*, and I wrote them all. Some of them are really good, and some of them could be improved.

LaGrandeur: I've always been fascinated by your conversion of your movies to musicals on Broadway. You did the same thing with *Young Frankenstein*. I was wondering if you could talk a little bit about how that came about.

Mel Brooks: I was between and betwixt. *The Producers* was such a big success and so naturally became a candidate for something more. And I also thought maybe *Blazing*

Saddles might work as a play, so I was caught between doing something with *Blazing Saddles* or *Young Frankenstein*. I thought that *Frankenstein* itself was operatic, was big, big stuff, and it had to do with a great father and son story. I feel that Dr. Frankenstein and the monster really are father and son. I said, "It's a great, big emotional story and a lot of it could be very funny with the right guy playing Igor." I thought it would work. Actually, between you and me, I'm doing it. I'm taking the musical and bringing it to London this coming fall . . . This coming late winter or fall. [Note: it is in fact opening at London's West End Theatre in Autumn 2017.]

LaGrandeur: You're going to revive it.

Mel Brooks: I'm going to revive it, yeah. It ran for over a year on Broadway, but it should have run for longer. I just think . . . I got some calls from some London theaters wanting it, so I asked Susan Stroman [director of the Broadway version of *The Producers*], who is a genius of a woman like Mary Shelley, if she would stage it. I would actually direct the comedy, and together we would find a great English cast, and we would have some fun. I love it so much. It will be a pleasure to see it again on the stage, and in London. It never played on the London stage.

When I do the musical version of *Young Frankenstein* onstage there, and when we get to the part in the laboratory scene where Victor throws the third switch on the machine that enlivens the monster, I'm going to have the theater explode with some sort of special effect. Not just on the stage, but in the audience, too, when Victor says, "Damn your eye. Throw it, I say. Now the third switch. Throw it . . ." The third switch is a very important moment in the creation of the monster. I'm going to have the effect of *papier-mâché* bits, exploding all over the theater, behind the people in the audience, on top of them. What will fall on them are little pieces of confetti that look like parts of the ceiling plaster, giving the effect the building has come apart. It might scare the hell out of them. Maybe I'd better think twice about that.

7

SINCE *FRANKENSTEIN*: EXPERIMENTAL SCIENCE AND EXPERIMENTAL FILM

Alexis Gambis

FRANKENSTEIN AND *CHIMERA* EXPERIMENTS

F rankenstein, the story written two hundred years ago by Mary Shelley, has become a media phenomenon. Beginning with the first film version made in 1910 by Thomas Edison, it has gone on to generate myriads of adaptations for film, television, and the stage, right up to the present day. The most famous of these is the 1931 film *Frankenstein* directed by James Whale, starring Boris Karloff as the monster created by the scientist Henry Frankenstein (renamed from Victor Frankenstein, the scientist in Shelley's book). In the film's most famous and powerful scene, Henry in his laboratory draws on a massive electrical jolt from lightning to animate the collection of body parts he has assembled. As Henry sees the first twitches of life appear in the creature, he is overcome and distraught, saying in amazement, "It's alive! It's alive! It's alive! . . . Now I know what it feels like to be God!"

This is one of the most dramatic scientific experiments ever to be put on a movie screen. In its audacious portrayal of the creation of life, the scene raises strong emotions. For the filmmaker and the scientist, it raises questions about science filmmaking and the many attempts, borderline delusional or freakish at times, to repurpose and re-create scientific experimentation for popular consumption. The experiment, in reality typically tucked away in a dark, obscure, or inaccessible laboratory, instead becomes a public performance, a ritual, a drama like the scene in *Frankenstein*—changing chameleon-like into myriad forms, identities, and meanings.

In 2017, on the tenth anniversary of Imagine Science Films—a nonprofit organization dedicated to promoting science through film— we introduced *Chimera Experiments*, a feature-length anthology by ten independent filmmakers built around stories told by the most influential scientists of our time. Each filmmaker contributed a chapter about evolution, in each case centered around a being with a chimeric identity. Like Frankenstein's creature, stitched together from body parts, the film's segments are joined by a connective tissue of three rules that define how they flow into each other. Continuing the Frankensteinian theme of creating new forms of life, *Chimera Experiments* is about both natural and artificial evolution, the random or deliberate modification of an organism. In genetics, a chimera is an organism containing at least two different sets of DNA, so the film also comments on advances in genetic and transgenic science. It examines as well how interactions with other beings shape our existence. As a mixed-genre, science-driven anthology film, *Chimera Experiments* was the very first of its kind.

But inherently, the focus is on the experiment and how to record, dramatize, and interpret it. Are the constructs of the experiment malleable? Can we subvert the very meaning of an experiment? These questions bring us back to the birth of cinema and scientific discovery through photography and early motion pictures.

THE FIRST "RECORDED" EXPERIMENT

Visual imagery has been an increasingly important part of how we present and communicate scientific ideas. Statistician and data visionary Edward Tufte claims, and rightly so, that visual information should be layered and organized for the viewer's understanding and engagement. It is precisely the singular, eye-catching packaging of data that will allow the viewer to process an image and give it meaning. Gaps are filled, areas are highlighted, and connections are drawn. Slowly 2-D images are transformed into 3-D experiences, simultaneously taking on a universal meaning for the many and a more subjective, personalized value tailored to, or derived by, the individual viewer.

In his book *Envisioning Information*, Tufte emphasizes the importance of "Small Multiples," where a series of images is laid out and structured to transparently reveal the movement over time of a data set. The panels come together and collectively form a narrative surface. The concept of Small Multiples, predating the birth of cinema, goes as far back as the photographic studies of motion in the late 1800s by Eadweard Muybridge. In his photographic plates, Muybridge displays exquisite studies of locomotion, from moving objects to animals and humans. These *études* led to the first films ever made, notably F. Percy Smith's use of time-lapse photography in *The Birth of a Flower*. They also stood as the precursors to today's rampant, time-bending clips and animated gifs. It is no surprise that the term "cinematography" coined by the Lumière brothers, the pioneers of early filmmaking, means the "art or science of motion-picture photography" (note the interchangeable "art" and "science" in the definition). Today, with technological advances, our fascination and experimentation with motion persists as it reflects our own time-sensitive existence. Whether it is a tree dancing in response to the weather, a father taking portraits of his growing child over fifteen years, or a baby recorded sleeping with the new iPhone time-lapse option, we marvel at the evolving (or revolving) of hybrid life-forms over days, weeks, or years that are condensed into a few seconds.

Hence, as we reflect on the role of the moving image in the context of scientific communication, we first make a detour and pay homage to its origins. Filmmaking was developed and arose from scientific fascination with the notion of movement, and was in its early form an extension of "the experiment." And yet over time, filmmaking moved away from its prestigious empirical and scientific value to become increasingly relegated to the ranks of entertainment and popularization.

THE EVOLUTION OF THE SCIENTIFIC EXPERIMENT

Filmmaking has recently been depreciated or undervalued as a means of disseminating scientific data. Perhaps the cinematographic format in the advent of the digital age has become so democratized that it has lost its rigor and its standards. Film steps down from its pedestal and becomes known as its lesser electronic counterpart: video. A film renamed as "video" takes on a more popular persona, and scientifically sound experiments "on tape" are hard to pinpoint in the infinite oceans of YouTube videos, where kids pretend to be Lady Gaga or cats play the piano. Concomitantly, the two words "scientific filmmaking" resonate with science fiction flicks or popular news coverage, where science is dumbed down, overly simplified, or sensationalized. The static rather than the moving image moves to the front row of scientific diligence.

And yet, in the past decade video has resurged and redefined itself. Web series are increasingly popular, and YouTube initiatives such as the international news channel Vice News are more respected and celebrated. In the scientific sphere, video has similarly come back in force. Byte-sized clips become the language for sharing data among scientists and directly with the public. Science videos even take on a "hip" factor as many scientific recordings go viral, such as one made to show the beating heart of a zebra fish embryo. Microscopes are hooked up to cameras, animated simulations are rendered from data sets, and scientists maintain web pages that give viewers dynamic interactive tours of their workspaces, though these may be as remote and isolated as Henry Frankenstein's laboratory. Through the medium of digital video, scientific data, once exchanged only among experts, is democratized, made widely and easily sharable through open access. Video tools have also propelled the Do-It-Yourself (DIY) movement in biology and other fields, where the public interacts directly with working scientists, often culminating in interdisciplinary projects that may not be feasible within the confines of an institution.

Moving from the popular front, video recently has made a few cameo appearances in the buttoned-up world of scientific publishing. For many research journals with high impact in the scientific community, video is present but relegated to the not-so-glamorous section called Supplementary Material, available only online to complement the printed article, which is still the main repository of the reported research. Thereby the videos awkwardly exist as "add-ons" in various web formats that frequently do not play correctly. This is slowly changing with more reliable web video platforms and the increasingly obsolete nature of printed material. The highly reputable journal *Cell* has introduced "video abstracts" that are produced by research scientists to complement their written abstracts that appear in print. *Nature* magazine frequently highlights research in its new section called Nature Videos—short, quirky films featured on the main site and promoted on social networks. Perhaps the most striking inclusion of "data as movies" is in the *Journal of Visualized Experiments* (JoVE), where video is the new metric for peer-reviewed scientific publishing and the presentation of methods and materials. Granted, JoVE submissions lack quality control, but they have the merit of positioning this digital format as the centerpiece for discussion.

It is to ride this "scientific new wave" that Imagine Science Films came into existence ten years ago. Since its beginnings, its objective has been to present and celebrate scientific visual data as "movies" and to organize a New York City–wide science film festival that previously had not existed. In these ways, the organization fosters a dialogue between scientists and artists. *Nature* and *Science* magazines, often considered rivals in the scientific publishing world, happily coexist as the founding sponsors of the weeklong film festival, a celebration of science and cinema. Continuing a ten-year-old tradition, films are selected based on their potential to be "hybrid"—a mix of aesthetics and accuracy in scientific storytelling. No restrictions are placed on form or source: documentary, fiction, home videos, lab footage, and music videos from anybody regardless of background are all accepted. But at its core, the aim is to present scientific experiments as cinematic experiences, and thereby scientists as filmmakers.

THE CONTROLLED EXPERIMENT

This all began a few years ago at the Union Hall bar in Park Slope, Brooklyn, which hosted the weekly Secret Science Club (SSC). Today, it is a mega event attracting on a weekly basis hundreds of people, who line up outside the Bell House in the Gowanus section of Brooklyn. Back in its early days at the Union Hall bar, SSC was more "secretive," when Nobel laureate Eric Kandel would come from uptown to Brooklyn and sneak onstage after hours to give a lecture on memory and his life story to a small, eclectic, inebriated group. It was marvelous, and it felt momentous as I stood in the back row with a small digital camcorder recording the event. One evening in the fall of 2008, after a few years of doing video recording for the SSC, I proposed an evening of short films entitled "Controlled Experiments." For over sixty minutes, the audience watched an experimental program composed of a mishmash of surreal medical animations, home videos acted and directed by scientists, model organisms in their experimental habitats, and microscopic avant-garde interludes. The audience seemed intrigued, concerned, fascinated—all symptoms of something new, strange, yet compelling.

It did not matter whether the experiments on the big screen were published or unpublished, finished or unfinished. Some videos were works in progress, defined as ongoing experiments by scientists or rough cuts by filmmakers. But terminology was not important in the dark theater. Scientific data unraveled on the big screen and took on a life of its own. The videos stitched together seemed like individual scenes of a feature film. Reminiscent of the Lumière brothers' fifty-second *Actualities* of everyday life, these scientific episodes took on a new dimension and became the staple food of the newly established Imagine Science Film Festival. Once upon a time, film was sequestered in Nickelodeon-type black boxes but then made its way to the big silver screen. Now, scientific videos, stored in out-of-the-way lab areas or on computer hard drives, are unpacked and presented as cinematic experiences.

A "STAGED" EXPERIMENT

Experiment is film and film is experiment. And with that interchangeable notion, the hope is to further explore the visual representations of scientific data, especially in the framework of the experiment. At Imagine Science Films, two initiatives were created after our first film festival. "Scenes" is a repository of scientific raw footage directly sourced from labs around the world and displayed online. "Live Stream" is a hack-the-city-type series, where we set up web cameras in labs and hook them up to optical instruments so that anybody in the world can probe the scientific process in a voyeuristic fashion, with the consent of the participating laboratories.

With these efforts, the objective is to bend the limits of "the experiment" and better understand how it is perceived by scientists, artists, and the larger public. And yet, as we do so, are we deviating from scientific rigor in these experiments? Or does it, quite to the contrary, broaden the possibilities of science and encourage interdisciplinary collaborations? I leave that to the spectator to decide. However, going back to early cinema and documentary filmmaking, Robert Flaherty's famous documentary film from 1922, *Nanook of the North*, was initially criticized as untruthful because it had some fabricated moments. But soon after, staged realities and the behind-the-scenes of filmmaking were embraced, leading to new languages in cinema, notably cinema verité. It was even proposed that reenactments and poetic experimentation could help us get closer to the objective truth about people and places. With this in mind, why can't recorded scientific experiments follow the same trajectory and make science more transparent by showing and enlarging the scientific method via new display techniques and fusion with other art forms?

To some extent this is already beginning to take place. Experiments are leaving the confines of the lab to happen all around us. For example, Noah Hutton's film *Bluebrain*, a product of his multiyear project tracking the iterations of a mysterious synthetic brain down to the molecular level, is projected at midnight on billboards in New York's Times Square. Filmmakers and performers are also collaborating with scientists and reimagining the conditions and output of an experiment. In one example, performance artist Marina Abramović is revisiting her show "The Artist is Present." In the original version presented at various sites, including New York's Museum of Modern Art, she simply sat in a gallery for long periods, totally available to the gaze and close inspection of any and all visitors to the gallery. The new idea is to couple her enduring presence with recordings of the neural activity of participants, including herself.

While some may deprecate the repurposing of scientific experimentation simply to produce the pleasures of performance or the cinema, the serious central purpose is to question the framework of an experiment, including its protocol, time line, process, variables, and expectations. After all, science is never completely objective. It is important to play with the form of documentary and storytelling experiments to pose the question of what is staged and what is real. I would argue that doing so increases transparency, making misconceptions, irregularities, and data fabrications less common.

FIGURE 1: An engraving by Theodor von Holst, which was the frontispiece to the 1831 edition, depicting the moment when Victor Frankenstein first looks upon his reanimated handiwork. It is a visual dynamic to be repeated many times. Symbols of learning, science, and rationalism are prominently featured alongside *memento mori*, or reminders of death. *Courtesy of the University of Toronto Library.*

FIGURE 2 (LEFT): This engraving by Nathaniel Whittock from a painting by Charles Thomas Wageman's depicts T. P. Cooke as the Monster in Richard Brimley Peake's 1823 play, *Presumption, or the Fate of Frankenstein*, which was the first stage adaptation of Shelley's novel.

FIGURE 3 (BOTTOM): Charles Ogle as the Monster in the first cinematic adaptation of *Frankenstein*, directed by J. Searle Dawley for the Edison Company in 1910. His version, which has the creature emerging from a steaming cauldron of chemicals, boils down the events in Shelley's novel to a film that runs less than fifteen minutes.

FIGURE 4 (ABOVE): In the midst of the Great Depression, celebrated American artist Lynd Ward produced a number of dramatic woodcuts for a 1934 edition of *Frankenstein*. This plate shows the Monster regarding his own hideousness in a pool, a crucial moment in the development of the creature's consciousness. *Copyright © 1934 Harrison Smith & Robert Haas.* FIGURE 5 (RIGHT): A testament to the growing popularity of Shelley's creation, this 1882 cartoon by John Tenniel appeared in the long-running satirical magazine, *Punch*, and presents the Irish pro-Independence Fenian movement as a Frankenstein's monster. *Drawing by John Tenniel,* Punch *Magazine.*

THE IRISH FRANKENSTEIN.

FIGURES 6 (ABOVE) AND 7 (BELOW): Dr. Frankenstein (Colin Clive) exults at the first signs of life in his creation in what is arguably the best-known adaptation of Shelley's novel, James Whale's 1931 film for Universal Studios. Boris Karloff's performance as the monster, and Jack Pierce's make-up effects, would become the definitive representation of Frankenstein's creature. *Copyright © 1931, 2004 Universal Studios Inc.*

FIGURE 8 (ABOVE): Another scene from James Whale's iconic film. FIGURE 9 (BELOW): Whale's sequel, *The Bride of Frankenstein* (1934), is in some ways truer to the spirit of Mary Shelley's story. Here, the mate (Elsa Lanchester) Frankenstein has been forced to create for his creature—demanded by the Monster, and never fulfilled by his maker in the novel—reacts less than enthusiastically at the sight of her Intended. *Copyright © 1934, 2004 Universal Studios Inc.*

FIGURE 10 (ABOVE): The Universal version of *Frankenstein* and the Pierce-Karloff version of the monster has been frequently referenced and parodied. In 1937, animator Frank Tashlin merged Dr. Frankenstein and his Monster into "Borax Karoff" in the cartoon *Porky's Road Race*, produced at Warner Bros.' animation unit. *Copyright © 1992 MGM/UA Home Video and Turner Entertainment.*
FIGURE 11 (BELOW): Familiarity breeds contempt, or at least comedy. By the end of the '40s, the monsters that had shocked audiences in the 1930s were becoming the stuff of juvenile entertainment and farce. *Abbot and Costello Meet Frankenstein* (Charles Barton, 1948) has the cross-talk duo butting heads with Dracula (Bela Lugosi), the Wolf Man (Lon Chaney, Jr.) and the Monster (Glenn Strange). *Copyright © 2000 Universal Studios Home Entertainment.*

FIGURE 12 (ABOVE): A monster superstar by any standard come the 1960s, Frankenstein's creature made numerous small–screen television appearances, many of them comic. *The Munsters* (1964) revived the Universal creature as a lovably goofy suburban dad, Herman (Fred Wynn), happily married to a vampiress (Yvonne DeCarlo). *Copyright © 2008 Universal Studios Home Entertainment.* FIGURE 13 (BELOW): A decidedly depraved Frankenstein (Peter Cushing) prepares to revive his creation a second time in *The Curse of Frankenstein* (Terence Fisher, 1957). True to the luridly violent tone of the Hammer series, the compulsively homicidal Monster (Christopher Lee) tried to throttle its maker within moments of its first rebirth and had to be executed (again). *Copyright © 1957, 1985 Warner Bros.*

FIGURE 14 (ABOVE): Echoes of Shelley's powerful ideas often resound in even the silliest of *Frankenstein* media adaptations. In a scene in *The Monster Squad* (Fred Dekker, 1987), echoing Mary Shelley and the work of Lynd Ward (see Figure 4), the Monster (Tom Noonan) looks with dismayed recognition at a plastic Halloween mask of the 1931 Universal monster. *Copyright © 1987 Taft Entertainment.* FIGURE 15 (BELOW): "He was my father," says the Monster (Robert De Niro) at the deathbed of Victor Frankenstein (Kenneth Branagh) in Branagh's lavish 1994 adaptation, *Mary Shelley's Frankenstein.* One of the most complete cinematic versions of the story, it is also one of the few occasions where a major movie star has been cast as the Monster. *Copyright © 1998 Columbia/ Tri-Star Home Video.*

FIGURE 16 (ABOVE): The 19th century monster gets a 21st century makeover using both digital visual effects and traditional special effects in *Van Helsing* (Stephen Sommers, 2004), another monster mash-up prominently featuring Frankenstein's creation. This is one of many pop-culture takes on the Monster, here played by Shuler Hensley, that redeem the creature through acts of heroism. *Copyright © 2004 Universal Studios.* FIGURE 17 (BELOW): In *Penny Dreadful* (2014–2016), a guilt-ridden and bewitched Victor Frankenstein (Harry Treadaway, center) is tormented by visions of his "hideous progeny:" the nameless Creature (Rory Kinnear, left), his second draft, Proteus (Alex Price, crouching below Victor), and Lily, the woman resurrected to be the Creature's bride (Billie Piper). *Copyright © 2016 Showtime Networks, Paramount.*

FIGURES 18–19 (RIGHT AND BELOW): Costumes, dolls and figures replicate movie and book characters, as "Frankenstein" figures from the "Universal Monsters and the Mad Monsters" series illustrate. *Courtesy of Figures Toy Company www.figurestoycompany.com.*

FIGURES 20–24 (ALL ON OPPOSITE PAGE): Artist Jason Freeny of Maryland produces something like scientific dissections within repurposed toys by creating skeletons inside popular children's toys. *Courtesy of Jason Freeny https://jasonfreeny.com.*

FIGURE 25: "Franklin to Frankenstein," the cartoon version of the connection between Ben Franklin's experiments with electricity and Mary Shelley's *Frankenstein*. *Courtesy of Dwayne Godwin and Jorge Cham.*

FIGURE 26 (ABOVE): A science experiment inadvertently affects gravity in town. Just another day for Sheriff Jack Carter to save in Eureka. *Copyright © NBC Universal Television.* FIGURE 27 (BELOW): Holly Marten (in hologram form) and Douglas Fargo watch the bio-printer build a perfect replica of Holly's body, cell by cell. *Copyright © NBC Universal Television.*

FIGURE 28 (ABOVE): Holly Marten (Felicia Day)'s "consciousness" is downloaded into her new bio-printed body. *Copyright © NBC Universal Television.* FIGURE 29 (BELOW): The Astraeus crew is held in suspended animation with their minds jacked into "Virtual Eureka" through a photonic computer. *Copyright © NBC Universal Television.*

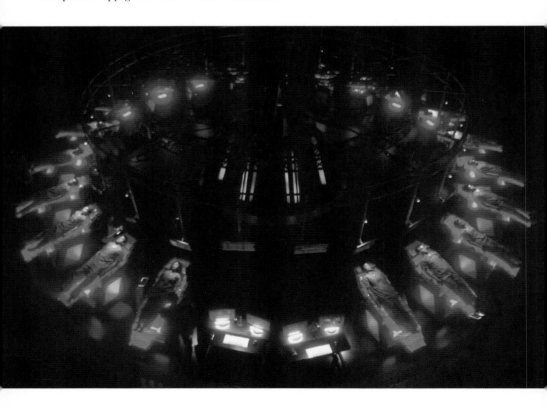

FIGURE 30 (ABOVE): Sen. Michaela Wen (Ming-Na Wen) un-plugs Holly Marten (Felicia Day) from Virtual Eureka, ending her life, and causing a permanent rift with mastermind, Beverly Barlowe (Debrah Farentino). *Copyright © NBC Universal Television.* FIGURE 31 (BELOW): *A rat's dream (or nightmare)* (Fabian Kloosterman, 2010): Hippocampal neurons called "place cells" are activated in distinct locations while a rat runs through a maze. *Copyright © Fabian Kloosterman, 2010.*

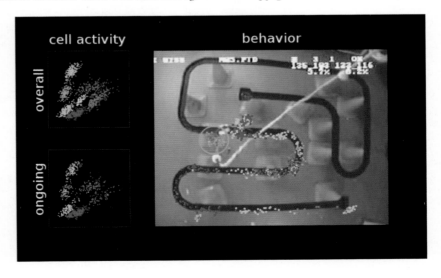

FIGURE 32 (ABOVE): *Blank* (Boris Hans-Tschacotin, 2011). A journey through memory loss. *Copyright © Boris Hans-Tschacotin, 2011.* FIGURE 33 (BELOW): *Carlitopolis* (Luis Nieto, 2006) scientific experiment or performance; confessions of Carlito the mouse. *Copyright © Luis Nieto, France, 2006.*

RODENT EXPERIMENTS: THREE CASE STUDIES

Experiments both stem from and cause accidental encounters and discoveries. In the pursuit of experimentation, there is always a strong sense of human relatability and the illusion of control.

Few people have made real science films that convey scientific ideas and experiments with the same immediacy as the fictional animation scene in *Frankenstein*. But scientists have made short experimental films that, while not reaching that level of drama, show how to directly present science on film. I present below three typical experimental films that Imagine Science Films would show as part of our Controlled Experiments program, which blur the lines between fact and fiction. With these films, one hopes to communicate the following driving message: one does not need to bend scientific facts to make them exciting and thrilling.

A rat's dream (or nightmare) (Fabian Kloosterman, 2010) (Figure 31, image insert)

As quoted in an article by Jay Lindsay published in the *Washington Post*, this work opened "a new door into the study of dreams," according to Matt Wilson, a neuroscientist at MIT and director of the lab where the study in the film was carried out. The article added that the researchers say "they have entered the dreams of rats and found them busily working their way through the same lab mazes they negotiate during the day," and went on to explain:

> The rats in this MIT study were hooked up to a device that measured the pattern of neurons firing in the hippocampus, an area of the brain known to be involved in memory. The scientists had the mice perform specific tasks in a maze that produced very distinctive patterns of brain activity. When [the scientists] repeatedly saw almost exactly the same patterns reproduced during sleep, they concluded the rats were dreaming about

running through the maze . . . The correlation was so great that scientists said they could place where in the maze the rat was dreaming it was.

Blank (Boris Hans–Tschacotin, 2011) (Figure 32, image insert)

How does one study Alzheimer's in model organisms? Rather than describe the results and findings of a new study using rodents, why not experience it firsthand and partake in the experiment as if you were the scientist? Over the voice of a scientist explaining the study and its methods, a mouse desperately tries to find a platform hidden right under the surface of the water in a basin. Children laughing faintly reverberates in the distance. *Blank* reproduces the sterile conditions of a genetic laboratory of molecular medicine. The room, the bodies, and the cells of the animals are subject to the strictest controls.

Carlitopolis (Luis Nieto, 2006) (Figure 33, image insert)

On a stage, artist–scientist and self-proclaimed "perversionist" Luis Nieto blows up a mouse in a black box using a straw. A mix of realistic takes and synthesized images makes us question the reality of these images and words. *Carlitopolis* reveals a student who presents his senior project in front of a jury: a simple act that slowly becomes an absurd and unusual performance, wherein a small lab mouse named Carlito goes through a number of experiences. What is real? What is not? A mixture of real images and special effects makes us doubt the veracity of images and words too.

SCIENTIFIC DATA IN MAINSTREAM CINEMA

The next big question is how to bring these experiments from the lab through the graffiti-covered corridors of underground cinema to mainstream cinema complexes—those frequented by your neighbors and relatives. Some films closer to the mainstream do already make direct use of scientific data. A few examples: Terence Malick supplemented his film *Tree of Life* (2011) with scientific data generated by supercomputers, interspersed in the story of a family in Waco, Texas, in 1956. And yet the imagery is not fully integrated; it still feels a bit too intentional and slightly disjointed from the rest of the film. Unfortunately, despite its cast of well-known stars, this indie film played primarily in art houses and never completely entered the mainstream film circuit. As preparation for the film *The Science of Sleep* (2006), its writer/director Michel Gondry studied dreams in Robert Stickgold's sleep research laboratory at Harvard, which influenced Gondry's representation of dreams in the film. In 2013, Alfonso Cuarón's film *Gravity* was applauded and rewarded for its hyperrealism and zero-gravity 360° spanning special effects. At the other end of the spectrum, IMAX films such as *Flight of the Butterflies* (2012) or *A Beautiful Planet* (2016) directly present science yet for the most part lack narrative appeal. They are targeted for educational purposes and play in museums or academic settings rather than mainstream movie complexes.

The real challenge is to create films that seamlessly fold scientific experiments into animal and/or human drama. By doing so, "science films" become simply "films." Adding the term "science" to "film" can often mute the cinematic attributes of a given film.

It is said that in 1895, at the dawn of cinema, people ran out of cafés and theaters when they saw a train coming at them on the movie screen, not yet understanding what film was and imagining that the train would tear through the screen. How will they react when genetic engineering reaches the point where it can create a new life-form and the reality of that breakthrough laboratory experiment is shown on film? That genuine scientific moment will be far stranger, more fantastic and dramatic than the fictional scene where Dr. Frankenstein's creature rises up.

8

LIFE AFTER DEATH:
A LOVE STORY, "WHEN FARGO MET HOLLY"

Jaime Paglia

From the moment *Homo sapiens* developed the capacity to ponder the meaning of life, our species has imagined ways to postpone death. The concept of reanimation has inspired some of our greatest science fiction writers to explore the potential wonders that modern science promises by extending or enhancing life and the moral questions that come with playing God. Mary Shelley's *Frankenstein, or The Modern Prometheus* set the standard for a genre that has inspired thousands of storytellers over the past two centuries, including a season arc by the writers of a little television show called *Eureka*.

In 2004, Andrew Cosby and I came up with a concept for a TV dramedy that would be something of a love letter to science fiction. The series follows Jack Carter (Colin Ferguson), a dry-witted US marshal who stumbles onto a hidden town in the Pacific Northwest that doesn't appear on any maps. Eureka turns out to be a secret government think tank comprised of the brightest minds in science that is decades ahead of the rest of the world technologically. Founded shortly after World War II by Albert Einstein and Harry Truman, Eureka was designed to be an idyllic safe haven where the world's greatest thinkers were invited to live and create in peace. The problem is, when you're constantly pushing the boundaries of science, that frequently creates chaos. That's where Carter comes in. After an experiment goes awry in the pilot episode, Carter uses his street smarts and keen investigative skills to save the town from disaster. As reward (or punishment), he finds himself reassigned against his will to be the new town sheriff. (Figure 26, image insert). Each week, our brilliant scientists at the top-secret Global Dynamics research facility create wonders that could save the world or destroy it. Sheriff Jack Carter is our modern-day Andy Griffith tasked with protecting Eureka's geniuses from themselves, and keeping the lid on Pandora's box. He is the lay audience's eyes into a world of infinite possibility where the scientists are more concerned with the question, Can we? than, Should we?

From the outset, we wanted to create a show that could play with the myriad concepts and ethical issues raised in classic science fiction stories and tropes but with a lighthearted, modern twist. Over seven years, we covered everything from artificial intelligence to zeta-waves. We paid homage to dozens of favorites, from *Close Encounters of the Third Kind* to *The Time Machine*, from *The Blob* to *The Invisible Man*, from *Night of the Living Dead* to *Invasion of the Body Snatchers*. In the final season, we did our version of *Frankenstein* with a long arc following the life, death, and reanimation of Dr. Holly Marten.

To give a little context for the significance of resurrecting Holly's character, you need to understand the unique background of the actress who played her. Holly was envisioned as a quirky genius love interest for a character named Douglas Fargo (Neil Grayston), the nerdy wunderkind director of Global Dynamics. Holly would be an adorably awkward rocket scientist with off-the-charts intelligence and effortless likability. The only person we considered for the role was Felicia Day. For those not schooled in Geek 101, Felicia created, wrote, directed, produced, and starred in the groundbreaking web series *The Guild*. She was a regular presence in Joss Whedon's universe with roles on *Buffy the Vampire Slayer*, *Dollhouse*, and, most pertinent to our *Frankenstein* theme, the cult favorite *Dr. Horrible's Sing-Along Blog*, playing Penny, the ill-fated object of Dr. Horrible's affection. SPOILER ALERT: Penny dies. Dr. Horrible weeps. And a super-villain is born. Fans around the globe still mourn Penny's heartbreaking demise. So . . . we thought, wouldn't it be crazy to cast Felicia Day in *another* lovable role, get the audience to adore her, then kill her again? But this time, we had the potential to give her a happy ending.

Okay, truth: we didn't know when we first cast Felicia that we were going to kill her character, much less bring her back to life. That would come later. The original contract was for a handful of episodes with an option for more. Lucky for us, Felicia was a natural fit for our show, and we extended her stay to the end. The main reason her character, Holly, had come to Eureka was to deliver the news that Global Dynamics had been awarded a multibillion-dollar research contract to mount the first manned space flight using faster-than-light technology (the somewhat unintentional by-product of a previous experiment gone wrong). This kicked off a season-long arc as our heroes prepared and trained for the Astraeus mission to Titan, Saturn's largest moon, a place real-life scientists believe may be capable of sustaining life.

For anyone who has considered watching *Eureka*, let me suggest that you stop procrastinating and come back to this chapter later, because there are MAJOR SPOILERS AHEAD.

At the end of Season 4.5, the *Astraeus* crew (including Holly and Fargo) enters hyper-sleep as the ship prepares to launch, but something goes terribly wrong. During the final countdown, someone outside of Eureka hijacks mission control and changes the destination coordinates for the space jump. The *Astraeus* and its crew disappear in spectacular fashion as Sheriff Carter and our genius heroes watch helplessly. The cliffhanger leaves everyone in shock, wondering where the ship has gone and who is responsible for the crew's disappearance.

This is where things get really diabolical. In Season 5, we discover that the *Astraeus* and her crew have been abducted by series antagonist Beverly Barlowe (Debrah Farentino) and her clandestine partners known only as "the consortium," a powerful group pledged to keeping disruptive technologies from disturbing the balance of power in the world. We later reveal that one of the leaders of the consortium is the woman who supported funding for the Astraeus mission, US senator Michaela Wen (Ming-Na Wen). This has been part of their grand plan all along. The big twist is that our genius crew-members don't realize they've been kidnapped. They are being kept in hyper-sleep with their brains jacked into a Matrix-like computer simulation that makes them believe their ship returned safely to Eureka after their mission went awry. But when they land, four years have passed since they disappeared. Having trapped our heroes in "Virtual Eureka," Beverly plans to monitor and mine their collective intellect in this virtual reality and co-opt any scientific advances they create for her group's real-world purposes. As Beverly says, "The greatest minds in Eureka are working for us now. And they don't even know it."

Whew! Now that you have some context, we can get back to the point of this chapter, which is to share how we approached paying homage to *Frankenstein* but with a Eureka twist.

To establish life-or-death stakes for our heroes, we made the decision in the writers' room that someone had to die. While the mortality rate in Eureka is three times higher than the national average (the potential risk of pushing the scientific envelope), we hadn't killed a major character since Season 3. That was when Carter's dry-witted foil, Dr. Nathan Stark (Ed Quinn), heroically sacrificed his life to help Carter save the town, leaving our audience stunned. Stark's death changed the dynamics of the characters as they came to terms with his loss, and injected the show with a renewed sense of unpredictability at a time when it was in danger of falling into the safety of formula. Now we had another opportunity to shake things up in Season 5. Given the heartbreaking death of Felicia Day's character in *Dr. Horrible's Sing-Along Blog*, we knew it would be unconscionable to kill her character again. Fans might never forgive us. After careful deliberation, we concluded that *we absolutely had to do it*. I mean, this was Eureka. A place where scientific miracles become reality every day. A world where Carter lives in an experimental smart-house named S.A.R.A.H. (Self-Actuated Residential Automated Habitat), which acts as his literal housewife and later falls in love with Carter's AI deputy, Andy (Kavan Smith). We had consistently tried to do unconventional things with conventional tropes. But we had yet to do a *Frankenstein* story. With Eureka's theoretical technologies at our disposal, we had the opportunity to bring Holly back to life in a completely unique and emotional way.

We laid out a season-long story arc for Holly that was divided into roughly three parts: death, recovery, and reanimation. The first four episodes showed the audience what Holly, Fargo, and the other crew members were experiencing inside Virtual Eureka while Sheriff Carter and our heroes searched for them back in the real world. Part of the challenge of Beverly Barlowe's kidnap plan was making Virtual Eureka feel real enough that the crew would not question it. By convincing them that four years had passed since their ship disappeared, they would be distracted by the emotional shock and less likely to question inconsistencies in their world. But we knew there would be technical challenges of computer processing power and real-time rendering as our unwitting crew-members interacted with the program. Consulting with our science adviser, Kevin Grazier, we saw an opportunity for this practical challenge to be the glitch that foils Beverly's otherwise perfect plan. Holly would be the one to figure it out, which would prove to be her tragic undoing.

In addition to being a genius rocket scientist, Holly Marten is also an avid video gamer (as is Felicia Day in real life). After witnessing a couple of bizarre rendering errors inside Virtual Eureka, she realizes that they must be in a Matrix-like construct similar to a video game. Before Holly can warn the other crew-members, the Senator pulls the plug on her, removing her character from the program and killing her in real life. The cold-blooded murder of Holly Marten leads Beverly Barlowe to break from Senator Wen and betray their cause. Beverly goes to Sheriff Carter to help him rescue the rest of the crew before they all meet the same fate.

With Beverly's assistance, the *Astraeus* ship and crew are recovered and Senator Wen is trapped in a virtual prison of her own, but Holly's death is a shock to the town. Fargo mourns the loss of the love of his life while our other characters manage the aftermath of their Virtual Eureka ordeal. Part of that process is running tests on the surviving crew–members to see if they've been physically or mentally altered by having been neural-networked to the Matrix mainframe. This being Eureka, Fargo tries to fast-forward through the stages of grief using a bioengineered grief patch, while an experimental high-tech fire-control tool called iFire wreaks havoc in town. They learn that the problem is being caused by the presence of the crew. Their EEGs show abnormal brainwave activity with a spike in bi-phasic delta waves, also known as zeta or *z-waves*. Once the Matrix computer is rebooted, another shocking discovery is made: the z-wave signature for Holly Marten is still present—*inside the Matrix mainframe.* Fargo reconnects himself to the neural network and finds that Holly has been wandering alone, stranded and scared inside an empty Virtual Eureka. Somehow her "consciousness" was trapped inside the computer mainframe when Senator Wen disconnected her body. Fargo is elated and geeks around the world rejoiced. Holly is "alive."

This kicks off the second part of Holly's arc as our heroes try to determine whether Holly is truly alive inside the mainframe or if she is simply a computer construct, a series of ones and zeroes, a ghost in the machine. And if she is essentially a software file, can she be recovered and given new hardware? With the Department of Defense coming to confiscate the Matrix computer, they don't have time to debate. They need to find a way to download Holly out of the mainframe before they lose her for good. Of course, it takes major storage space and processing power to house the digital file for a human being. Always looking to balance drama with humor, we decided to mine this dilemma for all it was worth. After being temporarily transferred into the Global Dynamics mainframe to escape the DOD, Holly "infects" the operating system, taking control of various high-tech equipment to relay messages to her rescuers before she is purged. In a race against time, Holly is downloaded onto the hard drive of the second most powerful artificial intelligence in town: Carter's smart house, S.A.R.A.H. Fargo could now interact with Holly as a holographic projection living in Carter's house. Fargo is thrilled, but life as a "Holly-gram" grows quickly frustrating for Holly and everyone else involved. It's awkward enough that Carter's robotic deputy has been dating his smart house (and having sleepovers plugged into her utility closet). They need a permanent, physical solution for Holly to rejoin the world. Thus begins Holly's humorous and emotional journey to reanimation as Eureka's geniuses try to figure out how to put Holly back into a working body. (Figures 27–30, image insert).

Mary Shelley's imagination was limited by the relatively primitive scientific tools available in the 1800s. Whereas in the famous 1931 Boris Karloff film *Frankenstein* Dr. Victor Frankenstein cobbled together body parts and reanimated the complete body through bioelectric galvanism, our scientists had the most sophisticated technology at their disposal. The writing staff always endeavored to ground our stories in cutting edge research that was at least theoretically possible. In the real world, scientists have been experimenting with bio-printers to create living tissue, bones, and cartilage. Using living cells instead of ink, they can literally print simple body parts like noses, windpipes, and ears that can be grafted onto human bodies. Soon scientists will be able to print complex organs, revolutionizing the need for transplants from donors. Taking biological fabrication technology to the next level, our Eureka geniuses, led by Henry Deacon (Joe Morton) and Zane Donovan (Niall Matter), plan to create an entire body for Holly. By combining a protein emulsion and undifferentiated somatic cells, they attempt to use Holly's DNA profile to print her a new body cell by cell, layer by layer, on an organic polymer lattice. Just a titch more sophisticated than Dr. Frankenstein stitching together random amputated extremities.

Of course, scientific experimentation being experimental, this is an incredibly complicated process, and early testing proves challenging. Fargo deems it too dangerous to risk losing Holly, so our heroes work in secret to bring his girlfriend back to life. Utilizing the best tech talk we could muster, they first attempt to outfit a body-blank test dummy with a spintronic microprocessor which will serve as a neural prosthetic into which they will download Holly's "brain." Sounds plausible, right? As Holly in hologram form watches hopefully, the processor overheats, melting the test dummy's head into a smoking pile of goo. "Ummm. We're gonna fix that, right?" she asks Zane and Henry nervously. When Fargo discovers their plan, he shuts the experiment down, accusing his friends of "trying to play Frankenstein" (our tip of the hat to Shelley). This leads to a fight between Fargo and Holly about what constitutes living. Fargo is content with having Holly back, even in non-corporeal form. Holly wants more. Just like Frankenstein's monster demanding that Victor create a mate for him, Holly won't settle for less with Fargo. A life without human connection and free will is not living. It's a prison sentence.

When Fargo finally agrees to move forward with the experiment, they reach the moment of truth. Like Dr. Frankenstein, Henry takes a moment to acknowledge the groundbreaking importance of what they are trying to achieve: "I was just marveling at the significance of what we are attempting. Holly is one in a billion. Like Henrietta Lax and the discovery of the immortal HELA cell. We are about to give her new life." Working with our incredible visual effects team led by Matthew S. Gore, Holly's body is printed on a bio-table, layer by layer, until a perfect copy is complete.

Then, in another homage to the electrifying moment of truth in *Frankenstein*, the switch is thrown and Holly's "consciousness" is transferred into the bio-printed body in a brilliant cocoon of pulsing electric energy. After a few tense moments, there are no vital signs. Just when Fargo thinks he has lost her for good, Holly sits up with a gasp, disoriented, but reanimated. She's *alive*.

As with Frankenstein's monster, Holly's reanimation does not go smoothly, which we played to both comedic and dramatic effect. At first, there is the childlike wonder of Holly acclimating to her new body. "Whoa! That was such a rush! Does my voice sound funny? These lips feel weird. Am I talking too much? I am, aren't I. Now it's awkward." They caution her to take things slowly while her systems acclimate and they keep her under observation in the lab. "Plus," Henry cautions, "we haven't prepared the town for your change in corporeal circumstances." Holly's reaction is a not-so-subtle acknowledgment that she is in fact a 21st-century version of Frankenstein's monster: "Ah. Yes. Don't want to spook the villagers." Indeed.

Like Frankenstein's monster, Holly relishes her new lease on life, wanting to indulge every appetite, both literally and figuratively. "There's nothing like dying to make you hungry to live. Oooh! Bring me some chocolate?" But it doesn't take long for the other proverbial shoe to drop. Holly begins having flashbacks to her ordeal in Virtual Eureka, including the memory of her death. Unable to distinguish memory from reality, she begins to unravel and becomes a danger to herself and others. In another little nod to *Frankenstein*, Holly goes on the run, but is found later by Fargo, hiding and terrified. With Holly's synapses misfiring and neural transponders degrading, they are left with no choice but to try and "reboot" her, running the neural transfer once again. The second time is the charm and Holly's systems stabilize. After going through the mountain of paperwork required to "undead" her, Fargo exclaims (with a nod to the 1931 movie), "You're alive!" Holly is officially back among the living, albeit with a few unique biotech enhancements. As the enormity of this scientific miracle lands on Holly, she is frozen by indecision. This is a second chance at life. An opportunity to do things differently. Should she continue the path she was on, or pursue something entirely new? After everything she's been through, what should she do next? Zane answers: "Whatever you want. You live your life." Even though their very definition of life has been forever changed.

For all of us in the writers' room, Holly's journey from death to reanimation was an opportunity to pay respect to a classic work of science fiction in our own Eureka-fied way. Whether one is a fan of Mary Shelley's book, the 1931 film, or any of the myriad adaptations that have followed, the subject matter and moral debate the Frankenstein story inspires are just as relevant for storytellers today as they were two hundred years ago. In the age of biotech, we are moving ever closer to the possibility of reanimation becoming a reality. The lines between life and death, man and machine, miracle or monster are being rewritten. For writers of science fiction, it is the gift that keeps on giving.

Kind of like life.

9

MONSTER NO MORE: A CONVERSATION WITH THE CREATORS OF *PENNY DREADFUL* AND *I, FRANKENSTEIN*

Eddy Von Mueller

In the two hundred years since its fateful first appearance in print, *Frankenstein, or the Modern Prometheus* has exercised a powerful hold on artists, authors, dramatists, illustrators, and creative professionals of every stripe. As the arts and media have marched ahead and new forms have emerged, at every stride, Frankenstein and his monster have been there. It comes as no surprise, then, to find Shelley's characters cropping up in some of the new century's most dynamic and popular media forms, including the serial cable drama, the graphic novel, and the contemporary big-screen special-effects spectacular. A conversation with the principal creative forces behind two noteworthy recent additions to the ever-growing body of *Frankenstein* content, the 2014 feature film *I, Frankenstein* and the cable television series *Penny Dreadful*, which ran for three seasons on the Showtime Network, highlights the ways in which screen artists today continue to mine a wealth of meaning and inspiration from Mary Shelley's remarkable book.

"It is amazing to me that this young person, essentially still a girl, wrote the book that has become, along with Sherlock Holmes and Dracula, one of our defining myths," said John Logan, the creator and showrunner of *Penny Dreadful*, who is effusive in his appreciation of Shelley's achievement. "I probably saw the Boris Karloff *Frankenstein* on black-and-white television," he recalls, and "the whole first and second generation Universal series, I watched them religiously." But it was the novel that most captured his imagination, and provided the spark for his ambitious series.

"I didn't read the book until after college," Logan recalls. "I assumed I had through osmosis seen every conceivable version of it on the screen [but] the book is so profoundly and shockingly different from the film treatments." Revisiting Mary Shelley's novel years later, during what he describes as a "deep dive into the works of Wordsworth, which led to Byron and Shelley and a study of all the romantics, just for pleasure," he was struck by the psychological complexity and linguistic beauty of the teenager's magnum opus. "It's a doppelgänger story: two separate people, two sides of the soul at war with each other—both eloquent, both fearful, both strangely innocent. The binary relationship between Dr. Frankenstein and his creature, and the eloquence of the creature, which I had forgotten since I read the book in the '80s, was so overpowering I thought, 'Oh my God, I want to do a *Frankenstein* version which really deals with that elemental issue, with the proper poetry.'"

That impulse to capture the depth and poetic richness of Shelley's book grew into a complex ensemble drama about Vanessa Ives (Eva Green), a "deeply religious woman" caught up in a web of dark supernatural forces in the Victorian era, which Logan describes as a "microcosm of our own world." Though the series draws on a dazzling array of 19th- and 20th-century sources—it is in some ways a grand pastiche of horror and the uncanny in film and literature, riffing on Oscar Wilde, Robert Louis Stevenson, Bram Stoker, and H. Rider Haggard, and involving witches, werewolves, vampires, voodoo, Colonial-era curses from Egypt and Africa and indigenous America—Logan puts the characters of Ives and Frankenstein's Creature at the center. Indeed, Rory Kinnear, who plays Frankenstein's first reanimate—in *Penny Dreadful*, the obsessive and occasionally drug-addled doctor (Harry Treadaway) creates three—was the first person cast, and the actor for whom the part was written. "I went into *Penny Dreadful* ten years ago thinking about these two characters, Vanessa Ives and the Creature, two pure, sad souls trying to find peace in some way," said Logan, adding, "one of them does and one of them doesn't."

The series is named for the inexpensive and frequently violent and sensational novels of horror, romance, adventure, and suspense that became popular in mid-19th-century Britain. The forerunners of later pulp magazines and the crucible of much contemporary horror literature, the dreadfuls were issued as serials, each chapter cheaply printed and priced at a penny, putting them in reach of the period's fast-growing, newly literate population of urban laborers. An early example of mass culture, the dreadfuls are in some ways an apt pre-screen analog of the serialized storytelling 20th- and 21st-century audiences would consume in movie theaters and especially on radio and television.

Serialization, Logan says, is a great boon to storytellers. "The great luxury of television is time," Logan observed. "If you said to me, 'Try to present your version [of *Frankenstein*] in two hours,' I would have been frustrated. If you say to me, 'You have thirty hours to tell that story' . . . for a dramatist it's the most liberating way to look at your characters." The freedoms afforded Logan by the format of *Penny Dreadful* go beyond the temporal. The late '90s and early 2000s have seen a kind of renaissance in television drama, driven in part by the profitability of the surging cable industry, which swelled production budgets, and the relative expressive freedom allowed especially to premium cable networks like HBO and Showtime. From *The Sopranos* and *The Wire* to *Game of Thrones* and *House of Cards*, cable (and later streaming) dramas can create the kinds of looks and worlds, and tackle the kinds of subject matter (ornamented, of course, with the smattering of violence, nudity, and sex that inevitably enlivens narrative for popular adult audiences) that previously had been the exclusive province of theatrical feature films.

This new golden age of television also draws A-list talent to the small screen, in front of and behind the camera. Logan himself, already an accomplished playwright before entering the screen trade, has written boutique dramas such as *RKO 281* (Benjamin Ross, 1999) and *Genius* (Michael Grandage, 2016), in addition to big-money, high-concept blockbusters such as *The Last Samurai* (Edward Zwick, 2003), *Sweeney Todd* (Tim Burton, 2007), *Skyfall,* and *Spectre* (Sam Mendes, 2012, 2015). He's worked with some of contemporary Hollywood's most renowned filmmakers, including Ridley Scott (*Gladiator,* 2002 and *Alien: Covenant,* 2017) and Martin Scorsese (*The Aviator,* 2004 and *Hugo,* 2011). A three-time Academy Award nominee, Logan has shown a deft hand at period material—he's written stories set in ancient Rome, pre-Meiji Japan, 1930s Paris, and, in Simon Wells's 2002 reboot of *The Time Machine,* C.E. 802701.

This flair for the past is much in evidence throughout *Penny Dreadful,* both in terms of its language and the realization of the plot and setting, which include numerous elements of late-19th-century culture, from the sensationalist London press and Victorian vogues for photography, phonograph recordings, and opium to popular entertainments of the era, like American Wild West shows (William "Buffalo Bill" Cody's show traveled to England in 1887, a turn that included a command performance for Queen Victoria's Golden Jubilee) and waxwork museums. "I love research, and I'm bookish by nature," says Logan. "Going into some other culture allows a writer a freedom of language. This is my version of Victorian language, filtered through Rilke and Charles Dickens, Robert Browning and Christina Rossetti."

The narrative scope permitted by the cable series format allows *Penny Dreadful* to delve more deeply into the lives of the characters ("to cast more shadows and shine more light," as Logan put it), and to further explore the possible ramifications of a successful Victor Frankenstein, who is able to go beyond his troubled "first draft" and refine his techniques. Frankenstein's last essay in the art of resurrection, Lily (Billie Piper), provided the showrunner with the opportunity to tackle some of the complexities of gender, femininity, and sexuality in the Victorian era—and ours.

Unlike the mate for the monster in Mary Shelley's story (which is scrapped on the slab by Victor in the Product Development Phase, before the horrified eyes of his watching and enraged firstborn) and James Whale's dumbstruck, feral female creature in *The Bride of Frankenstein,* Logan's Lily has both a fully developed narrative arc and a powerful voice. "She has some of the longest speeches in a cast filled with wordy characters," he laughs, "it's such an extreme arc . . . [from] a Belfast tart, an innocent woman who turns out not to be so innocent because of all the degradations heaped on her by men, . . . who becomes an avenging angel." Logan clearly relished the opportunity to "write to the extremes" of the character. "She's like a pirate, she's like writing Long John Silver."

The character of Lily allows *Penny Dreadful* to lustily tread into a very wide range of generic and psychological territories, and provides a platform to critique the plight of women and the poor: her existence creates a pseudo-incestuous love triangle between herself, Victor, and the Creature, and even before her reanimation, she is already one of the millions of "walking dead" slowly succumbing to the scourge of tuberculosis. According to Logan, Lily Frankenstein is a deliberately and complexly feminist character. "There was always in my political consciousness an awareness of two sides of what it means to be an empowered woman," he says. "In a way Lily gets to accomplish both. She's my Gloria Steinem *and* my Andrea Dworkin!"

Like the "prestige" cable series, the graphic novel came into its own in the 1990s and 2000s, and is built on conventions and genres pioneered in a medium previously seen as lowbrow or at the very least more ephemeral and unpolished: comics. In the late 1970s and into the 1980s, television miniseries such as the television adaptation of Alex Haley's *Roots* (1976) and Gerald Green's *Holocaust* (1978), as well as the occasional groundbreaking series (Steven Bochco's *Hill Street Blues*, which ran on NBC from 1981 to 1987, may be the best example), broke long-established rules of small-screen storytelling, paving the way for *Penny Dreadful* to come. During the same period, the American comic book industry saw the emergence of similarly trailblazing titles, some mini-serialized (such as Art Spiegelman's *Maus*, issued between 1980 and 1991, and Alan Moore and Dave Gibbons's *Watchmen* in 1986 and 1987), some stand-alone projects (Will Eisner's 1978 *A Contract With God and Other Tenement Stories* is considered by many historians of the form the first modern graphic novel). By the turn of the 21st century, the graphic novel was firmly established as a contemporary literary form and a wellspring for screen adaptions.

While *Penny Dreadful* takes advantage of contemporary television's new freedoms to explore more deeply the characters and themes in Shelley's novel and the particularities of her century, *I, Frankenstein* draws on ideas and aesthetics important in contemporary comics and graphic novels, and situates the majority of its action in our time. The film also makes use of a range of powerful digital tools that have become indispensable in commercial cinema, and that have allowed filmmakers to create spectacular, and spectacularly "realistic," visual effects that have produced a boom in what might be called "fantastic cinema." One reason, in short, that so many films made today are based on comic books, graphic novels, and tales of magic and the fantastic is that CGI (computer-generated imagery) and various kinds of digital animations allow directors to do so.

Despite the cutting-edge technology employed in its production, *I, Frankenstein* has its foundation set firmly in Shelley's original story. "We wanted to keep the heart of the *Frankenstein* story, and write the second chapter," says director Stuart Beattie, who also wrote the screen adaptation of Kevin Grevioux's 2012 graphic novel of the same name. "We pick up where Mary Shelley left off." This is literally the case: the film opens with a montage sequence that gallops through the key moments in the novel, narrated by Frankenstein's creation (Aaron Eckhart), concluding with a scene that finds his maker (Aden Young) frozen to death in the snow. In Beattie and Grevioux's version, however, the monster does not expire on some ice floe, cradling the corpse of his maker, but carries the body—and Victor's journal, a kind of how-to manual for making monsters—to the Frankenstein family cemetery.

I, Frankenstein then veers in a direction wholly unanticipated in Mary Shelley's text, but very much in keeping with trends prominent in contemporary comics and graphic novels. Beattie's film reimagines Frankenstein's creature as a kind of superhero, or super-antihero (think Batman with sutures), caught up in a supernatural battle between Good and Evil, or in this case, literally between Heaven and Hell. Pursued by demons who want to unlock Frankenstein's secrets to make an army of superhuman reanimated corpses to serve as hosts for fallen angels, the monster chooses to "go his own way" rather than join the good guys, a corps of living gargoyles, who nevertheless give him magic weapons and a new name: Adam.

I, Frankenstein's Adam is ostensibly strikingly different from the creature in *Penny Dreadful*. Though capable of horrific violence, Logan's extrapolation is an eloquent, sensitive, even compassionate being, more prone to melancholy than to rage; "a creature of poetry," Logan calls him (it is worth noting that Shelley's monster, too, had a passion for literature), "who believes in John Clare more than he believes in God," referring to the 19th-century working-class poet whose name he adopts.

Whatever sentimentality might have been in the creature at the beginning of *I, Frankenstein*—much of his interaction with Victor was evidently cut from the film ("there was a lot more there," Beattie said), and his ambivalent anguish at the death of Victor is still evident—has long since been beaten out of him when the film picks up his story in the present. Even the longing for companionship that drives Shelley's and

Logan's creatures has curdled into snarling misanthropy. "He's given all that up; he doesn't trust anyone, he doesn't care about anyone," Beattie explains, "he's like a wounded animal."

Acrobatic fight scenes, fast cutting, and outlandish images of animated stone gargoyles battling demons who erupt like human torches and burrow into the earth as they are "descended" back to hell aside, Beattie's principal concern is character, and the redemption of a being who, despite his crimes, is himself a victim. "Adam didn't ask for this, to be made," he observes, "he's been alone for two hundred years, and he doesn't even know how long he'll be alone. That's the cruelest thing Victor Frankenstein did: he [Adam] has been given a life sentence, and he's immortal. . . . Aaron [Eckhart] and I talked a lot about what that would do to a person, being alone and knowing you'll be alone forever . . . You can't just play angry, you need deeper human emotions."

Beattie is an accomplished screenwriter—his script for the Tom Cruise-Jamie Foxx thriller *Collateral* (Michael Mann, 2004) garnered wide praise and earned him the BAFTA award for best screenplay—and he has a solid track record with fantasy and horror: he penned the script for the first installment of the blockbuster *Pirates of the Caribbean* franchise, *The Curse of the Black Pearl* (Gore Verbinski, 2003) and adapted the arctic vampires-on-the-loose comic book *30 Days of Night* for David Slade's 2007 film. His second outing as director, *I, Frankenstein* presented Beattie with the challenge of balancing the demands (and constraints) of genre and adaptation with his appreciation for, and fascination with, the *Frankenstein* story.

"I saw the films first, of course," said Beattie, who vividly recalls watching the Hammer studio's cycle of *Frankenstein* films, "and I've always felt for the monster. I think Mary Shelley's [monster] is the loneliest being created in all of literature." Beattie and Eckhart worked to make sure that this loneliness was not lost in the midst of the kinetic and stylistic brio of 21st-century action cinema. Asked why Shelley's story has such staying power, Beattie flatly claims, "*Frankenstein* is a love story, it's about finding love, finding someone like you . . . that's what the Monster wants. That's what we all want.

"A love story is sometimes a distraction in an action film," he notes, but he maintains the centrality of the theme to the development of Adam's character: it is the monster's willingness to accept his own isolation, to give up on that quest for "someone like himself," that redeems him and transforms him from monster to hero. "[Victor] Frankenstein is a villain, it's his obsession that drives the plot, his desire to cheat death," says Beattie. "Victor absolutely believes in what he is doing. . . . It's Adam who ultimately understands that it's inherently morally wrong, that he himself is a mistake." Adam finally rights this wrong by destroying Victor's journal (a book, the leader of the Gargoyle Order says, that is "proof that God is no longer the sole creator of man"), preventing the rise of an undead army and dooming himself to singularity. "He makes a choice . . . to become human, he sacrifices his own happiness, gives up the one thing he wants most."

Indeed, as different as *Penny Dreadful* and *I, Frankenstein* are, stylistically, tonally, and formally, there are nevertheless striking similarities in terms of the moral or, perhaps better to say, philosophical dynamics of Shelley's story, and how both Logan and Beattie understand the inner life of these synthetically reborn creatures. For both creators, these emotional and thematic depths are the reason why *Frankenstein* has never staled. Part of the project of his series, according to Logan, confronts the dilemma of "unloved people, and how do they find some sense of community . . . of kinship."

"There is a theological imperative in *Frankenstein*," says Logan, "which is: 'Did I, master, ask you to create me out of clay?' Meaning: why do I exist? What is my purpose here? What is my artistic purpose? My personal purpose?" Different characters, he acknowledges, and different people inevitably frame such questions in different ways and come to different answers, but the questions remain inextricably woven into the fabric of the story.

For Logan, the story so often cited as a watershed early work of science fiction is not about science at all. "People are always so disappointed when they read the book because they expect there to be a big creation scene," he says, "they think there's going to be lightning, there's going to be a big storm . . . but in the book it's 'well, there he is!' It's a beautiful wink from Mary Shelley saying that part doesn't matter; what matters are the moral underpinnings."

If Beattie's film is ultimately about the *un*making of a monster, the vengeful Creature, the "wounded animal" becoming "Adam Frankenstein," Logan rejects the category of monstrosity outright. "I have no interest in branding anything 'monsters,'" he says. "When you are working with characters or extrapolating from characters you have to look at them with unbelievable compassion . . . the whole point of being an artist is just to celebrate, as Seneca said, 'Nothing that is human is alien to me.' Artists and writers and poets and playwrights and actors and musicians have to stretch themselves to the limits of what it is to be human. What interests me as a dramatist is creating . . . complicated characters that keep turning around. One moment you love them and then you hate them but you're always striving to understand some wounded part of them."

It is remarkable that to the present day, the characters that people Shelley's tale continue to inspire the creative community, and keep finding new expressions and new forms in so wide a range of retellings.

"I think the provocation of Mary Shelley," Logan says, "and the provocation of probably every version in one way or another is who do you want to be? Do you want to be the creature or the doctor? Make your choice."

10

THE FACE OF THE FIEND:
MEDIA, INDUSTRY, AND THE EVOLVING IMAGE
OF FRANKENSTEIN'S MONSTER

Eddy Von Mueller

UNIVERSAL *FRANKENSTEIN*

If modern fan culture needed a Founding Father, it would almost certainly turn to Forrest J. Ackerman. Forry was a literary agent specializing in science fiction, who at various points represented some of the genre's greats, including Isaac Asimov, Ray Bradbury, and future Scientology guru, L. Ron Hubbard. He was also the founder and, for twenty-five years, the editor of *Famous Monsters of Filmland*. The magazine debuted in February 1958, and was the first publication focused exclusively on horror, science fiction, and fantasy media, presenting profiles, reviews, interviews, commentary, and production histories. During the 1950s, these fantastic genres were in something of a slump, associated primarily with low-budget B-features and exploitation pictures aimed at the teenagers swarming America's drive-ins. By the time *Famous Monsters* folded in 1983, blockbusters like *Jaws, Star Wars, Close Encounters of the Third Kind,* and *E. T.* had made monsters, robots, and alien invasions mainstream. Fans of these genres were beginning to gather by the thousands for organized conventions and could choose from among half a dozen competing magazines.

The cover of the first issue of this groundbreaking periodical shows a glammed-up blonde in tightly fitted dress, smiling up at a tall, gaunt, flat-headed apparition, incongruously dressed in velvet jacket and ascot. Both these figures are *iconic*, in the most literal sense. They are images that function not only as pictures *of* something but as pictures that represent a range of meanings that are highly conventionalized and widely understood by certain groups of people. In the same way that an iconic image of the Madonna and child is far more than just a picture of a woman with a baby, the couple on the cover of *Famous Monsters*, though anonymous to the overwhelming majority of readers (in fact, it is a photograph of *Famous Monsters*' publisher, James Warren, wearing a store-bought rubber mask, and his model girlfriend, Marion Moore), nevertheless signifies a great deal. The woman is a stereotypical starlet, a cute, curvy, cookie-cutter "Hollywood blonde." She is as it were a walking cliché; "Filmland" made flesh. Her companion is equally familiar, a veritable embodiment of an entire genre (or at least a sub-genre), the most famous movie monster of them all: the creature stitched together from spare parts in Universal Studio's 1931 film adaptation of Mary Shelley's 19th-century novel *Frankenstein, or The Modern Prometheus.*

More than half a century later, Pulitzer Prize–winning editorial cartoonist Steve Benson ran a cartoon in the February 16, 2016, edition of the *Arizona Republic*, depicting a lumbering, flat-headed caricature of then-candidate Donald Trump, clomping away with an apparently unconscious woman labeled "G.O.P." in his arms. A figure in the lower right-hand corner of the panel, dubbed "Dr. Ailes FOX," wails, "I've created a MONSTER!" The entire composition is tagged "The Bride of Trumpenstein." Benson's cartoon is hardly unique: in the run-up to, and aftermath of, the 2016 presidential election, the story of *Frankenstein* and more specifically Frankenstein's Monster, were frequently evoked in editorial cartoons, satirical monologues, and op-ed columns. But we can see at a glance that the creature in this cartoon isn't referencing Mary Shelley's monster, a tormented, blackmailing voyeur who so eloquently holds forth at points on the morality and metaphysics of his own existence. It is rather another iteration of the *Famous Monster* cover-creature, another version of Universal's shambling, flat-headed hulk.

One of the "Little Three" studios in Hollywood, which, along with the "Big Five," dominated the American screen trade until the early 1950s, Universal had a long and proud history. Its founder and former head, Carl Laemmle, who had passed the studio down to his son Carl Jr. in 1929, had been one of the original "moguls" and one of the principal architects of the business model that long served as the foundation of the Hollywood studio system. But in the early '30s, with the entire industry grappling with the collapse of the American economy and the transition to sound, Universal was far from the biggest or most prolific of the studios. It didn't have a vast stable of shining stars or a sprawling national network of affiliated theaters, like those maintained by its larger rivals. Nor was Universal's 1931 effort the first time *Frankenstein* was brought before the public. If anything, the story was old hat: the novel was more than a century old when the Universal film appeared. It had already been reprinted, translated, abridged, serialized, and illustrated in myriad editions in a dozen languages. Versions of *The Modern Prometheus* had already appeared onstage, in Europe, Britain, and the United States. Several filmed versions, too, already existed.

How is it that a single performance in a single film based on so widely known a work came to be so indelibly associated with it? How is it that, scores of film adaptations later, when everyone involved in its making and even the industry that produced it has passed away or been transformed beyond recognition, the figure of Frankenstein's monster as depicted in Universal's 1931 film can serve as visual shorthand for the novel, the story writ large, with the very *idea* of science, technology, human activity run monstrously amok? How, in short, did this Frankenstein's monster become *the* Frankenstein's Monster?

Answering these questions demands that we look anew at both the Universal film and at the source material on which it was based, and also that we look beyond them, to the ways in which Shelley's story, and Whale's film, were made available to their consumers, as well as the various uses to which both have been put. We must also attempt to assess the myriad ways in which changing technologies and industries shape how stories are told and understood.

IMAGERY, IMAGINATION, IMAGE

As everyone knows who has ever seen, to their delight or dismay, the cinematic adaptation of a beloved piece of literature, from any author, era, or genre, reading books and watching films are vastly different experiences. Entire literatures, in fact, and several sub-disciplines we might very broadly encompass under the heading "adaptation studies," have emerged to explain and explore these differences and their consequences. In the act of reading (absent, of course, illustrations), any visualization of the events, places, and people in the text is left entirely to the reader's imagination, or more precisely, to the reader's imagination as cued, limited, and shaped by the information supplied by the writer. The imagination is not then wholly free; there are parameters and conventions established within the text, which may, or may not, provide an abundance of detail about how things and people would appear were they made visible, as well as a complex range of cultural, social, and generic factors that work to determine the kinds of pictures likely to emerge before the mind's eye. Some authors may provide an abundance of imagery, or visually descriptive language, while others may give us none. Most often, literature provides a smattering of specific visual information and leaves us to infer the rest.

Consider this passage from Shelley's novel, in which Victor Frankenstein gives us an adoring (and condescending description) of his foster-sister and future bride, Elizabeth:

> She was docile and good-natured, yet gay and playful as a summer insect . . . Her person was the image of her mind; her hazel eyes, although as lively as a bird's, possessed an attractive softness. Her figure was light and airy; and, though capable of enduring great fatigue, she appeared the most fragile creature in the world . . . I loved to tend on her, as I should on a favourite animal; and I never saw so much grace both of person and mind united to so little pretension.

This passage *tells* us a lot about Frankenstein's attitude—and perhaps Shelley's attitude or those of the men of the romantic era—towards women and femininity. It tells us, too, about Elizabeth's personality, about the part she plays in the moral and ethical worldview presented in the novel. Yet reading it, what do we *see*? Who do we picture in the role of this hazel-eyed, airy-figured "summer insect" of a girl? "Fragile," "docile," and "playful" are powerfully descriptive terms, but also markedly *subjective* ones. What constitutes an attractive and playful young woman, should an adapting filmmaker choose even to attempt to retain these traits as described by Shelley, might look quite different in 1931 from what it would in 1985 or 1994. In any case, whoever is sent up from the Casting Department in any given reader's mind is in all likelihood *not* going to look like Mae Marsh or Carrie Fisher or Helena Bonham Carter (all of whom played Elizabeth in various screen adaptations).

And what of the Monster, as described by the author? Aside from a few specifics—yellow skin, black hair (and black lips), gigantic stature—Shelley is again evocative but vague. We know the Monster is unlovely:

"hideous," "horrible," "wretched," and "detestable" are all repeatedly used. "A mummy again endued with animation," Frankenstein recalls, describing the Monster's visit to his chambers after he had fled from the Monster in his laboratory, "could not be so hideous as that wretch." But these terms too are subjective and as mobile in meaning as the positive adjectives used to describe other characters. Moreover, some of the terms assigned to the Monster, such as "wretch" and "daemon," are now so tinted by their archaism as to call to mind no images at all but rather a sense of a somewhat creakily distant time. For the contemporary reader in particular, Shelley does not paint a very clear picture of what the creature at the center of the story *looks* like as much as she conveys to us who he is. We come over the course of the novel to know his personality far better than we do his person. Textually, the Monster is idea, not image. Victor Frankenstein is therefore not the only one making monsters in *Frankenstein*—we are, as we conjure up creatures that match the character as we come to understand it, without clashing too violently with whatever direct descriptions we have read and recall.

The adaptation of Shelley's story to cinema and other media forms demands monster-making of a more material kind. If, as consumers of Shelley's novel, we translate her words into images that are filtered by the limits of her language and our culture, as discussed above, the adaptation or illustration of *Frankenstein* presents to us, fully formed, the monstrous progeny of other "authors"—artists, directors, actors—who come to the act of translation with their own filters, agendas, and understandings. It is as if we outsource the work of imagination to others, whose visualizations we then consume as spectators. It is no longer up to the reader to conjure any details not provided by the prose. In cinema, an arctic waste or blasted heath or ruined crypt can no longer be any (and therefore every) arctic waste, blasted heath, or ruined crypt the reader happens to dream up: it must be a specific, actual arctic waste, blasted heath, or ruined crypt, authentic or synthetic, one that we can point a camera at and put actors into. Inference becomes observation. The act of adaptation, at least in visual media, is necessarily one of definition and constraint. When the filmmakers have chosen their Elizabeth and made their Monster, they become, within that particular media experience, the only such ones. Whatever mental pictures you as a reader may have formed fade before the evident "fact" displayed on the screen.

The first images of the Monster seen and in some cases circulated in the 19th century were not of course cinematic. The first illustrated edition of the novel, the third, was published in 1831, and included a number of engravings by Theodor von Holst, a prolific illustrator and literary painter of the romantic period. Other visualizations took place onstage. The first dramatic adaptation of the story, Richard Brimley Peake's *Presumption or, the Fate of Frankenstein*, was staged in London in 1823, and the first parodies, Peake's own *Another Piece of Presumption* in 1823, and the comic operetta *Frank-in-Steam, or the Modern Promise to Pay* in 1824. In popular culture, parody is the surest measure of relevance, and such theatrical lampoons were 19th-century London's versions of *Saturday Night Live*. Mary Shelley, who published the first edition anonymously, held no power of copyright, which doubtless helped accelerate the adaptation process (and deprived the author of any royalties), but as Lester D. Friedman and Allison B. Kavey have pointed out, the popularity of the stage play gave *Frankenstein*, and Shelley, a huge boost, prompting the second printing of the novel. At least fifteen theatrical adaptations were staged in England, Europe, and the United States in the 19th and early 20th centuries.

Neither Holst's admittedly portentous illustrations, however, nor any of the designs, performances, or performers in the 19th-century theatrical adaptations produced any images that echoed into the 20th in the way the 1931 *Frankenstein* has reverberated to this day, regardless of the popularity of the individual works or the waxing and waning prominence of the original novel. This has little to do with either the quality of any of these efforts in and of themselves, or with the degree to which they were faithful to Shelley's work. It was a consequence rather of how these adaptations and interpretations functioned within the media environment of the time. It would be over thirty years before a new edition of *Frankenstein* appeared in England, without Holst's illustrations; as for the plays, most 19th-century theater—indeed, virtually *all* theater prior to the advent of sound recording in the late 1870s—was invariably idiosyncratic and ephemeral. A printed copy of a play could be acquired, preserved, and read, and playbills, posters, and even photographs of popular plays and players were printed and sold, particularly in the latter years of the century, but it was impossible for anyone to see the same play more than once (since every live performance will differ from every other one), or for anyone who could not be physically present in the theater at the time of a play's performance to see it. For both print illustrations and theatrical presentations of *Frankenstein*, then, circulation and repetition were sharply limited, making it difficult to create lasting associations between the source material and any particular visualization.

If *Frankenstein* had not spawned over the course of the 19th century any enduring images, it had seen great success in terms of disseminating the author's ideas. The 19th century saw a steady climb in literacy throughout the Western world and a concomitant boom in print media, thanks to rapidly expanding urban populations and the advent of steam-powered paper mills and printing presses. Over the course of the century, newspapers, magazines, and novels all became more widely available, more widely read, and more profitable. Mary Shelley died in 1851, having sold the copyright to the publishers of the illustrated edition, Henry Colburn and Richard Bentley, for their Standard Novel series of reprints. British publication was suspended after two runs, but new editions continued to appear in America and on the Continent. It was, after all, a timely tale for a world convulsed by massive changes in culture, technology, politics, and demography. Industrialization itself, the scientific inquiry that sustained it, and the unintended and often grotesque consequences of it—from job loss to hideous and maiming factory accidents and the mechanization of warfare—all made Shelley's work resonate with readers in the Victorian era. Susan Tyler Hitchcock, in her book *Frankenstein: A Cultural History*, notes that by 1900, "Frankenstein," referring interchangeably to the Monster or his creator, had become a widely used metaphor in many kinds of popular discourse. For example, though the creature had as yet no fixed appearance, the famous Frankenstein name, combined with a general hugeness and hideousness, was sufficient to make the Monster as ideal a bogeyman for 19th-century political cartoonists as he is for those working today.

If the explosion in print media helped make the central themes and figures in Shelley's novel part of a kind of conceptual commons in the mid-1800s, another explosion, this one in image-based media at the turn of the 20th century, would permit Shelley's fiend to find a face it would wear into the next millennium. In the 1880s and '90s, while *Frankenstein* was making its way into the hands and minds of a rapidly expanding reading public, George Eastman was revolutionizing photography with celluloid film and the first "point and shoot" cameras; the half-tone printing process was putting photographs on the covers of newspapers; Eadweard Muybridge and Étienne-Jules Marey were conducting their landmark experiments in motion photography; and in France and the United States, a small group of entrepreneurs and industrialists was laying the foundations of the cinema. The new century was going to be an age of images.

IMAGE, INDUSTRY, ICON

The first cinematic adaptation of Shelley's novel was made in 1910, at the Edison Studios. Edison was at the time the biggest and the oldest name in movies. In the early 1890s, he had patented in the United States the first viable motion picture camera, as well as a coin-operated machine for viewing films, and he had remained a dominant force, culturally, politically, and economically, in what had become by 1900 an international motion picture industry. But by the end of the first decade of the 20th century, it was already an industry in crisis. Reformers and the "uplift" crowd, worried about the effects of sensational cinema on what was at the time a primarily lower-class, primarily urban, audience, were putting pressure on filmmakers to make a safer, more refined product. What's more, the industry had, in 1909, lost a landmark infringement case over an unauthorized adaptation of Lew Wallace's 1880 novel, *Ben-Hur*. Henceforth, filmmakers were actually going to be expected to *pay* for the right to adapt other people's intellectual property.

This combination of forces sparked a stampede on the part of the fledgling film industry towards the kinds of material that would attract and entertain their customers without risking either censorship or costly copyright litigation. Historical films were a popular choice, as were Bible stories and "classic" literature—all of which lay safely in the unguarded public domain. Better still, much of this content allowed filmmakers to indulge in special effects, suspense, violence, and sex, all under the comfortable cloak of education, faith, and art. From 1909 to 1912, viewers saw silent, short (most movies at the time were contained on a single reel, about fifteen minutes; some were far shorter) cinematic adaptations of everything from the life of Napoleon and the story of Moses to the poems of Longfellow, the plays of Shakespeare, and novels by the likes of Dumas, Defoe—and Shelley.

James Searle Dawley, who produced and "directed" (the term was not widely used in the film business at the time) the *Frankenstein* project for Edison, had been a protégé of Edwin Porter, one of the pioneers of cinematic storytelling, and the film contains many elements familiar to period audiences from the popular "trick films" that had been a dominant mode of filmed entertainment at the turn of the century, including double exposures, primitive pyrotechnics, and a very nicely done special effect sequence in which the Monster slowly materializes, from the bones out, in Frankenstein's cauldron (the creature here is chemically, rather than surgically, constructed). Despite these details, aesthetically, performatively, and in terms of the visualization of the monster, the 1910 *Frankenstein* remains essentially theatrical. The film consists almost entirely of long and medium shots (the shot of the materializing Monster effect is somewhat closer), and the acting, particularly that of Augustus Philips as Frankenstein, is broad and gestural, even considering the histrionic style favored in films at the time. The Monster, played by a wild-eyed

Charles Ogle, is dressed in some kind of tattered tunic, has grotesquely large hands and feet, and sports a wild mane of false hair, all details easily read at a distance, as would be the case in a stage play.

It is true that, given its fleet fourteen-minute running time, there isn't much of Mary Shelley's *Frankenstein* in Dawley's *Frankenstein*. Only the broadest strokes of the story are retained: the hubris of the ill-advised scientist, the malice of the Monster (here, "evil" from the time of his creation), the threat to Frankenstein's beloved. While it is certainly consistent with *Frankenstein* as it was popularly understood through the kinds of usages and references seen in print and, to some extent, onstage, the Edison film is only an adaptation in the most rudimentary sense, a rough sketch. But it is not for that reason that the Edison Company film left so slight a mark on the popular imagination. As with the earlier theatrical adaptation, the conditions under which films were made and shown presented significant obstacles to the creation of an enduring legacy for the first *Frankenstein*. While the film business was booming in the first decade of the 20th century—hundreds of storefront "nickelodeons" (so called for the standard five-cent cost of admission) were attracting millions of customers every week—films were shown not as stand-alone entertainments but in mixed bills or programs, which were generally changed several times a week, or even daily, again limiting exposure. What's more, early films were shot on and projected from combustible, fragile nitrate stock. Every time a film was run, there was a good chance it would be scratched, scorched, or destroyed. By some estimates, as many as three fourths of all films made during the silent period have been lost, including the first filmic *Frankenstein*, which was known only from fragments until the 1970s.

If factors largely unrelated to the adaptations themselves had prevented earlier images of Frankenstein's Monster from reaching a threshold of discussion and familiarity that would stabilize them within popular culture, similar factors can be said to have created conditions favorable to the 1931 Universal *Frankenstein* achieving its iconic status. Filmmaking and filmgoing in the United States are dynamic processes, and both the industry and the audience had changed dramatically by 1930. What had been an ephemeral experience in 1910, and associated primarily with lower-class patrons in urban nickel theaters, had evolved by the end of the 1920s into the premier mode of national entertainment, consumed by all classes and in every corner of the country. Nearly every small town in America had at least one purpose-built movie house, and in large cities, patrons could choose between several lavish studio-owned "dream" palaces, some of them seating thousands. During the period of economic expansion that preceded the stock market crash of 1929, weekly admissions had soared to over sixty million, and even in the early years of the Great Depression, a trip to the movies was a weekly ritual for 65 percent of Americans. Longer, "feature-length" running times and star-making close-up shots brought patrons face-to-face with their favorite players for hours at a time. Proximity bred popularity: from the introduction of named actors in the movies in 1909, right around the time Edison was commissioning his *Frankenstein*, movie stars became the most widely recognized people in the world and the best guarantors of a film's financial success. Edison, interestingly, had held out against crediting his workers on-screen, fearing, correctly as it turned out, that celebrity would drive up costs. By the 1930s, stars routinely commanded salaries in the hundreds of thousands of dollars.

The Hollywood studios had moreover been the beneficiaries of decades of disruption to European film markets following the Great War. This gave American films unprecedented reach and longevity. Supported by a well-oiled publicity machine and expert advertising, motion pictures opened in major coastal cities, moving slowly from larger markets and theaters towards the more remote and rural areas in the interior, and then on to audiences abroad. Tight control over the exhibition sector by the vertically integrated and collusive studios and well-developed foreign partnerships meant that a major motion picture could count on being seen by a lot of people, for a very long time. Some Hollywood productions might consistently be playing on some screens, somewhere, for years on end. Victor Erice's superb *Spirit of the Beehive* (1974), in which a young girl's experience of seeing Whale's 1931 *Frankenstein* in Franco's Spain is central to the plot, has the film still touring rural Spanish communities in 1940. Moreover prints of the 1931 *Frankenstein* were still being exhibited in France in 1943.

Universal's decision to bankroll an adaptation of Shelley's novel in 1931 was also based on solid industrial logic. Monsters and the macabre had enjoyed wide popularity in the late 1910s and '20s, with American audiences responding well to a spate of German-made thrillers like *Nosferatu: a Symphony of Horror* (F. W. Murnau, 1922), an authorized adaptation of Bram Stoker's *Dracula*, then still under copyright, and *The Golem* (Paul Wegener, 1920). American-made examples of the genre had even spawned a star: the versatile former circus-performer Lon Chaney, "the Man of a Thousand Faces," who headlined such hits as *The Hunchback of Notre Dame* (Wallace Worsley, 1923) and *The Phantom of the Opera* (Rupert Julian, 1925), both of which had been produced through Universal. Onstage, both *Dracula* and *Frankenstein* enjoyed a comeback, thanks to actor and impresario Hamilton Deane, who commissioned a script for the latter from Peggy Webling. Horace Liveright brought Deane's versions of the Gothic classics to Broadway in 1927. A Hungarian matinee idol, Bela Lugosi, who would play both Dracula and the Monster over the course of his career, played the title character in *Dracula*.

After success of *Dracula*, which used the Deane play as a foundation, *Frankenstein*, based on Webling's play, was the logical follow-up. When several other players passed on the role—Lugosi famously demurred for fear that playing a horribly disfigured monster would dim his growing reputation as a sex symbol—the studio cast Boris Karloff, a British-born émigré who had been a stock company stage actor first in Canada and then in the United States. Karloff arrived in Los Angeles in 1916, where he worked for years as a bit player and second-string heavy, appearing in over sixty films. His height, his swarthy complexion, and gaunt features made Karloff a go-to for playing Native Americans, Asians, Gypsies, and other "exotics," and it was reportedly his unusual appearance that helped land him the role. Those unconventional features were made more striking by Universal's veteran makeup man, Jack Pierce, who designed a look for the creature unlike anything that had ever been seen before on-screen or onstage.

It is important to note the nuances of Karloff's performance, and the particularities of Pierce's work in *Frankenstein*, in light of the long afterlife and eventually iconic stature Karloff's turn as Monster would ultimately attain. Unlike the 1910 film, with its broadly gestural acting, long takes, and relatively loose, distant framing, Whale's 1931 version makes frequent and effective use of close-ups, in which both the subtleties of Karloff's expressions and the virtuosity of Jack Pierce's appliances and makeup are clearly to be seen. The men worked closely together, not least because Karloff spent nearly four hours with Pierce every day getting into and out of character. The Monster is, like most of the characters we see on-screen, a hybrid creation, arising from the collaborations and collisions of multiple technologies, technicians, and creators: the writer, the director, the editor, and the actor all play pivotal roles in crafting the ultimate experience of the performance. In this particular case, both make-up artist and actor were personally deeply invested in the process. According to Pierce, he did six months of research developing the Monster, studying dissection practices, creating the custom makeup to make Karloff's dark complexion read as a corpse-like pallor for the camera, and designing a wardrobe that would exaggerate the tall actor's height. It is Pierce who conceived of the distinctive patchwork of scars and the metal appliances affixed to the Monster's head and neck, to carry the reviving jolt of electricity to the creature's borrowed brain.

Karloff, for his part, sought the advice of Lon Chaney. The script for the film, by John Balderston, deviated from both Shelley's novel and Webling's play in a number of ways, most conspicuously, by muzzling the Monster: despite the notable loquaciousness of the character throughout the novel, the Monster in the film is not given a single line of dialogue. Robbed of speech, the Monster's consciousness becomes far more cryptic to the viewer, his complaints and entreaties, so essential to the relationship between the Monster and the man who made him in the novel and in the adaptations for the stage, remaining trapped inside him. Encouraged by Chaney to embrace the potential of pantomime—both Chaney's parents were deaf, and the actor made only one talking picture in his career—and to find something in the character that "only you can do," Karloff makes the Monster's bewilderment, his frustration, palpable. At first nearly catatonic, the Monster struggles to understand the strange world in which he has awoken, and to make himself understood by it. In *Frankenstein*, notwithstanding the fact that sound was now standard throughout the American film industry, Boris Karloff gives us the last, great dramatic performance of the silent cinema.

The effectiveness of this amalgamation doubtless does much to explain the long-lasting legacy and relevance of what we might call the Pierce-Karloff Monster. The pair teamed up again twice, for 1935's *The Bride of Frankenstein* and for *Son of Frankenstein* in 1939, which marked the last of Karloff's theatrical appearances as the character. While *Bride* and *Son* are very different films from the first of Universal's *Frankenstein* films, and the Monster displays in them to some extent a different temperament and capabilities, the dramatic impact and moments of subtlety are still there. We cannot, in this case, separate the man from the makeup; it would have been an utterly different character in the hands of a different artist or another actor. It is true that others would wear the makeup after *Son*, and that other technicians would imitate Pierce's Monster makeup after the abrupt dismissal of the temperamental artist in 1946, but none of the reproductions and knock-offs of Pierce's makeup effects have stood so well the test of time, and no actor since has generated the emotional mileage Karloff did out of his dead-eyed, flat-topped look.

Though the film was originally conceived as a vehicle for Colin Clive, the man cast as the scientist Dr. Frankenstein (in this film, christened "Henry"), the monster was the movie's biggest draw. When the film opened in November 1931, the image of the Pierce-Karloff Monster was already in wide circulation in advertisements and other promotional material. Posters, lobby-cards, reviews, interviews, articles, and "puff pieces" in magazines and newspapers, trailers and newsreels, and guest appearances on the radio were essential to generating sustained interest. It's clear from Karloff's prominence in and out of makeup in these kinds of media that *Frankenstein* and the man behind the Monster had become hot commodities for Universal. The Monster and Karloff even showed up in material made by the competition. The Merrie Melody and Looney Tune cartoon series produced by Leon Schlesinger's animation unit at Warner Bros., like the musical comedies of the Victorian theater, made a good barometer of contemporary popular consciousness. You were definitely trending if they took a potshot at you, and there were more than a few aimed at the Monster. Frank Tashlin inserted the Monster as "Borax Karoff" in *Porky's Road Race* (1937) and in a lineup of movie fiends in *Have You Got Any Castles?* (1938). Tex Avery sets the Monster clomping his way through a chic nightclub filled with caricatured celebrities in *Hollywood Steps Out* (1941). Bob Clampett's *The Great Piggy Bank Robbery* (1945) features among its rogue's gallery of grotesques a glowing outline of the Pierce-Karloff Monster called "Neon Noodle," and the Universal-style Monster continued to make occasional cameos through the mid-'60s, when the practice of producing animated cartoons to accompany theatrical films was coming rapidly to a close. The Monster makes a final appearance in Robert McKimson's *Doctor Devil & Mr. Hare* in 1964. It is not a particularly distinguished swan song. The Monster, though recognizable, has been reimagined as a metallic robot, probably to avoid legal trouble, and Warner Bros. has added a laugh track, a convention borrowed from television, which was increasingly becoming the native habitat of animated cartoons (and of Frankenstein and his Monster).

So familiar had the face of the Pierce-Karloff monster become that Universal continued to exploit it, despite the absence first of Karloff and then of Pierce. The films of the 1940s, however, suggest that widespread familiarity had its downsides too. With the exception of *Ghost of Frankenstein* (Erle C. Kenton, 1942), the films of the 1940s—*Frankenstein Meets the Wolf Man* (1943), *House of Frankenstein* (1944), *House of Dracula* (1945), *Abbot and Costello Meet Frankenstein* (1948)—are multi-monster ensemble films, as if the Monster alone could no longer carry a feature. The character of the Monster, too, becomes progressively less complex, the performances less nuanced and distinctive, seeming to reflect a level of indifference, as if, since the "look" of Universal's version of Frankenstein's monster had become sufficiently fixed in the minds of the public, it didn't matter so much who actually wore the outfit. Three different actors, Lon Chaney Jr., Bela Lugosi, and Glenn Strange appeared as the Monster during the 1940s, none of them investing the character with a tithe of Karloff's sensitivity.

The films also become less horrific over time, ending in outright farce in *Abbot and Costello Meet Frankenstein*. The Monster looks the same, more or less, but it seems less monstrous, perhaps because the world had collectively faced things far more frightening than any movie monster. Whatever the reasons—indifference, incompetence, or collective trauma—the Universal *Frankenstein* films of the 1940s neither attempted nor achieved the eeriness and thrills attained in the 1930s. Still, albeit as a figure of fun rather than fear, the Monster proved profitable. Through circulation and repetition, the Pierce-Karloff Monster had become a modern mass-media icon, instantly recognizable to millions, but it had also become generic, its original meanings shifted. Moving forward, the Monster might not be scary (and, perhaps, might not be technically monstrous), but it could still make money for its masters. When the studio system collapsed in the 1950s, broken up by federal antitrust actions and bedeviled by new competition from television, the cash-strapped former giants had to scramble to stay solvent. Universal began to actively police its intellectual property. Shelley's original novel was clearly in the public domain, but the image of the Pierce-Karloff Monster had been created by the studio. With other filmmakers beginning to trade on the "Frankenstein" name, Universal began to take action to protect the monster they had made.

FRANKENSTEIN™

Finding ways of monetizing content became a crucial concern for Hollywood's once-mighty studios in the 1950s. The so-called Paramount

Decrees issued in 1948 had forced the divestiture of a studio's associated chain of theaters, and in some markets with access to multiple television stations, theater attendance dropped by two thirds between 1952 and 1954. The new media environment compelled innovation.

The rerelease of films was once a relatively rare occurrence. Only the Walt Disney Studio routinely sent its pictures back out on the road, an innovation originally intended to help the company recoup the colossal losses on some of its pricier failures like *Fantasia* and *Pinocchio*. This meant that while most Americans went to the movies far more frequently than they do today, each individual film had a finite window in which it could be accessed by any individual viewer. In 1954, however, Universal bucked this trend and rereleased *Dracula* and *Frankenstein* as a theatrical double feature. With the franchise trending toward comedy and self-caricature over the course of the 1940s, the repackaged originals proved viable as a draw both for the new adult "arthouse" audience that was beginning to take a second, nostalgic look at the films of their childhood, and the surging teen audience that was learning to consume older thrillers as camp.

Other studio tactics involved fraternizing with the enemy. Beginning in 1951, the studios began selling the broadcast rights to their extensive film libraries to television networks and syndicates. Television brought American audiences decades' worth of films that most people had probably never seen, or had seen once, in the theater. Far cheaper to license than newer films or original content, such films often aired late at night or on weekend afternoons, outside the lucrative "prime-time" blocks. Genre pictures were especially popular, since television in the 1950s was evolving, as the cinema had, as a genre-oriented medium (this is in part because as the theatrical market shrank, underutilized production capacity in Hollywood became available for television production). Programs like *The Vampira Show* (1954), featuring Maila Nurmi as the black-garbed titular host, and John "The Cool Ghoul" Zacherle's *Shock Theater* (1957) targeted the adolescent audience and presented studio-era thrillers and horror pictures with tongues firmly in cheek. *Shock Theater* was in fact built around the package of horror films and thrillers Universal had been compelled to sell through the Screen Gems syndicate in 1957, which included *Frankenstein* and *Son of Frankenstein*.

The Monster invaded the small screen in other versions as well. David Levy brought Charles Addams's gently macabre print cartoons to television in 1964 as a situation comedy. *The Addams Family*, which had debuted in the pages of the *New Yorker* in 1938, included a cadaverous, towering butler, Lurch (played on television by the six-feet-nine Ted Cassidy), who bore a striking (but non-infringing) resemblance to the Pierce-Karloff Monster. The program ran for two seasons on ABC and has enjoyed a long afterlife including holiday specials, animated cartoons, and feature films. Simultaneously, in 1964, the Monster appeared in person (so to speak) as one of the principal characters in another sitcom on CBS, *The Munsters*. The show was produced by Universal's television division and made the most of the studio's trademark monsters, featuring Fred Gwynne as the Monster, reimagined as a bumbling, good-natured family man, trying to live out the American dream with his vampiress bride, her *Dracula*-like dad, and their two children, a budding werewolf and his shockingly normal, blond-haired sister.

After three decades of growls and groans, *The Munsters* restores to the Monster his voice—or *a* voice, anyway. There is no caveman grammar in the Munster's house on Mockingbird Lane, but neither is there any trace of the eloquence or agony of Shelley's writing. This is a Frankenstein's Monster without a Dr. Frankenstein; all the motivating dilemmas of its existence have been miraculously erased. Everything that tormented his literary prototype, everything that made such a misery of the short second life of the creature in the novel and the 1931 film, has been fixed. No more unscratchable itch to confront his creator and make him long for death. No more rejection or solitude, either: Herman Munster has a loving mate, adoring children, a purpose, and a place (even if the neighbors aren't terribly happy about it). While he is the spitting image of the Monster visualized through the fusion of the makeup talents of Jack Pierce and the pantomimic virtuosity of Boris Karloff, Gwynne's

Herman Munster is nevertheless the antithesis of the character they created together. After three decades of diffusion, reproduction, and reprise, the image has been unmoored from the idea, the symbol severed from the story. The icon, now a global brand, has become so expansive in potential meaning that it can accommodate even its own negation.

The Monster also appeared on television in numerous animated cartoons. By the late 1960s, animation, initially part of prime time, had become the cornerstone of children's television experience, in particular, as part of the lucrative block of programming presented on the previously desolate Saturday mornings. A superb vehicle for selling toys, candy, and sugar-laden breakfast cereals, Saturday morning cartoons quickly became a ritual for millions of kids, and companies like the one founded by studio-era animation alums Joseph Hanna and William Barbera (the pair had previously headed MGM's animation unit) scrambled to crank out content to meet demand. Cartoon "kidvid," as it was known, was not noted for its emphasis on originality; if anything, seeking to maximize audience and minimize risk, cartoon makers often recycled familiar film, television, and cultural properties. Laurel and Hardy, the Three Stooges, the Little Rascals, Charlie Chaplin, Evel Knievel, Hulk Hogan, Mr. T, to name but a few, all had animated avatars on Saturday morning, not to mention the countless cartoon takes on movies and TV shows, from *20,000 Leagues Under the Sea* to *Star Trek*.

In 1965, Hal Seeger, another veteran of the grand days of theatrical shorts, created the first of the Monster avatars, Milton the Monster, for ABC. Unlike the Universal-produced *Munsters*, Milton could not exactly mimic the Pierce-Karloff creature, but the flat-headed, good-natured and none-too-bright creation of "Professor Montgomery Weirdo" is clearly close kindred, as is the gigantic robot featured in Hanna-Barbera's 1966 *Frankenstein Jr. and the Impossibles*. The Universal monster, green skin, neck bolts, and all, has also made numerous licensed guest appearances in various iterations of Hanna-Barbera's impressively long-lived Scooby-Doo franchise, beginning with a cameo during the first season *Scooby-Doo, Where Are You?* in 1970. The same year, and the same network, CBS, saw another Pierce-Karloff clone in Filmation's *Groovie Goolies*. This Monster, in the Milton/Herman Munster vein, is a likable buffoon who speaks with a Karloffian lisp, runs a gym, and plays xylophone in a rock 'n' roll band with his monster pals, including a mummy, a wolf man, and Dracula. This list is far from exhaustive: as a principal character, "guest star," or visiting villain, monsters all recognizably referencing the Universal paradigm continue cropping up in children's cartoons to the present day.

There was even an animated monster feature made. During its postwar "economic miracle," Japan became a principal outsource market for American manufacturers of electronics, toys, and animation. Arthur Rankin, Jr. and Jules Bass's Videocraft International Company produced a number of animated holiday specials in Japan, including the beloved 1964 *Rudolph the Red-Nosed Reindeer*, largely executed by stop-motion pioneer Tadahito Mochinaga using a puppet-animation process they dubbed "animagic." Mochinaga's technique was used as well for the 1967 feature *Mad Monster Party*, which featured the usual suspects of Universal monsterdom—Dracula, the mummy, and a particularly oafish version of the Monster (inexplicably called "Fang"), with the voice and a caricatured likeness of Boris Karloff. The film did not perform particularly well, but it resurfaced regularly during the next decade as the Halloween equivalent of *Rudolph* or *The Year Without a Santa Claus*.

When we add these to a mix that includes reprints, abridgements, and adaptations of the novel, extensive appearances in comic strips and comic books, and the toys, masks, models, games, and other material cultural artifacts associated with the Monster (as discussed elsewhere in this anthology), it may not be going too far to say that the Pierce-Karloff Monster has become ubiquitous, at least in Western popular culture. This pervasive presence across media not only reinscribes the image of the Monster as definitively associated with the Frankenstein name and brand; the prevalence of this Monster in *children's* media ensures that long before young people could possibly be expected to encounter or understand Mary Shelley's *Frankenstein*, the central figure in the novel has already become inextricably associated with a range of responses utterly unrelated, if not antithetical, to those presented in it. Even the most successful *Frankenstein* feature of the 1970s, Mel Brooks's exquisite *Young Frankenstein*, is a comedy. Kids meet the Monster first as a clown; everything else it may be—killer, victim, Byronesque antihero—must come after and compete with that first impression.

REJECTION, REVISION, RESTORATION

Contrasted with the progressive shift of the Monster towards content aimed at younger consumers evident in American media in the '50s, '60s, and '70s, the movies made by Hammer Films in Britain during the same period go for a much more grown-up audience, and go for the throat. Hammer's horror films, including their numerous *Frankenstein* pictures, are replete with visual excess. Shot in Technicolor, Hammer borrowed shamelessly from the same stable of public domain monsters Universal had made famous (Dracula, Frankenstein and his monster, werewolves, walking mummies), and added plenty of carnage, cleavage, and bright red blood. The quality varies widely across Hammer's thirty-plus years of horror cinema, but even the most accomplished of the films produced by the studio are ultimately exploitation films. Interestingly, unable to trade on what had come to be universally recognized as *the* Monster, for fear of legal action by Universal, Hammer's focus shifts from the creature to the creator, emphasizing the character of Dr. Frankenstein. Indeed, Hammer's Victor Frankenstein is in most of these films the *real* monster. A cold and frequently sadistic figure, he is far more likely to do something horrific to a peasant child or a buxom barmaid than are most of his creations.

Since, as we have seen in the case of the Pierce-Karloff Monster, repetition and circulation are crucial to establishing an image as iconic in the popular imagination, it is not surprising that despite the cult status Hammer's *Frankenstein* films have come to enjoy, it is Hammer's Frankenstein, rather than their Frankenstein's monster, that winds up standing out. The *image* of the monster and, more or less, its "character" are consistent in every Universal feature, from *Frankenstein* in 1931 to *Abbot and Costello Meet Frankenstein* in 1948. The mad scientists in the Universal films, on the other hand, are far more fluid, played by six different actors—Colin Clive, Basil Rathbone, Cedric Hardwicke, Ilona Massey, Boris Karloff (becoming his own grandpa in *The House of Frankenstein* in 1944), and Onslow Stevens—only one of whom, the 1931 *Frankenstein*'s Colin Clive, appears twice in the role. In the Hammer series, in contrast, the creature is not only played by different performers in every film, it *looks* different in every film, from *Curse of Frankenstein* in 1957 to *Frankenstein and the Monster From Hell* in 1974. A single performer, however—the delightfully serpentine Peter Cushing—holds unshaken the role of the monster-maker. So relatively undistinguished are Hammer's Monsters that even Christopher Lee, who plays the role in *Curse*, could not make it memorable, despite the fact that he would soon become, along with Cushing, the most popular of Hammer's stock players. Both men would grace many a cover of *Famous Monsters of Filmland*, and Lee would go on to cult stardom playing Hammer's *Dracula* in eight films, and later appearing in George Lucas' second round of *Star Wars* films and Peter Jackson's adaptations of *The Lord of the Rings*.

Hammer's *Frankenstein* films can be seen as a kind of rejection of or resistance to tendencies already clearly emerging in the meaning, style, and approach associated with the iconic Universal market. This resistance may not have been entirely voluntary: the real or imagined threat of legal action harried the Hammer productions almost from their inception, and numerous changes were made to everything from settings to costumes to the plot in order to protect the smaller studio's investment and its access to the essential American market. Hammer's *Frankenstein* franchise is almost the anti-Universal. Instead of accelerating its turn toward the juvenile market, Hammer's films became increasingly explicit, the last two films, *Frankenstein Must Be Destroyed* and *Frankenstein and the Monster From Hell*, earning an R rating in the United States. Universal-style Monsters can be anywhere—cartoons or sitcoms, the past or the present—while Hammer's creatures are firmly situated in a more-or-less Mary Shelley–like Britain. The American Monster consistently lists into parody. The British films remain stubbornly serious.

Perhaps the most explicit act of resistance to the Universalist Frankenstein came in 1994, with *Mary Shelley's Frankenstein*, directed by Kenneth Branagh. This production plays against the fact that most decisions made in the movie business are based in one way or another on economics. Take the case of Universal Studios and its iconic Monster. While Karloff *was* the Monster, the popularity of the *Frankenstein* films raised the performer's profile (and his pay), and the actor's A-list status helped enhance the films' performance at the box office. This is the basic star equation: stars bring the audience, the audience brings the cash. When, by the end of the 1930s, the Monster had become a kind of star unto itself, a screen personality familiar enough to the filmgoing public to be caricatured alongside all those other famous faces in Warner Brothers' *Hollywood Steps Out*, the equation changed. It's true that none of the other men who played the Monster for Universal played it nearly as well as Karloff had, but they played it well enough. The fact that the monster had no dialogue to speak of (or to speak), and, in succeeding films, a less complex set of motivations and personality, made moot the question of who was under the makeup. It *looked* like the Pierce-Karloff creation, and that was sufficient. In the case of Universal's monsters, the studio quickly recognized the value of having "stars" in their stable who could work regardless of who was available to actually wear the costume.

While this state of affairs has caused some viewers to overlook the occasionally fine performances, like Karloff's, that have appeared in films featuring the Monster or other entities like it, it has also led some filmmakers to assume that audiences are wholly indifferent to the many bad ones. In any event, there are clearly strong disincentives to putting an expensive or expert performer in the role of a Monster in the Universal mode—a creature represented as inarticulate and shambling, much of its residual humanity and pathos eroded by long dissociation from the heady conflicts that drive the novel and the cartoonish and camp associations the figure of the fiend has accrued over the decades. There just doesn't seem much for a serious actor to *do* with the iconic creature.

Mary Shelley's Frankenstein gives us the sole instance in over a century of Frankensteinian cinema of a major motion picture star known for his acting ability playing the part of the Monster. As the title suggests, Branagh's film strikes a literary note and hews closely (or at least, far more closely than has been typical) to the novel. Ornate, at some points overwrought, the film seeks to balance high seriousness and lurid adventure, and features the renowned Italian-American actor Robert De Niro as the creature, playing opposite Branagh as a Victor Frankenstein rather more vigorous and virile than has been typical. De Niro is a curious choice. De Niro, though unquestionably adept in his craft, is associated primarily with decidedly urban, decidedly American films—his breakout role was as the young Vito Corleone in Francis Ford Coppola's *The Godfather Part II* in 1974, for which he won an Oscar for Best Supporting Actor. This was followed by an Academy Award nomination for his lead performance in Martin Scorsese's *Taxi Driver* (in which he does play, it's true, a kind of monster). It is a bold move, casting two icons against type: De Niro in a bizarrely unexpected role, and the Monster with a strikingly strange new personality to go with a shocking new look.

Branagh's film also breaks ranks with the other adaptations insofar as it includes a significant amount of material usually excised in other adaptations. The novel's framing story that takes place in the Arctic is retained, as well as the Monster's acquisition of language and philosophy, and the wrongful execution of the innocent servant Justine for the creature's murder of Frankenstein's younger brother, all of which are crucial to understanding the psychological and moral development of the character. On the level of performance and presentation, it is clear that adding more Shelley to the Monster in *Mary Shelley's Frankenstein* effectively shows how little Shelley was left in Universal's *Frankenstein*. Designed by Paul Engelen, Carol Hemming, and Daniel Parker, the makeup effects in the film suggest the results of a visit to a Civil War surgeon—the skin is sallow, rather than green or gray, and the far more extensive stitches look raw and inflamed.

There are no bolts in the Monster's body, and perhaps most significant, no hint of the trademark flattened skull. These flourishes were not only specific to the Pierce-Karloff Monster that Universal still holds under copyright; they were also details forcefully connecting the Monster to the long legacy embodied in that iconic image. Yet, since we have known it since childhood, that legacy still haunts Branagh's film, even as Branagh's film rejects it. So much more familiar to us is Universal's *Frankenstein* than Mary Shelley's *Frankenstein*, so much more vividly imprinted is the image of that movie monster than are the powerful questions raised in the novel, that *Mary Shelley's Frankenstein* becomes more cinematic revisionism than an exercise in adaptational fidelity. Ironically, the *Frankenstein* films have drifted so far over a century from the wellsprings of the book that inspired them that an attempt at restoration is almost revolutionary, and a reimagining is the act of an iconoclast.

11

FRANKENSTEIN'S CREATURES:
THE PLEASURES OF TOYS, GAMES, AND COSTUMES

Carol Colatrella

Understanding that play represents an essential dimension of human nature, Friedrich Schiller (1759–1805) argued in his 1794 treatise on aesthetics that "man only plays when he is in the fullest sense of the word a human being, and he is only fully a human being when he plays."[1] Born a generation after Schiller, Mary Shelley elaborated in *Frankenstein* (1818) how human characteristics of ambition, invention, and creativity combine with those of trust, care, and compassion. These essential topics have helped make her novel a rich source text for media representations and popular culture objects, including horror toys, games, and costumes that are involved in forms of play and creativity. Shelley subtitled *Frankenstein* "The Modern Prometheus"; the Greek myth tells of the trickster who gave humans the gift of fire and was punished by Zeus. The classical reference to human invention and creativity as overreaching acknowledges that the novel establishes a modern myth detailing the terrible consequences of ambitious scientific attempts to create new life.

Shelley's text describes the scientist-inventor Victor Frankenstein, his unfortunate creation, his university professors, his family members, and his romantic interest, Elizabeth. *Frankenstein*'s primary narrative dynamic concerns the conflict between the creator of a new being and that creature who shows remarkable powers of self-invention. Mourning his mother, Victor Frankenstein cobbles together new life from human body parts he scrounges from graveyards. He acts as God to satisfy his ambition of becoming a famous scientist, but he is repulsed at the first sight of the living creature and abandons the creature to an inhospitable world. After a period of observing others to learn the ways of the world, the creature approaches Victor to beg "his parent" for a mate, but the scientist fears accommodating the creature with a companion. The monster and his creator are doubles; their characterizations combine creativity, compassion, and revenge, and both represent unforeseen, deadly dangers incurred by scientific experiments and technological innovations.

Connecting the creator and creature, Leo Braudy classifies various types of "monsters of modernity"; his taxonomy encompasses "the monsters from nature (like King Kong), the created monster (like Frankenstein), the monster from within (like Mr. Hyde) and the monster from the past (like Dracula)."[2] Braudy's typology conflates the creator and created in identifying the essence of the Frankenstein myth. One contemporary Facebook meme similarly references this popular confusion of scientist and creature while acknowledging the moral lesson of the novel: "Knowledge is knowing that Frankenstein was not the monster. Wisdom is understanding that Frankenstein was the monster."

Shelley's novel illustrates how ambitious creativity without rational judgment costs lives, suggesting that scientists should carefully consider material and ethical consequences of technological innovation before proceeding to invent and innovate. Scientific ambition should be tempered with a sense of moral responsibility to society; this message invokes feminist principles of equity and cooperation to critique Victor's misguided ambition to become a famous scientist. Victor's secret experiments to produce the creature and his abrupt abandonment of it reveal his selfish ambition and refusal to admit what he has done, actions contrasting with behavior described in the framing story of Robert Walton's aborted exploration in the polar region. In contrast to Victor, Walton exemplifies scientific responsibility: the explorer explains his aims in letters to his sister, acknowledging that Victor's ambitions have destroyed him and his loved ones. Walton turns back from risking the lives of his crew and protects them by ending his mission of scientific discovery. The explorer gives up his expedition rather than endanger the lives of his crew. In this way, Walton serves as a practical and cautious example, as well as a mediator for readers judging Frankenstein.

Adaptations of and references to Shelley's book are ubiquitous in many written and visual texts. But cinematic adaptations generally do not include Walton's story, preferring to focus on the moment of creation and the ensuing battle between Victor and his creature rather than on examining the motivations and heroism of the explorer who makes a practical, moral decision to retreat from scientific discovery when the human cost becomes too high. Since the novel's publication in 1818, it has been commonly invoked to illustrate public concern about the consequences of science gone awry or dangerous technological innovations. Adaptations of Shelley's *Frankenstein* feed on one another, adopting some elements and reconfiguring others. As visual media, most stage and film versions offer spectacle and special effects concentrated on depicting the creation of the monster, his scary visage, and his destructive revenge against his creator. Publicity for Thomas Edison's 1910 short film documents monster makeup typical of earlier stage versions of the story. Some dramatic films, including Ken Russell's 1986 film *Gothic*, provide historical context in conveying Shelley's writing of the novel.

Allusions to the novel abound in diverse media. Playing on the idea of combining odd elements to create new ones, genetically modified foods are called "frankenfood," a term adopted by a Spike reality television show using that title. The Internet Movie Database summarizes this show's formula: "Each episode features local amateur food innovators competing head-to-head in order to get their unexpected food concoctions onto the menu of a popular local restaurant."[3] Adopting the term to recognize a different kind of innovation, the *New York Times* in 2015 applied the term "frankenfood" to heritage foods brought back into existence.[4]

A number of material culture items are based on Shelley's characterizations of Victor Frankenstein and his creature and on the related cinematic adaptations. The past half century has birthed a wide selection of children's books, figures, toys, games, and costumes that represent characters and themes from Shelley's novel. Many physical items reproduce characters without referencing the moral lesson of *Frankenstein* that illustrates Victor's lack of scientific responsibility; instead figures and games reproduce or suggest the act of creation and its results. Video games generally follow conventions of adventure stories and highlight the conflict between the two central characters (Victor and the creature) in Shelley's novel. According to the description of one *Frankenstein*-based game released by the CRL Group in 1987, "*Frankenstein* is a standard text adventure with static graphics in some locations to set the scene. It is similar to the earlier game *Dracula*, which was produced by the same author. It is divided in three parts; the player takes the role of Dr. Frankenstein in the first two, and of his monster in the third."[5] The 1994 multi-platform *Frankenstein* game was a tie-in with Kenneth Branagh's film *Mary Shelley's Frankenstein* of the same year. In the game,

> The player controls Frankenstein's monster as he stomps through the streets of Ingolstadt, Bavaria, in the year 1793 seeking revenge against a certain man named Victor for rejecting him once he was created . . . The player uses a wooden stick to ward off enemies. The stick that Frankenstein's monster carries can be

put on fire if swung towards fire. Frankenstein also has an additional attack; a blue ball of negative energy that pops up when the player releases the button. Peasants in the game can either be male or female; soldiers are always male. The female peasants attack with pots while the male peasants attack with melee weapons. However, the soldiers (men dressed in red) attack the player with musket shots. Simple puzzles involving switches and pulleys must be solved in order to progress within the levels.[6]

At least one game player has archived his playing of the game in an hourlong YouTube video depicting attacks and puzzles.[7]

In an article published in 2010 in *Educational Researcher*, Sasha A. Barab, Melissa Gresalfi, and Adam Ingram-Goble explain how transformational play can occur within a video game. They elaborate their theory with reference to observations of children playing *Modern Prometheus*, a game based on *Frankenstein*, that includes the character of "Doctor Frank."[8]

Modern Prometheus focuses on persuasive writing, as students are asked to convince others to share their perspective on particular ethical dilemmas. In particular, students grapple with the role that ethics play in science and technology; in this case they consider whether and when ends justify means in a battle with a bacterial plague, as well as the notion of companionship. The game culminates with students' making a decision about whether Doctor Frank's creation is "human" and trying to persuade others of their views on whether "it" should be used for experimentation . . .

Players are positioned in an important role, working as writers who engage and develop persuasive writing skills. They have to reflect on the happenings in the town and on their own beliefs, and then use both evidence and their own opinions to craft an argument supporting or opposing the doctor's experiments. They aim to convince even the most committed dissenters. Experiential consequentiality is threaded throughout the unit.

Modern Prometheus references Shelley's novel and employs entertainment conventions to enhance students' communication skills and develop their ethical understanding. The game offers players opportunities to enact an entertaining experience that enables ethical and educational development.

Mass media communication scholars studying the pleasures of horror have determined that "young males, individuals with low empathy, and those higher in sensation seeking and aggressiveness report more enjoyment of fright and violence"[9] in media content:

One explanation for why people enjoy such presentations relies on the conversion of negative affect to euphoria following a satisfying resolution to a threat. According to Zillman (1996), suspenseful drama, in which liked characters experience or are threatened with victimization, arouses dysphoric emotional reactions or empathic distress . . . Consequently, arousal from suspenseful scenes should carry over and intensify the viewer's positive response to a satisfying resolution, thus producing a rewarding, enjoyable emotional experience. Conversely, if the resolution is unhappy and produces sadness or disappointment, resident arousal from suspense should intensify viewers' dysphoria. (209)

Toys and games based on films and television shows allow players to reenact and reconfigure what they have seen on the screen. Playing with Frankenstein figures or games provides children and adults opportunities to continuously transform and adapt the Frankenstein story, which is itself a myth about human creativity and transformation.

Game players adapting Shelley's story follow in the footsteps of those who produced cinematic adaptations and who frequently revise elements of plot, characterization, and setting. Each adaptation offering innovative shifts in the *Frankenstein* myth can inspire a proliferation of other adaptations. The classic film version of *Frankenstein* directed by James Whale and distributed in 1931 introduces new elements, such as depicting Victor's laboratory, introducing an assistant, and changing characters' names (Victor becomes Henry Frankenstein and the scientist's friend Henry becomes Victor). The director took pains to make the monster and his actions appear as frightening as possible, although audiences, producers, and censors toned down the film by eliminating some scenes deemed too violent, such as the monster's drowning of a little girl. Victor's relationship with Elizabeth is prominent in Whale's film, and an epilogue allows a happy ending for the scientist and his bride. Boris Karloff's gruesome makeup and his portrayal of the creature in the 1931 film inspired numerous costumes, toys, and games. These material objects sometimes represent the creator as mad scientist but more frequently reference the monster, now also dubbed "Frankenstein."

Other collectibles depict the scientist and the monster's bride; some figure toys and settings illustrate the creation of the monster in Dr. Frankenstein's lab. According to reviews posted on websites from vendors such as Amazon, horror figures are purchased as models by collectors seeking authentic representations of characters appearing in various *Frankenstein* films such as those produced by James Whale, the Hammer Film company, etc. Other purchasers use them as Halloween decorations or as amusing figures for science fair projects.[10] Figure toys embody the creature as either a frightening sight with stitches around his face or as a less threatening, humorous monster, following in the wake of TV shows such as *The Addams Family* and *The Munsters*. These two popular 1960s family situation comedies, which are annually rebroadcast by the Boomerang television network in October, feature caricatures of characters adapted from Shelley's novel and rebirthed in Hammer horror movies, such as those starring Christopher Lee as the monster and Peter Cushing as the scientist. *The Addams Family* includes Lurch, a tall butler with deep-set eyes, a craggy face, and stiff gait, features similar to

Karloff's portrayal of the creature. *The Addams Family* television show has also had renewed life in popular films distributed in 1991 and 1993. In *The Munsters*, Herman Munster is a typical genial yet clueless situation comedy dad who resembles the creature; he shares the facial features, physiognomy, and clothing with Frankenstein's monster. Herman is married to the vampire-like Lily. Grandpa and young son Eddie share vampire qualities although daughter Marilyn is conventionally pretty.

Fans of horror films often become collectors of associated movie memorabilia. Actor-comedian Gilbert Gottfried loves the film *Frankenstein* and explained his long-standing interest to an interviewer:

> As a horror-movie-obsessed child—he's now a horror-movie-obsessed adult—Mr. Gottfried sent away for the poster when he came across an impossible-to-resist offer in the back of a comic book. "The way it was described I thought Frankenstein's monster would actually be coming to my house in Brooklyn, which I was looking forward to," he recalled. "But it was this rolled up 6-foot poster that I kept in the back of a drawer for years. And my wife had it framed for my birthday a few years ago."[11]

Musician Chris Cornell of the Seattle band Soundgarden amassed a large comic book, figure, and toy collection related to the *Frankenstein* story and horror media. Ownership of such collectibles offers another opportunity to reenact or reconfigure the *Frankenstein* story, albeit by means of an extremely expensive hobby. As Ty Burr has written in the *New York Times*, "Purchasing a $6,000 limited-edition bronze bust of Frankenstein from Universal Studios, or a $7,500 replica of C-3PO from Party Professionals, indicates that you have devoted your life to the worship of one entertainment property, and also that you might be better off with a skilled stockbroker."[12] One can admire, build, and/or play with objects; these activities can allow one to control fear and to experience the pleasure of managed suspense inducing satisfaction, if not euphoria, as one can stop playing with the toy, poster, or figure.

Even those of us who do not collect objects are surrounded by popular toys and texts referring to Frankenstein's monster. There are numerous wind-up toys from Lucky Penny—pumpkin, skeleton, Dracula, and Frankenstein's monster—that share the same stiff gait.[13] The social media site Pinterest offers a plethora of Halloween *Frankenstein* crafts.[14] Puppet shows can be aimed at children and adults. A 2015 puppet show offered on the Isle of Skye illustrated "a gentle horror"; according to an advertisement, *Little Frankenstein* tells the story of "Semi-famous puppeteer Frank Stein," who "has had enough with his badly made puppets. He'll never be really famous because his puppets keep falling apart! However, taking inspiration from the scientist Dr. Frankenstein, and with the help of the audience, he creates a new real live puppet that is destined to change the world forever! A gentle horror for little horrors!"[15] Puppet shows based on *Frankenstein* have also popped up on college campuses, including in Texas and Ohio.[16]

Popular culture examples of science fiction characters circulate in different genres across age groups. Teens and adults observe the supernatural strength, incredible persistence, and intelligence of Frankenstein's creature as these characteristics appear in video games requiring the player to chase the monster or, in a variation based on the *Frankenstein* adaptation *The Rocky Horror Picture Show*, to save young lovers from the mad scientist's experiments. For example, *The Adventures of Dr. Franken* (1997) features Franky, a cartoon Frankenstein's monster on a mission to collect the scattered body parts of his girlfriend to bring her back to life.[17] The quest is similar to that followed by the reader of Shelly Jackson's *Patchwork Girl*, an electronic feminist hypertext fiction based on Shelley's novel and released by Eastgate Systems in 1995 that requires readers to stitch together parts of a girl's body to navigate through the text. iPad apps based on Shelley's *Frankenstein* link images of texts, such as letters and writings of Mary Shelley and her husband, Percy, to a "choose your own adventure" game.[18]

Children's media, including toys, share many of the themes that dominate adult books, television shows, and films about aliens, zombies, vampires, and *Frankenstein*. A long-running popular show for pre-schoolers, *Sesame Street*, normalizes the story of nonhuman figures such as a cookie monster, a two-headed monster, Martians, and a Dracula-like count teaching numbers. Gobbling cookies and counting objects are common toddler activities along with learning the alphabet and the names of body parts. *Sesame Street* produced animated videos with Dr. Frankenstein and the creature that are now available on YouTube. One *Sesame Street* cartoon shows the scientist's assistant, Igor, listening at the castle door as the scientist announces the names of the body parts he puts together to make another Igor.[19] An early cartoon shows the scientist teaching F words (Fred, foot, Friday) to the monster strapped in a chair in the lab.[20] Another animation has the scientist explain back and front to the wind-up creature.[21] In addition to offering children information about body parts and words, these animations introduce the major characters associated with Shelley's novel and versions of it: Franken-stein the scientist, the monster, and Igor. (Frankenstein employed an assistant named Fritz in the 1931 film directed by James Whale, but Igor is the name assigned the assistant in many other adaptations.)

A number of children's books represent versions of the *Frankenstein* myth,[22] sometimes riffing on other well-known books. *Frankenstein: A Monstrous Parody* begins by echoing Ludwig Bemelmans's classic, *Madeline*: "In a creepy old castle all covered with spines, lived twelve ugly monsters in two crooked lines"; "Frankenstein is the scariest of all the monsters in Miss Devel's castle."[23] In Patrick McDonnell's *The Monster's Monster*, three little monsters make a "MONSTER monster" by putting together various items and by causing the giant monster to be struck with a lightning bolt. "The growling giant" has a flat head, large facial features, and neck bolts like Frankenstein's monster. He at first seems scary to the little monsters until they chase him to the beach, where the giant monster gives jelly doughnuts to the little ones.[24]

Children learn by play and incorporate life into play and play into life. Freud's description and analysis of *fort-da* ('gone'-'there') show how a child deals with his separation from parents by managing the disappearance and the reappearance of a toy. Etienne Benson acknowledges creative play with toys as education. "Children learn from people. A child never plays with the same toy twice: it is transformed."[25] Scott Barry Kaufman and his collaborators agree, describing pretend play as "a vital component of normal child development."[26] Jeffrey Goldstein cites "psychiatrist Stuart Brown (2009)" who "discovered that the absence of social play was a common link among murderers in prison. They lacked the normal give-and-take necessary for learning to understand others' emotions and intentions, and the self-control that one must learn to play successfully with others."[27] Equally compelling are observations of the ways that young children make up their own play and objects even from construction sets designed to produce a certain object. For example, one reason Lego blocks and other construction building toys are popular is that children can design their own creations, take them apart, reconfigure, and/or destroy them at will. Children develop autonomy in such play and enjoy taking on pretend roles in playing with figures or wearing costumes that allow them to adopt powerful personae.

The theme of reanimating life reflects human anxieties about death and losing loved ones that also pervade Shelley's novel, so it is not surprising that popular adaptations of it take up themes of anxiety and unresolved mourning in homage and parody. Mel Brooks's film *Young Frankenstein* (1974) faithfully reproduces the setting of Dr. Frederick Frankenstein's lab and scientific activities while changing the protagonists' personalities and adding new characters and scenes. For example, when Dr. Frankenstein praises the creature and forecasts their partnership, the monster cries, and the doctor hugs him, telling his creature:

This is a nice boy. This is a good boy. This is a mother's angel. And I want the world to know once and for all, and without any shame, that we love him. I'm going to teach you. I'm going to show you how to walk, how to speak, how to move, how to think. Together, you and I are going to make the greatest single contribution to science since the creation of fire.

Brooks also famously represented the scientist (played by Gene Wilder) and his creation (played by Peter Boyle) as wearing top hats, white ties, and tails while singing and tap dancing to "Puttin' on the Ritz."[28] Their elegant attire and smooth performance wow their audience until a stage light blows out and frightens the creature, who cannot continue performing. The event erupts in chaos as the audience boos them off the stage. Brooks juxtaposes elements drawn from Hollywood horror films and movie musicals to show a bond between inventor and his creation. Comedy, sentiment, and many jokes about sex combine to make this version of *Frankenstein* a celebration of human creativity, ambition, and compassion rather than dwelling on destruction and death: "The film ends happily, with Elizabeth married to the now erudite and sophisticated Monster, while Inga joyfully learns what her new husband Frederick got in return from the Monster during the transfer procedure (the Monster's gigantic penis)."[29]

Director Tim Burton stylishly intertwines Halloween-ish themes of death and life in several popular films, including *Beetlejuice* (1988), *The Nightmare before Christmas* (1993), and *The Corpse Bride* (2005). Burton's film *Frankenweenie* (2012) adapts Shelley's novel and Hollywood *Frankenstein* films to create a story about bringing a dead pet back to life. Victor Frankenstein is a young boy who uses electricity from lightning to reanimate his beloved dog, a scientific endeavor creating chaos but one that brings together his community. Burton made a short, live-action version in 1984 before rewriting the script, and in 2010 began filming the 2012 stop-motion version using puppets. *Frankenweenie* domesticates the Frankenstein myth, lovingly referencing images of characters and settings used in the classic Hollywood film *Frankenstein* while reconfiguring the plot so that it culminates in peaceful acceptance of reanimation technology rather than ending in tragic chaos.

Halloween costumes based on the Frankenstein story include those representing the creature, his bride, and the scientist for adults and children. Costumes incorporate the human, yet not quite human, aspects of Frankenstein's creature by including odd-looking hair, bolts in the head,

stitches across the face, and green skin. Costumes for men tend to hor-
rifically represent the creature, while those for women tend to emphasize
sexiness over scary features. Shelley's tale of dangerous scientific ambition
and agonistic conflict between doubles inspires features of the characters
in toys, games, and costumes; overcoming fear and repulsion, players find
joy in projecting themselves in these media as Frankenstein's creature
or bride. Costumes and figures replicate movie and book characters,
as "Frankenstein" figures from the Universal Monsters and the Mad
Monsters series illustrate (Figures 18, image insert). Adopting the role
of technological innovator and humanized product as disguises in safe
realms, we allow ourselves to manage nature and to teach ourselves to
cope with unintended consequences of scientific ambition and experimentation gone awry.

Today, we tend to admire the powerful opportunities enabled by
innovation, so it is not surprising that we are drawn to artistic representations of inventions made possible by scientific and technical skills. For
example, images by the German photographer Thomas Struth allow us
to peek into laboratories, to be impressed by their scale and detail, and to
be fascinated in considering these settings as technological playgrounds.
Struth's recent show "Nature and Politics" incorporates images of laboratories and other scientific facilities alongside those of theme parks,
notably Disneyland and the Georgia Aquarium. Struth's show includes
works "that examine how human ambition and imagination physically
manifest in the highly complex constructions that shape our world."
The images, published in *Nature and Politics*, "uncover sites of scientific
development—typically kept from public view—where the heights of
human knowledge are enacted, debated and advanced. Struth's images
also reveal the layers of politics and the influences of the past and present
often found in human-crafted environments."[30] The most playful image
in Struth's show is his 2013 photograph of adults and children in front of
the Tropical Reef exhibit at the Atlanta Aquarium, a technical achievement. The tunnel's curved wall arches over the people, encapsulating
two "natural scenes," one the curated fish swimming around the reef

and the other the social interaction taking place in front of the reef and within the marvelous tunnel, a social scene highlighting caregiving and childhood wonder. There is no Frankenstein in this image; however, when the image appears in a photography show alongside images of scientific labs, viewers regard it as a technological marvel of human abilities to manage nature and to offer a packaged natural scene that represents human ambitions to create and care for life.

Other genres of art and artistic craft play with the elements of the *Frankenstein* myth concerned with human management of nature. Anatomizing toys—putting skeletons and other body structures inside toys—is a variant of Frankenstein-type manipulation of bodily organs. Maryland-based artist Jason Freeny produces something like scientific dissections within repurposed toys by creating skeletons inside popular children's toys (Figures 20–24, image insert). The website that displays photographs of Freeny's creations acknowledges he "plays Frankenstein with anatomical children's toys," noting that "Freeny started making sculptures from old toys by taking them apart and designing a skeleton along with realistic organs from your favorite popular toys. The result is pretty freaking amazing! Look in awe as your favorite character's anatomy is revealed in a unique, creative way."[31]

Other artists also adopt the Frankensteinian technique of assemblage. According to the *Urban Dictionary*, "Frankenpets" is used as the name for genetically modified pets, for pets dressed as characters or as other animals, and for reconfigured photographic images or stuffed animals stitched together from parts from other stuffed animals.[32] The heavy stitching of a patchwork bear resembles the dog's stitching in Tim Burton's *Frankenweenie*. Multiple references to Shelley's novel and its Hollywood adaptations mean that Halloween blow-up figures, like costumes and toys, need no labels or captions to be recognized (Figure 18, image insert). The blow-up figures have softened, generic features, resembling the images of the monster in the children's books, while a *New Yorker* cartoon reproduces Karloff-like features in the monster, whose anatomical feature of a flat head makes him an ideal member of a yoga class doing headstands.

In sum, adapted versions of characters and themes in Shelley's novel have influenced a plethora of popular culture objects and texts: toys, costumes, games, films, television shows, art, and crafts. Reflecting on human capacities to invent and reconfigure, many objects and texts resonate with references to the novel *Frankenstein*, which may be more frequently acknowledged as a text that shapes other texts than it is itself read. Shelley's story has become incorporated into modern US culture via objects and adaptations. Along with Bram Stoker's novel *Dracula* (1897), Shelley's characters and themes constitute framing myths that contribute to our *modern* American celebration of Halloween, which "emerged from the Celtic festival of Samhain (summer's end), picked up elements of the Christian Hallowtide (All Saints' Day and All Souls' Day), arrived in North America as an Irish and Scottish festival, and evolved into an unofficial but large-scale holiday by the early 20th century."[33] Given the hegemonic influence of American culture, it is not surprising that the modern celebration of Halloween showcasing a mix of costumes emphasizing ghosts, goblins, and monsters such as Frankenstein's creature has spread to continents beyond North America. Anyone with an Internet connection and a credit card can purchase Halloween costumes based on Shelley's novel that enable one to take on a new identity as the scientist, the creature, or one of their brides.[34]

PART THREE

THE CHALLENGES OF *FRANKENSTEIN:* SCIENCE AND ETHICS

You are my creator, but I am your master . . .
—The Monster, demanding his mate
from Victor Frankenstein.
Mary Shelley, *Frankenstein*

As many and diverse as are the potential meanings and interpretations of the *Frankenstein* story as presented by its original author and in the many derivative works made since its publication, one central theme emerges as very nearly universal. In almost every version, revision, and homage, in almost every medium, from *Bride of Frankenstein* in 1934 to *Frankenhooker* (Frank Henenlotter) in 1990 to *Ex Machina* (Alex Garland) in 2014, the progress of scientific research and discovery outstrips the ethical sensibilities of the persons or institutions conducting it, with disastrous if not catastrophic results. If there is any shared "moral" among all these stories, it is this: however miraculous its potential results, science unchecked is a threat.

It's easy to see why this one foundational element of the *Frankenstein* narrative is so immovable in an otherwise highly adaptable and accommodating framework. Throughout the late 19th and the 20th centuries, individuals, nations, and indeed the entire world confronted again and again the sharp side of science's cutting edge: from mechanized munitions and chemical weapons to technological job loss and the toxic and environmental side effects of the revolutions in agriculture, pharmaceuticals, and energy production.

Still more momentous and appalling, Victor Frankenstein's innovations produce not a dangerous machine but a living, breathing, and (most troubling of all) a thinking *being*. Whether this experiment is conceptualized in metaphysical terms, as a usurpation of divine prerogative, or in terms of a secular ethical understanding, as a titanic failure of science to take account of its ethical responsibility to its subjects and the community, the myriad fictional Frankensteins and Frankenstein stand-ins embody a real, and increasingly urgent, issue within modern culture as our science becomes capable of achieving what Mary Shelley only imagined.

While we push ever back the frontiers of knowledge, of life, of death, of consciousness, while our understanding and control of biology, heredity, and evolution continue to grow, what potential monsters are we making? What kind of monsters might we become?

To answer these questions, physicist and science writer Sidney Perkowitz traces the human preoccupation with creating life, from antiquity to today's world. He shows how science has evolved through many steps in the chemical, biological, and physical understanding of life until now we have the potential to seriously modify humanity and create new synthetic life-forms by manipulating the human genome. At the same time, he considers myth, folklore, and fiction over the centuries to show that the scientific community still struggles with the millennia-old challenge of tempering knowledge with wisdom, of combining scientific progress with enlightened and ethical concerns about what that means for our society and all humanity. These anxieties are becoming not only theoretical but real and urgent as dramatic new developments offer us an opportunity to one-up Victor Frankenstein, if we can. But perhaps, if we are wise enough, we can also learn from him, as he himself implores another character and the reader in Shelley's novel.

Chemists Jay Goodwin and David Lynn, who study the molecular basis of life, extend the scientific story by showing how research at this scale illuminates the origins of life and its development, enlarging our understanding of how we might manipulate and change living things, including ourselves. Referring to Shelley's novel, they show how current molecular research represents a modern version of Victor Frankenstein's ideas based on the known science of the time; and they circle back to Shelley herself, wondering what that prescient, precocious teenager might make of all this. If Shelley's night-born story was both a celebration of the discoveries of her times and a cautionary tale for ours, Goodwin and Lynn's article likewise excites and horrifies, showing us how far we've come, and warning us—yet again—that some technological monsters are already here and could grow unless we successfully blend the drive for knowledge with the wisdom to apply it well.

12

FRANKENSTEIN AND SYNTHETIC LIFE: FICTION, SCIENCE, AND ETHICS

Sidney Perkowitz

INTRODUCTION

The creation of synthetic life may seem a project that could be realized in a 21st-century laboratory, or it may seem merely a fiction that began with Mary Shelley's story about Victor Frankenstein and his creature. In reality, making synthetic life is both science and fiction and even science and myth, with roots far older than this century or the 19th, when Shelley wrote. She understood this, for the full title of her story is *Frankenstein, or The Modern Prometheus*. In Greek mythology, Prometheus was a Titan, one of the powerful divinities who preceded Zeus and the other Olympian gods. In some versions of the myth Prometheus creates mankind, and in all versions he steals fire from the Olympians for the benefit of humanity. These actions angered Zeus, who punished Prometheus by sentencing him to eternal torment.

In Mary Shelley's novel, Victor Frankenstein creates a living being with the hope of creating a superior version of humanity, but like Prometheus, he pays a price for his aspirations. Stories like these raise timeless issues and express significant truths. At the deepest level, they reflect our own feelings about life and death. Furthermore, they present the long-standing moral questions that synthetic life would raise. A modern scientist could still share the same goals and fears as Victor Frankenstein, but with one great difference: now we truly have the scientific tools to modify and perhaps even create living things.

Some observers believe that life has already been synthesized in the form of bacteria that have been radically altered in the laboratory. Scientists have also already attempted to genetically modify non-viable human embryos, and in the latest work seem to have achieved a high success rate in repairing a genetic deficiency that could lead to death. The scientific community is now taking seriously the possibility of engineering genetic changes in humanity that could be inherited, and has called for a moratorium on such work until we better understand its consequences. These could be unpredictable for future generations and could lead to serious abuses by governments, supporters of the discarded idea of eugenics, special interest groups or commercial enterprises. Yet if this same technology were to obtain wide approval and were wisely applied, it could give humanity better health, greater longevity and increased abundance, and improve us as a species.

At the two hundredth anniversary of Shelley's story about the creation of synthetic life, we need to understand the science that could now make these different outcomes possible. Fiction and myth offer a first step. Long before there was a science of synthetic life, artificial life-forms were being imagined in myth and legend, then later in literature and the theater, and finally in film, television, and the Internet.

These efforts, including Mary Shelley's story, add up to a fantasy history of synthetic life that illustrates the motivations for creating it, the means to achieve it, and the deep ethical concerns it raises, providing an introduction to the real science of synthetic life and how society might respond to it.

IMAGINARY SYNTHETIC LIFE

Since humanity's early days, different cultures have wondered about the beginnings of life and have expressed the desire to create it, typically in human form. Why? Perhaps to challenge the gods, or to outwit death, or to improve humanity, or simply driven by the so-called techno-logical imperative: "because we can." When science had advanced suf-ficiently, its practitioners began trying to imitate, modify, or create life by different means—first mechanically, in the form of early automata and robots, and now, within the emerging sciences of genetic engi-neering and synthetic biology.

At the same time, writers and thinkers imagined how humankind could create life. Often these imaginings expressed deep concerns about replacing God or the gods as the creators of life. These concerns have different roots. One is based on fear: divinities reserve for themselves the power to make life and, like Zeus, become angry when humanity challenges this right. In the Judeo-Christian tradition, another factor is that God created humanity "in His own image," giving human life a unique value and sanctity. A different view sidesteps such issues. It is the purely materialistic and scientific approach that holds that during the multibillion-year history of the universe and our planet, atoms became simple molecules and then complex ones that self-replicated. In a complicated process whose origins and details science does not yet fully understand, these eventually took on the characteristics we associate with "life" to become all the life-forms we now know.

The history of imaginary synthetic life embraces both the divine and the scientific approaches. An early example of the divine creation of a living being is the Greek legend of Pygmalion, made famous in the work of the Roman poet Ovid. Pygmalion was a sculptor who made a statue of a beautiful woman. He fell in love with this ivory imitation and one day, he found that it had turned into a real woman, brought to life by the goddess Aphrodite in response to his wish.

Greek mythology also shows a god using technology to create what can only be called the first robotic synthetic being. The god was Hephaestus (Vulcan in Roman mythology), who worked with fire and metals to make devices such as Apollo's chariot. His greatest artifact was Talos, a giant, bronze, manlike construction that defended the island of Crete from enemy ships by hurling rocks at them. Talos's metal body, however, still needed a divine spark in the form of ichor, the blood of the gods, that ran through a vein in its body. When the ichor drained out of the vein, Talos was destroyed.

Other early metallic creations were also said to have lifelike qualities. Two 13th-century religious figures and philosophers, Albertus Magnus and Roger Bacon, were each reputed to have made a talking head out of brass. Later a more humble material, clay, became the source for the golem, a synthetic creature from Jewish legend. The most famous of these was said to have been created in the 16th century by the rabbi of Prague to protect the city's Jews from pogroms, that is, violent organized attacks directed at them. This artificial being required another kind of divine spark. In the Old Testament, God fashions Adam from dust or clay and breathes life into him. Similarly, after the rabbi constructs the golem, it is animated by calling on the power of God.

One feature of the golem legend would continue throughout the saga of imaginary synthetic creatures. Though made to protect the Jews, the creature eventually goes violently out of control and must be deactivated. The idea that synthetic beings might run amok, turn against their creators, or be made for evil purposes raises fears that persist as we approach the possibility of really making them. Frankenstein's creature follows this tradition in turning on its maker.

In one crucial aspect, however, Mary Shelley's vision departs from earlier ones: Dr. Frankenstein makes his creature purely through scientific knowledge rather than by supernatural means.

Shelley's story gives few details about the creation of this synthetic creature—the Being, as Mary's husband, Percy, called it—but it does tell us that it is made of parts taken from "the dissecting room and the slaughterhouse." And though the Being is ugly, it has some favorable features. Its limbs are in proportion, it is agile, and it displays a good brain as it speaks eloquently and reads classic literary works. (Director James Whale's definitive 1931 film version of *Frankenstein* makes Boris Karloff into a more monstrous Being. Its brain comes from a dead murderer, it emits only animal-like cries, and it lurches rather than walks.)

Shelley's fictional Being, with its intellectual and physical capacities, made not by God but by science, follows new discoveries of her time. In 1780, the Italian scientist Luigi Galvani had observed that the muscles in a frog's legs twitched when voltage was applied. His discovery of what he called "animal electricity"—what is now known as bioelectricity—generated huge interest before either electricity or life processes were well understood. It was not then a big step to believe that electricity might reanimate the dead, and experiments were made to revive hanged criminals by applying voltage to the dead body (as described elsewhere in this anthology)—needless to say, unsuccessfully. Nevertheless, Shelley's introduction to the 1831 edition of *Frankenstein* alludes to these beliefs, stating, "Perhaps a corpse would be reanimated; galvanism had given token of such things."

Certainly Victor Frankenstein has the background to perform a scientific reanimation. Shelley writes that as a boy he studied electrical science and moved on to chemistry and anatomy, using this knowledge to learn how to animate dead matter. After constructing the Being on a "dreary night in November," he collects "the instruments of life . . . that I might infuse a spark of being into the lifeless thing that lay at my feet." Shelley does not tell us what these instruments are, but clearly this is a scientific process.

Yet for all the neutral scientific approach, something deeper pulls at Victor when he beholds the Being he has created. After animating it, Victor says:

> I had worked hard for nearly two years, for the sole purpose of infusing life into an inanimate body . . . I had deprived myself of rest and health. I had desired it with an ardour that far exceeded moderation; but now that I had finished, the beauty of the dream vanished, and breathless horror and disgust filled my heart. Unable to endure the aspect of the being I had created, I rushed out of the room . . .

Similar emotions appear in James Whale's *Frankenstein*. When Dr. Frankenstein (Colin Clive) first sees the body he has energized with a lightning bolt actually twitch, he is overcome, crying with a mixture of hysteria, exultation, and fear, "It's alive! *It's alive!* IT'S ALIVE! . . . Now I know what it feels like to be God!"

These visceral reactions represent a realization that despite the scientific trappings, the creator of synthetic life may sense that he or she is transgressing forbidden boundaries—simultaneously feeling pride in the achievement and fear that it will be punished. There are psychological factors too, as noted by the pioneering psychoanalyst Sigmund Freud in 1919. In his essay "The Uncanny," Freud wrote that humans feel dread in the presence of a dead body because that awakens hidden but intense feelings about our own mortality. Yet once we accept that a being has reached that final stage of nonexistence, it is a new shock to see it again cross the boundary from death to life, becoming a person and not a thing—the shock that Dr. Frankenstein feels when he says, "It's alive!"

Freud's "uncanny" border between living and nonliving is echoed in a modern possibility, the creation of robots that look and act human—androids, which, if they were self-conscious, would represent a type of synthetic being. How human-like they seem depends on our reactions, because much of our willingness to see a synthetic being as truly alive depends on projecting our own characteristics onto it. In 1970, that led the Japanese robotics professor Masahiro Mori to the concept of the "Uncanny Valley." As robots evolve from lumbering metal machines to human-like appearance and behavior, people make emotional connections with them. But if an android becomes nearly but not quite indistinguishable from a person, empathy turns into revulsion, like a dip or "valley" in the empathetic link to the android. This may be why Dr. Frankenstein feels horror at his creation: it is somewhat human, yet not human enough.

Other fictional synthetic creatures appeared in the 19th century, starting just before *Frankenstein* was first published. In 1817, the German author E. T. A. Hoffman wrote "The Sandman," a Pygmalion story about a young man who falls in love with an imitation woman called Olympia, a clockwork automaton or early robot. She and similar artificial beings appear in the ballets *Coppélia* (1870) and Tchaikovsky's *Nutcracker* (1892), and the opera *The Tales of Hoffman* (1881).

Only in the early 20th century did really widely known synthetic beings appear, in the stage play *R. U. R.* and the film *Metropolis*, both of which introduced beings made for use by humankind. Karel Čapek's *R. U. R. (Rossum's Universal Robots)* became a worldwide sensation after its premiere in Prague in 1921. It remains famous today because it gave us the word "robot," which derives from the word "robota," which means "forced labor" in Čapek's native Czech and describes these entities made only to work for humanity.

The robots were made of an artificial organic material that "behaved exactly like living matter." It was used in "vats for the preparation of liver, brains . . . and a spinning mill for weaving nerves and veins" to mimic human bodies. Decades before the discovery of the role and structure of DNA, before genetic engineering and synthetic biology, Čapek foresaw the creation of organic rather than mechanical synthetic humans, and also gave them reason and emotion. They resent their slave status and desire revenge against humanity but also display the capacity for love.

Another enslaved being appeared in the remarkable film *Metropolis* (Fritz Lang, 1927), which portrayed a futuristic city of that name. The story features a noticeably female mechanical robot built by the scientist-wizard Rotwang (played by Rudolf Klein-Rogge), as the first of many that would replace human workers like the robots in R. U. R. Later Rotwang transforms the robot into what we would now call an android. This is an exact physical replica of Maria, a real woman, but it lacks her moral sense (the robot, the real Maria, and her android copy are all played by Brigitte Helm). Through their synthetic beings that are more or less human, R. U. R. and Metropolis raise the still relevant moral questions, how should we treat our own creations? and its corollary, how would they treat us?

Other imaginary synthetic life-forms followed. Many were mechanical robots, most famously in Isaac Asimov's science fiction story collection I, Robot (1950), which introduced the Three Laws of Robotics, a guide to robotic behavior toward humans (there was no corresponding guide for human behavior toward robots). Other media creations included the mechanical robots Gort and Robby in the films The Day the Earth Stood Still (Robert Wise, 1951) and Forbidden Planet (Fred M. Wilcox, 1956), respectively.

Mechanical entities like these could never be mistaken for people, but later, two stories showed manufactured synthetic beings made to look and act human—that is, androids. In Ridley Scott's classic futuristic cult film Blade Runner (1982, based on Philip K. Dick's 1968 novel Do Androids Dream of Electric Sheep?), engineered "replicants" can pass as human but nevertheless know they are artificial with a deliberately limited lifetime. Led by the exceptionally strong and intelligent replicant Roy Batty (Rutger Hauer), they display the human trait of self-preservation. They violently rebel against their preset termination until a special policeman, Blade Runner Rick Deckard (Harrison Ford), destroys them. Another replicant, the advanced model Rachael (Sean Young), has a deeper level of self-awareness. She believes she is human and has difficulty accepting that she is not.

Another significant android character is Lieutenant Commander Data (Brent Spiner) in the television series Star Trek: The Next Generation

(1987–1994). Like Roy Batty, Data is in many ways a physically and mentally superior being. As an officer in the United Federation's Star Fleet, he earns the respect and friendship of his human shipmates. Though initially he does not experience human emotions, an "emotion chip" implanted into his artificial brain later helps him do so, but he still struggles with the complexities of human feelings and behavior.

The quandaries that Roy Batty, Rachael, and Commander Data face illustrate the difficulties in creating engineered synthetic beings. Even with a degree of self-awareness, their inability to become fully "human" highlights how hard it would be to artificially reproduce self-consciousness and the human condition, let alone create beings with superior abilities.

There is another approach, which is to modify or create life, including human life, through genetic manipulation. Once, such efforts to "improve" humanity came under the heading of eugenics, the social philosophy that aims to promote reproduction among "desirable" people while preventing the "undesirable" from reproducing. This approach is now discredited, not least because of the vile role it played under the Nazis. Instead, we are considering how to genetically change people for laudable goals like fighting disease, and with the added realization that genetic manipulation is the modern science that might actually also be able to create new beings.

As fiction has explored synthetic humans, it has explored the consequences of genetic manipulation. In 1931, Aldous Huxley's novel *Brave New World* described a future society based on an advanced form of eugenics, where reproductive technology is used to put people into five castes, from the highest Alphas to the lowest Epsilons. To create these categories, fetuses are cloned and chemically altered so they develop into people with either enhanced or limited abilities. The former dominate this future world; the latter are fit only for inferior roles in a stagnant, shallow, and corrupt society.

Decades later, writer-director Andrew Niccol's film *Gattaca* (1997), which NASA called the most plausible science fiction film ever made, foresaw a future dominated by eugenics and DNA (the title *Gattaca* combines the initials of guanine, adenine, thymine, and cytosine, the compounds crucial to how DNA functions). In a society focused on people with the "best" genes, the wealthy pay for enhanced "designer children," while genetically "inferior" people face limited lives and prospects. The story, however, has a redemptive element. By manipulating the system and through sheer persistent effort, Vincent Freeman (Ethan Hawke) soars above his genetic deficiencies to realize his dream of becoming an astronaut.

These stories, along with Shelley's *Frankenstein* and the many other tales about modified or wholly synthetic beings, point to two questions we must face as fiction becomes reality: the scientific one, Can we truly modify living things and go on to build synthetic beings? and the ethical one, which asks simply, Even if we can, should we?

REAL SYNTHETIC LIFE

We are still a long way from making *Blade Runner*'s replicants or a modern Frankenstein's Being, but we are now creating the science that might make this possible. One set of tools comes from advances in digital technology, robotics, neuroscience, tissue engineering, and more. These are already contributing to the design of devices and systems that compensate for bodily damage or decline: brain-machine interfaces that provide direct mind control for a paralyzed person to operate a computer or a person with a missing limb to manage a prosthetic replacement; and artificial bones or organs that successfully replace the natural versions. These could even someday go beyond replacing physical abilities to augmenting them and perhaps also to creating neural prosthetics for conditions such as the deterioration of memory with age. We are also beginning to see real growth in the power of artificial intelligence in applications like computer assistants that listen, interpret and reply, and self-driving automobiles.

These abilities to create synthetic versions of the human body and brain point to the possibility of someday creating a complete synthetic being, an android, as human-seeming and as capable as Commander Data. But for now, we do not know how to even begin building a fully functioning self-aware brain—indeed we do not even understand our own consciousness, one of the great puzzles of current science. Judging by the present state of our technologies and our still limited knowledge, the construction of an android based on computer chips, artificial eyes and skin, and so on that would qualify as a true synthetic being will not happen soon; nor does this approach offer a direct way to broadly improve the human condition, because artificial augmentations or beings do not naturally reproduce but can only be manufactured.

However, another set of new tools—the rapidly developing techniques of genetic engineering and synthetic biology—offer the real possibility of creating "improved" people, whatever that may mean, and even wholly constructed humans or human variants.

This continues an old quest that began with seeking the origins of life. Probably the earliest idea about how life begins is spontaneous generation, the theory that living things can arise from inanimate dust or dead flesh. Aristotle was the great expositor of this idea, and it was widely accepted until it was unequivocally disproved in the 19th century. In 1864, the great French scientist Louis Pasteur announced experimental results showing that when microorganisms were prevented from entering a sealed environment, it remained sterile without spontaneously producing life. Instead, he concluded, life as we know it proceeds by the law of biogenesis—living beings arise only when other living beings reproduce.

But though life comes only from life, in the 19th century chemical analysis showed that living things are made of nonliving components, and later, that life could be affected by purely chemical means. In 1899 the German researcher Jacques Loeb, working at the Marine Biological Laboratory in Woods Hole, Massachusetts, used saltwater solutions to induce sea urchin eggs to reproduce without fertilization in the process called parthenogenesis. This achievement was overhyped in the media of the time as the "creation of life," but it supported Loeb's dream of truly controlling life. As he was quoted in an article in *McClure's Magazine* in 1902,

> I very early came to the belief that the forces which rule in the realm of living things are not other than those which we know in the inanimate world. Everything pointed that way . . . I wanted to take life in my hands and play with it. I wanted to handle it in my laboratory as I would any other chemical reaction—to start it, stop it, vary it, study it under every condition, to direct it at my will!

In 1912, Loeb's book *The Mechanistic Conception of Life* underscored these ideas and his vision of creating "a constructive or engineering biology in place of a biology that is merely analytical," that is, a science and technology that could successfully manipulate living things.

Loeb anticipated today's genetic engineering, but before that could develop, scientists had to learn more about the materials of life. Some of that knowledge came from the 19th-century development of organic chemistry, the study of the carbon-based molecules that also contain hydrogen, oxygen, and nitrogen and are ubiquitous in living things. Then in the 1930s, the new science of molecular biology began examining the molecules of life in detail, particularly the proteins that perform living functions. The powerful tool of X-ray analysis, which uses short-wavelength electromagnetic radiation to determine the atomic structure of intricate molecules, aided this development. The most significant of these efforts was the determination of the structure of deoxyribonucleic acid, DNA. When that complex biological molecule was first isolated in 1869, its function was unknown, but later there were hints that it passed on genetic information. In 1952 researchers confirmed that it did so, but exactly how was not understood.

The answer came in 1953, when the American scientist James Watson and the British scientist Francis Crick used X-ray data to show that the DNA molecule consists of a double helix, chains of smaller units that twist around each other like a double spiral staircase. These units include adenine, guanine, cytosine, and thymine (A, G, C, and T), appearing in "base pairs"—always A with T, and C with G—whose arrangement encodes genetic information. The pairing ensures that this information is copied and passed on when an organism reproduces and its cells divide. The importance of the discovery was recognized when Watson, Crick, and a third researcher, Maurice Wilkins, were awarded the Nobel Prize in Physiology or Medicine for 1962 (questions remain about whether a fourth researcher, Rosalind Franklin, has received proper credit for the important role of her X-ray data).

In establishing how heredity operates, the discovery of the structure of DNA was a major step in understanding life processes. The discovery also opened the possibility of characterizing an organism by examining its DNA or "genome," since particular sequences within the DNA—the genes—act as instructions to make the proteins that determine how an organism functions. This laid the basis for genetic manipulation. As Jacques Loeb had dreamed, DNA "blueprints" could be chemically altered to engineer the resulting life-form. Victor Frankenstein had to stitch together body parts to build his creature, but a modern scientist could in principle modify or design an organism by changing or creating its DNA.

To understand and manipulate an organism's genome, a scientist must first determine how the base pairs of its DNA are arranged to form its genetic code, a process called "sequencing," then find connections between specific genes and the bodily features and functions they control. Human DNA contains some three billion base pairs and over twenty thousand genes, so sequencing it is a daunting task. But in 2000, Francis Collins, director of the US National Institutes of Health (NIH), and the pioneering geneticist J. Craig Venter announced that human DNA had been sequenced through the efforts they led. This was done jointly through the Human Genome Project, supported by the NIH and an international scientific consortium, and a parallel, privately funded effort by the Celera Corporation, spearheaded by Venter. The full genome, published in 2003, was described by the NIH as "nature's complete blueprint for building a human being."

Progress has also been made in determining the connections between human genes and the bodily traits they define, which is essential for genetic knowledge to produce true medical benefits. This is not simple, because genes and what they control may not be connected in a direct one-to-one way. A given gene may influence more than one trait; a given trait such as autism may be related to genes scattered throughout the entire genome; and environmental and other factors can influence how cells actually interpret the genetic instructions. Nevertheless, it has been possible to identify, for instance, genes that determine blood type, play a role in resistance to infection, and are linked to early-onset breast cancer, along with about eighteen hundred other diseases.

In some cases, researchers now know enough about the human genome to carry out targeted genetic engineering. An early example resulted in a better way to make insulin, the protein that controls the amount of sugar in the bloodstream. Diabetics lack this natural compound and must receive it by injection. This injectable insulin used to be derived from cows or pigs; but in 1973, scientists developed a better approach using recombinant DNA, which was constructed in the lab from other DNA sequences. They isolated the part of human DNA that produces insulin and inserted it into the DNA of certain bacteria by chemical means. As the bacterial cells divided and reproduced, they produced insulin that could be harvested. Today this engineered insulin is used by millions of diabetics.

Recombinant technology that splices desirable genes into existing DNA has other applications in medicine, such as producing human growth hormone, and elsewhere. In agriculture, for example, the technique has created crops like corn and soybeans modified to resist pests, disease, and herbicides, which are now widely grown. Beginning ten thousand years before the advent of modern bioscience, humanity obtained similar desirable results through the selective breeding of plants and animals, a completely accepted method of manipulating genetic outcomes. Nevertheless, some consumers emphatically reject genetically modified "frankenfood" as unnatural or insufficiently tested, illustrating the strong negative reactions that genetic engineering can generate even when not applied to people.

Both the beneficial and worrisome aspects of genetic engineering are amplified with the rise in the last decade of synthetic biology, an advanced approach that provides greater control over living things. Synthetic biology is so new that it lacks a universal definition, but a core element is that it is an engineering approach to manipulating biological systems. One definition is that it deals with "the design and construction of novel artificial pathways, organisms or devices, or the redesign of existing biological systems." Another formulation, made by a group of experts for a European Commission report, defines synthetic biology as "the synthesis of complex biologically based (or inspired) systems, which display functions that do not exist in nature . . . at all levels of the hierarchy of biological structures—from individual molecules to whole cells, tissues and organisms."

The "systems" aspect of synthetic biology also draws on digital and computational science. In a recent review, Simon Auslander of ETH Zurich and Martin Fussenegger of the University of Basel point out that like transistors, which control the flow of electrical current and can be connected in circuits to perform digital operations, "biomolecules can control the flow of biological signals and are connected to complex circuits that organize cellular operations."

An example of synthetic biology in action is the production of the anti-malarial compound artemisinin, discovered as a plant extract by the Chinese scientist Youyou Tu, who in 2015 shared a Nobel Prize for her work. With its natural origin, the cost and availability of this extract suffered undesirable fluctuations. In 2004 biochemical engineer Jay Keasling at the University of California, Berkeley, began developing an artificial, multistep "metabolic pathway" to make artemisinin cheaply and reliably. His team synthesized the gene that made an enzyme necessary to produce the compound, inserted the gene into yeast cells, which

then made artemisinin, and optimized the process for large-scale production. By mid-2015, the method had supplied fifteen million doses
to African countries where malaria is a serious issue and is projected to
provide treatment to one billion people by 2025. Other applications of
synthetic biology are emerging. In 2015, scientists at the J. Craig Venter
Institute (JCVI, the research establishment founded by Venter) showed
how to modify diatoms, a type of microalgae found in watery environments, to produce bio fuels.

Despite its real or projected benefits, synthetic biology raises doubts,
such as the concerns about frankenfood, and inspires fears of "making
monsters" and "playing God." In 2006, an article in the *Economist*
magazine introducing this new science was provocatively titled "Playing
Demigods" and showed an image of Frankenstein's monster contem-
plating DNA's double helix. The article reasonably asserted that "synthetic biology needs to be monitored, but not stifled," yet also exploited
fears of what would happen when the first living thing "created from
scratch by the hand of man" begins to reproduce. These fears persist a
decade later, as in a 2016 article from The Institution of Engineering and
Technology entitled "Frankenstein Redux: Is Modern Science Making
a Monster?"

Apocalyptic language aside, the rapid advances in genetic manipulation force us to ask whether we can indeed radically modify people or
even make artificial versions. The closest we have come so far is with a
life-form far simpler than a human: a radically re-engineered microbe. In
2010, Venter and a team of researchers at JCVI built an entire genome
in the lab, made to be similar to that from a natural bacterium, *Mycoplasma mycoides*. This DNA was inserted into cells of a related bacterial
strain, *Mycoplasma capricolum*, to replace its natural genome, which had
been removed, like changing a computer's operating system while leaving
the hardware in place. The modified bacteria continued to function and
reproduce, and following the instructions encoded in the new DNA created proteins characteristic of *Mycoplasma mycoides*. Effectively *M. capricolum*
had been changed into *M. mycoides*.

According to the researchers, this experiment was carried out to learn how to manipulate DNA more effectively, not to create a synthetic being. In any case it produced only a synthetic genome, but like Loeb's work on parthenogenesis, it was presented in the media as the creation of a complete synthetic organism. Some religious groups denounced the result, and Venter was accused of "playing God." Still, this achievement, remarkable as it is, does not match the complexity of dealing with the human genome. Syn 1.0, the artificial version of the *M. mycoides* genome, contains 901 genes, compared to the more than twenty thousand in the human genome.

In practice the brave new synthetic world contains many pitfalls in editing or making a genome, even a relatively simple one, and putting it into an organism; and even if that can be accomplished, it is still difficult to know exactly what genes control which of an organism's traits and functions. In early 2016, Venter's team at JCVI reported on efforts to engineer a bacterium with the smallest genome and fewest genes that would support life. Two different attempts to build this minimal DNA for *M. capricolum* from scratch did not produce a viable microbe, though through trial and error the team did produce a pared-down version of Syn 1.0 with only 473 genes.

But genomic knowledge is growing fast, and so is the push by entrepreneurs and investors, as well as scientists and clinicians, to rapidly explore, develop, and exploit the area. This heightens concerns about how, whether, and when we should manipulate the human genome, and who, if anyone, should do so.

These issues were raised by researchers, clinicians, technologists, and bioethicists, led by the Nobel Laureate David Baltimore, in the leading research journal *Science* in April 2015, and at a summit conference in December 2015 convened by the United States National Academy of Sciences and other institutions. In both venues, the focus was on the new gene editing method called CRISPR, an acronym for "clustered regularly interspersed palindromic repeats." Named the scientific breakthrough of 2015, CRISPR makes it relatively simple to cut open a DNA sequence at a precisely targeted site and splice in a new sequence—for instance, to eliminate a sequence that is known to control a harmful disease and replace it with a corrected set of DNA instructions. In general, as the *Science* article states, this throws gene editing wide open by allowing "any researcher with knowledge of molecular biology to modify genomes, making feasible experiments that were previously difficult or impossible to conduct."

CRISPR has already shown its value, for instance, in developing therapies for cancer and AIDS. Its great potential to treat disease and even improve human capabilities has been quickly recognized by commercial interests. The profit-making possibilities for the technique have led to contentious disputes over patent rights. In early 2017, the U.S. Patent and Trademark Office decided between competing claims for the invention of CRISPR from the Broad Institute, an arm of MIT and Harvard that explores genetic knowledge for the treatment of disease; and from the University of California. The Patent Office decided in favor of the Broad Institute, but the University of California may appeal the decision. Despite this lingering uncertainty, an estimated billion dollars of start-up capital has poured into firms that make up what has been called CRISPR Inc. These corporations plan to develop the technique for applications that promise revolutionary advances in areas from medicine to agriculture.

REAL SYNTHETIC LIFE AND REAL ETHICS

There is, however, one great issue with genetic manipulation that sets it apart from the technology that could produce mechanical and digital android versions of people. Genetic technology could be used to change the DNA in the reproductive cells that carry genetic information to an organism's offspring, its so-called germline. If this is done in sperm, fertilized eggs, or embryos, every cell in the organism is altered and the changes, for good or ill, are forever passed on to succeeding generations. This possibility greatly raises the stakes for what genetic manipulation could do to the human race and therefore raises serious ethical issues.

With these questions in mind, David Baltimore said at the 2015 summit that "the unthinkable has become conceivable." He and his colleagues believe it would be "irresponsible to proceed" without further evaluating the risks for humanity and gaining a "societal consensus" about how to continue. As a temporary solution, they called for a moratorium on making inheritable changes to the human genome.

But by the time the moratorium was proposed, its spirit had already been violated. Earlier in 2015, a Chinese research group became the first to openly report an attempt to alter human DNA with CRISPR. The experiment was carried out on abnormal non-viable embryos from in vitro fertilization clinics, so there was no intention to produce a baby; nor did the experiment directly raise issues according to current ethical protocols. Still, the effort was controversial and its outcome disturbing. The researchers hoped to produce embryos with a precisely altered gene in every cell, but they met utter failure. Every one of the eighty-five embryos either died, lacked the altered gene, exhibited a mixture of altered and unaltered cells, or suffered damaged DNA.

This failed attempt and a similar effort proposed in the United Kingdom motivated the December 2015 summit conference and the resulting recommendation for a moratorium. But in February 2017, the National Academy of Sciences and the National Academy of Medicine— leading commenters on and arbiters of scientific and medical policy in the United States—issued a lengthy report, *Human Genome Editing: Science, Ethics, and Governance*, which further examined the ethical questions. An international group of nearly two dozen scientists and physicians, bioethicists, and representatives of the legal, cultural, and commercial worlds reviewed the tools available for genetic editing and the consequences of such alterations.

The report notes first that as a society and as a matter of public policy, we have not really begun to address the many human implications of genetic technology. One concern with heritable genome editing is to find the balance between the benefits that would come to individuals such as parents and children, and the harms that could affect an entire society and culture. "This is a complicated ethical analysis," says the report, "because the individual benefits and risks are more immediate and concrete, whereas concerns about cultural effects are necessarily more diffuse . . . and because any cultural changes resulting from a new technology take time to develop."

Nevertheless, we must find a way to weigh the individual benefits against the wider costs. These include unintended genetic consequences and the impact on the ideal of a "level playing field" for all the members of a society. In the former instance, if people could be physically and mentally enhanced via gene editing as in the film *Gattaca*, that would change human DNA with unknown long-term outcomes for descendants. In the latter, if enhancements were limited to those who could afford them, that would only make worse the inequalities in a society where lack of equal opportunity is already an issue. Even if gene editing were used not to enhance people but only to eliminate disease, that too could become available only to the "haves" in our society within the present system of distributing medical care. Overall, the potential split between those who would benefit from gene editing and those who would not or would even be relatively diminished by it carries an uncomfortable whiff of eugenics.

For reasons such as these, the report recommends that genome editing should not proceed without more consideration of the issues; but to the surprise of many observers, the report does not support a full moratorium. Instead, it proposes that after more studies of risks and benefits, clinical trials of embryo editing might be allowed for couples if both have a serious genetic disease that might be passed on to a child for whom embryo editing is "the last reasonable option." Predictably, illustrating the weight of the unresolved ethical issues, this engendered a diversity of responses from the scientific community. They ranged from approval of the limited clinical use to dismay that the report seemingly supports any use whatsoever of genetic editing before a full public discussion and consensus have taken place.

Meanwhile experiments continue in human genetic editing when they do not violate the restriction that the genetic changes cannot be heritable. In early 2017, a team of Chinese scientists reported using CRISPR to correct genetic mutations in six human embryos. Unlike the embryos used in the earlier failed Chinese effort in 2015, these were normal except that they were immature and so could not develop into babies. The researchers were able to correct the mutation, which would have led to a hereditary disease, in all the cells of one embryo and in some cells in two others—a limited but better success rate than in the 2015 attempt.

In August 2017 however, embryologist Shoukhrat Mitalipov of Oregon Health and Science University and his team announced an apparently far more successful effort that could be an important step toward clinical use of gene editing to repair problems in human embryos. The researchers used CRISPR to target and cut a particular gene at the site of a mutation that produces an enlarged heart, which can cause sudden cardiac arrest and death, and added pieces of DNA containing the healthy gene sequence. This eliminated the mutation in 42 out of 58 embryos formed from donated eggs and sperm by in vitro fertilization (none were implanted in women) apparently without damaging any other part of the genome.

Like the report *Human Genome Editing: Science, Ethics, and Governance* with its limited endorsement of clinical use, this effort raised varied reactions in the research community. Jennifer Doudna at University of California, Berkeley, a pioneer of the CRISPR method, found herself "uncomfortable" with the study, saying that "It's not about research . . . It's about how we get to a clinical application of this technology." Others think that Mitalipov's results show that there may be a relatively low level of risk in clinical use and that an increase in healthy embryos from in vitro fertilization justifies the use of CRISPR. But illustrating that this is far from settled science, soon after the Mitalipov paper was published, still other researchers raised questions by noting reasons why CRISPR gene editing may not have happened at all in this case, or not in the way that was reported.

Nevertheless, it has also become clear that scientists are ready to go beyond gene editing tools like CRISPR with still bolder approaches to modifying the human genome. In 2016, twenty-five academic scientists and figures in the biotechnology industry, led by Jef Boeke at New York University and George Church at Harvard, proposed what was called either the Human Genome Project–Write (HGP-write) or simply the Genome Project–Write (GP-write) in an article its originators wrote to describe its goals. The first title honored the Human Genome Project under the NIH and the Celera Corporation that had sequenced or "read" the human genome. Now this new project aimed to create from scratch, or "write," the entire human genome with its three billion base pairs, and other huge genomes, within a decade at a cost of billions to be raised and managed by the nonprofit Center of Excellence for Engineering Biology.

Considering that so far the only lab-built genomes are the small bacterial ones from JCVI and a portion of a synthetic yeast genome made by Boeke, this was a remarkably audacious proposal. It met with mixed responses from the scientific community. Some researchers called it "brilliant" with "unlimited potential"; others questioned its scientific rationale and whether existing technology can really design and build enormous genomes. But the project's originators thought this approach is essential if we are to make genetic change on a big scale. "Editing [of genes] doesn't scale very well," said Church, adding, "when you have to make changes to every gene in the genome it may be more efficient to do it in large chunks."

Though the founders of HGP-write pointed to its scientific and medical benefits, observers raised ethical concerns. For instance, Drew Endy, a bioengineer at Stanford, and Laurie Zoloth, a religion professor at Northwestern University, asserted that questions such as "whether and under what circumstances we should make such technologies real" should have been broadly addressed before the project began and not decided by a small group without seeking wide consensus; nor was it clear that the federal research establishment would support the concept. Tellingly, NIH director Francis Collins was not enthusiastic. The NIH encourages research in DNA synthesis, he said, but "has not considered the time to be right for funding a large-scale production-oriented" project like this, adding that such projects "immediately raise numerous ethical and philosophical red flags."

In response to the ethical questions, the project's founders were quick to discount fears that it would directly affect the human germline or lead to the creation of new kinds of humans. Jef Boeke stated that any synthetic products from HGP-write would be engineered to make reproduction impossible, adding, "We're not trying to make an army of clones or start a new era of eugenics. That is not the plan." But after further ethical concerns were raised, and the researchers reconsidered the technical difficulties of building large-scale genomes, they substantially scaled back the project. "Human" was dropped from its title, which is now definitively "Genome Project–write;" and rather than immediately try to build a human genome, the scientists will first draw on expert opinion and public comments to decide whether this is a worthy goal.

After a full-speed ahead approach focused on the human genome, these changes illustrate again that the desire to quickly develop, apply, and exploit the new science of the human genome needs to be tempered by thoughtful consideration. Along with the proposed moratorium on modifying human DNA except for limited clinical use, this would help allay fears that CRISPR and synthetic biology will soon lead to a world like that in the film *Gattaca*, dominated by genetic destiny and a kind of new scientific eugenics. The scientific potential certainly remains for improved or completely new kinds of beings to be created using these methods, but Frankenstein-like moments of creation are still far distant, according to two leading scientists involved in these efforts. After the failure in 2016 to design and make a minimal bacterial genome at JCVI, Craig Venter summarized the state of the art when he said, "Our current knowledge of biology is not sufficient to sit down and design a living organism and build it." And responding to the original HGP-write proposal to construct the entire human genome, NIH director Collins said,

"Whole-genome, whole-organism synthesis projects extend far beyond current scientific capabilities."

This does not mean that synthetic life will never come, because the pressures to continue exploring and using the relevant science and technology will continue; but if it does, it will not appear as living goo crawling out of a test tube or a Frankensteinian creature suddenly rising up from a laboratory bench. Rather it will be the result of modifying humans or other organisms over succeeding generations. This long-term approach to Victor Frankenstein's dream of "infusing life" may give us time to understand what we are doing and why we are doing it. If so, we may hope to someday make and deal with synthetic life-forms without the "breathless horror and disgust" that Victor Frankenstein felt, but with the knowledge that we have achieved something good for humanity and for the new beings themselves.

13

WHAT WOULD MARY SHELLEY SAY TODAY?

Jay Goodwin and David Lynn

Venter is creaking open the most profound door in humanity's history, potentially peeking into its destiny. He is not merely copying life artificially . . . or modifying it radically by genetic engineering. He is going towards the role of a god: creating artificial life that could never have existed naturally.[1]

In 2010, the pioneering bioscientist J. Craig Venter and his colleagues reported stripping the genetic material from one bacterial cell and replacing it with an artificial genome, that is, a complete set of DNA instructions constructed by chemical synthesis.[2] The resulting "synthetic life," launched in the second decade of the 21st century, was the realization of an idea introduced almost two hundred years earlier in Mary Shelley's *Frankenstein*. This landmark of horror and science fiction literature tattooed the social and moral dilemmas of synthetic life onto our collective cultural psyche; an image that continues to echo through our scientific and technological endeavors to this day.[3]

Creation stories are often passed down through mythology and storytelling as a dynamic mingling of philosophy, religion, and science. This blending of supernatural forces that are not for us to know with the commitment to reason creates a tension and motivates wonder and imagination around some of our most fundamental questions: What does it mean to be human? Why do we love? Why are we here? How did life begin and how did it evolve? Why does it continue to do so? What specifically misfires to cause illness and disease? Why do we age and not live forever? Are we alone in the universe? These questions provide a muse for literature and art, as well as scientific inquiry, innovation, and technological development. Much has been learned since Shelley wrote her tale of creating life from deathly remains, but the nature and the context for the big questions we face have only become richer and more inspiring. To understand that context, we consider this question: what would Mary Shelley say today?

Shelley, a young writer born in the romantic period, was likely responding to the empiricism and deconstructionism within science, literature, and the arts from the preceding era, the age of reason. Romanticism embraced a holistic perspective of human beings connected to and engaged with nature—perhaps what today might be called a systems-focused scientific lexicon. While the romantic movement spawned a remarkable catalog of literary works, Shelley's *Frankenstein, or The Modern Prometheus* perhaps claims the greatest and longest-lived impact. Her tale threads the creation mythology in a dialectical fashion, developing the tension, if not outright conflict, between the natural philosophers—the scientists of her time—and other contemporary social, philosophical, and political forces. While it was perhaps intended primarily to entertain, a horror story to thrill the reader, it has also yielded to many other deeper and wider interpretations. We have chosen to view it through the lens of the science of her time, how that science is reflected in many of the fundamental questions of human existence, and how the story reverberates as a continuous through-line to many aspects of present-day science and technology. Where might that narrative idea lead us in the future?

SCIENCE IN THE ERA OF *FRANKENSTEIN*

From this day natural philosophy, and particularly chemistry, in the most comprehensive sense of the term, became nearly my sole occupation. I read with ardour those works, so full of genius and discrimination, which modern inquirers have written on these subjects.

—Victor Frankenstein in Mary Shelley,
Frankenstein, chapter 4

Decades before Darwin's introduction of the remarkable and transformative concepts of biological evolution, the natural philosophers of Shelley's time were exploring galvanism—the effects of electrical currents upon deceased tissues in biology—and, through that science, developing an ever-deepening understanding of chemical bonding and organic synthesis. They were also detailing the concepts of inheritance as it was then understood. Shelley distilled this milieu, along with the moral and ethical implications of Promethean mythology, into her narrative. The science of Shelley's time viewed life in terms of holistic systems, imbued with some unknown vital force. Frankenstein constructed his creature not from the foundational molecular components of living matter—fats, sugars, proteins, nucleic acids, water, and minerals—but rather from pieces of previously living and pre-organized anatomical parts. While the molecular processes by which these anatomical pieces developed, grew, and worked were not yet understood, the basic "road maps" for how they fit together were relatively well explored. All that remained then was to compel them through some initial input to reengage, to retrace through their inherent memories, the established conduits and functional pathways of a previous life, so that life could reemerge.

Through the literary genre of horror and in an early example of another genre, science fiction, Shelley has been able to entertain and engage a broad public for two hundred years by addressing through narrative the big questions that humanity asks about life itself—what are the origins of life, how does life emerge, what is consciousness, and what does it mean to be human? And in her narrative we can read new answers that come out of science, not only from myth, religion, and philosophy.

CREATING THE CREATURE

Shelley's description of the scientist Victor Frankenstein, raiding mortuaries and slaughterhouses for the materials for his Creature, conjures up graphic social images. A creature stitched from parts of multiple human and possibly animal parts, a patchwork quilt of skin, organs, and limbs most assuredly would have appeared uniquely grotesque to the naïve eye and repulsed even its creator. Looking back, we can imagine the implications of corporeal decay and the immunological host/donor rejection that would have doomed the Creature. Modern biochemistry and medical science have shown us that the viability of deceased organisms and transplanted parts is remarkably time-sensitive; it is a battle against the decay favored by increasing entropy and disorder at the molecular level. Not only are tissue and organ transplants subject to host rejection on the basis of subtle differences in molecular identities but they are also at the mercy of cascading chemical reactions upon reperfusion of oxygen-ferrying blood—that is, subject to tissue damage when the blood supply returns to tissue that has for some time lacked oxygen. These complications would not have been understood in Shelley's time, but they continue to drive medical research in the present. We can also see the faint echoes of this hybrid creature foreshadowing the emergent work in human/animal chimeric biology in present times, which is often branded as "Frankensteinian" in its pursuit and ethical implications.

If we look closely, Shelley also wove in origins-of-life themes, how to bring about life from inanimate matter, and the synthesis of a whole being by analogy, using component parts from different sources. These themes reemerge today in the disciplines of systems and synthetic biology. While chemistry and electricity are both critical determinants of the genesis, function, and reproduction of living matter, they in turn depend on the fundamental blueprints for life, ensconced at the molecular level, that underlie the central dogma of molecular biology. This can be stated briefly as DNA encodes RNA, and RNA encodes proteins. The dynamic molecular chemical networks connecting the "digitally encoded" genetic information within DNA are transcribed into new instructions in the related compound RNA, which ultimately directs the translation of digital information into proteins that define the functions and structure of a living organism. The advent of recombinant DNA technology, which makes it possible to combine DNA from different organisms, to form modified DNA with specified properties; and the ability to robustly and economically synthesize DNA to exacting standards of purity and sequence—that is, the exact arrangement of its encoded genetic information—have given us the potential to directly interrogate and modify the molecules making up living matter.

Neither Shelley nor the scientists of her time could have imagined the molecular scale we now understand to be so critical to ultimately designing new forms of life, now within the domain and promise of systems and synthetic biology. The parts have changed, but the basic questions and themes have not; rather, they have merely moved downward in scale to a molecular level.

REANIMATING THE INANIMATE

With an anxiety that almost amounted to agony, I collected the instruments of life around me that I might infuse a spark of being into the lifeless thing that lay at my feet.

—Victor Frankenstein in Mary Shelley, *Frankenstein*, chapter 5

Although in her story Shelley describes the construction and composition of the Creature from parts of previously living beings, she does not explicitly describe the process by which the Creature is reanimated. We can, however, infer that her descriptions were strongly influenced by the state of scientific knowledge and research at that time, since the introduction to the later 1831 edition of her original 1818 publication explicitly refers to "galvanism." Luigi Galvani and his nephew Giovanni Aldini had both demonstrated that application of electrical currents to recently deceased tissues could bring about movements that gave the appearance of restoring living function. The literary device of the "vital spark" has informed subsequent retelling and reinterpretations of the *Frankenstein* story, particularly its cinematic adaptations. These take dramatic license with the use of electricity as the sine qua non to create life. This may be in no small part due to the visual impact of arcing light and showering sparks, the crackle and pop of electrical currents, and even the vast power of lightning, displayed most spectacularly in the classic 1931 film *Frankenstein* starring Boris Karloff as the Creature. Certainly by comparison, the application of chemical solutions to induce (re)animation would likely seem pedestrian. In any case, at that time the understanding of how such processes function at the molecular and nanoscales would have been unknown to scientists and the readers of Shelley's novel.

A STATE OF MIND

The "vital spark" anticipated in many ways what is now known as fundamental to the biological and chemical workings of the brain. We understand that living matter requires manifold electrical processes, from electron transport in respiration and in the processes that harvest chemical energy from sugars, to the voltage differences across cell membranes that transmit signals along our neural pathways, and finally in the brain itself as the origin and foundation of consciousness. In *Frankenstein*, the Creature's brain seems to have been considered by Shelley as a tabula rasa, in the sense that the process of integrating the brain and body parts together and providing the spark of life to this patchwork creature effectively "erased" its cerebral hard drive, remapping new experiences, new knowledge, and presumably a new personality and consciousness to this reanimated and yet brand-new being.

Modern cognitive science and computational neuroscience suggest that the physiological structures and biochemical dynamics of the brain, the enormous and complex network of synaptic connections among neurons, represent a mapping of the emergent consciousness and the accumulating memories of a particular person. It is challenging to consider how much of that "hard-wiring" might be retained in a transplanted brain and would in fact manifest the persona of its previous owner. The *Frankenstein* narrative suggests that the Creature's mind and personality are due mainly to its nurture, to how its creator and others socialize with and respond to it, and very little, if at all, to its own intrinsic composition. These challenging questions of the origins of consciousness, of memory, and of individual agency in engaging with the world around us remain very much a rich source of scientific inquiry.

TWO HUNDRED YEARS OUT

Shelley wove the known science of her time into a captivating human story, but our scientific understanding of chemistry, physics, and biology have changed substantially since then. Indeed many of those advances have been driven by the very questions implicit in Shelley's Promethean story. As is clear in Venter's work, like the creation of Frankenstein's creature, the creation of a bacterium used existing parts, the bacterial cell, and added a synthetic construction of the new bacterial genome from organic, pre-animate molecular materials.

PLUG AND PLAY

The complexity of the operational networks fundamental to living matter suggests that merely placing the simplest components of living matter in combination and expecting the spontaneous emergence of life is folly. Shelley's contemporaries did not know the biochemical rules for life, and even now we continue to explore and reevaluate these rules to answer the most fundamental questions about life. Darwinian theory implies that every cell of every living organism on earth today is a direct descendant of that last universal common ancestor (LUCA). Once the processes that synthesized the molecular components of cellular life were in place—the lipids, nucleic acids, and proteins—they were "shoplifted" from the external environmental niche in which they had originated and then incorporated into a new collaborative and self-contained entity. Thus, our biosphere was born. But precisely how those components came about, and how they came together, still remains a mystery to science.

REWRITING THE BOOK OF LIFE

In Shelley's story, Dr. Frankenstein seeks to create new life by exercising control over what constituent parts are selected and integrated into the resulting Creature. In modern biology, the ability not just to replace the genetic foundations of an organism, as with Venter's synthetic bacteria, but also to exercise more direct control over the flow of information from genotype to phenotype—from the genetic makeup of an organism to its observable characteristics—has become a primary goal. Bacteria themselves have shown us new ways to exercise such control. The recent discovery that some bacteria have an innate immune response to viral attacks has given us new ways to edit genetic material in situ. This technique, called CRISPR/Cas9, has opened new research vistas for genetic control over living matter, and once again forces us to contend with the ethical, moral, and safety considerations that such abilities raise. The echoes of Victor Frankenstein's struggles reverberate still.

STRANGER IN A STRANGE LAND

The central dogma of molecular biology tells us that the inherent, fundamental flow of molecular genetic information is at the core of living matter and gives us a deeper understanding of the origins of life and its possibilities. The protein-producing processes that define how living matter functions are the products of prebiotic, dynamically evolving chemical networks. It may be that alternative molecular systems arose early in the history of the Earth, prior to the explosion of living matter that came from a common ancestral network—the aforementioned LUCA. It may also be possible that such alternative systems could still be emerging to this day, in places hidden as well as in plain sight. How might such alternative biochemistries function, and how might we identify them? Much as Frankenstein's creature was made from an amalgam of similar parts into a distinct being, these alternative genetic systems might be composed of similar components that lead to DNA, RNA, and proteins, but in ways just distinct enough to evolve and function separately from one another. Scientists are expanding the genetic code we know with new compounds and reaction pathways, suggesting the possibility of entirely new chemical networks which might have evolved, collaborated and competed with the genetic systems we currently understand.[4]

FROM STARDUST TO US

Dr. Frankenstein's creation is not the only fictional being that represents a certain approach to creating life. The golem is a being out of legend that in some ways mirrors Frankenstein's Creature but differs in not being composed of previously living tissue. It more nearly resembles the homunculus of ancient times and was made of purely inanimate earthen clay, lacking any physiological residue. In different versions of the legend, this clay figure was brought to life by a mystical or religious "spark," typically in the form of an incantation. In an intriguing twist, the origins of the golem might be thought of as an analogy to the processes that led to the emergence of life on earth through the evolution of simpler chemical systems that led to the central dogma. This is the realm of one modern area of research on the origins of life: systems-based chemical evolution. In this scenario, chemical inventories of basic organic gases, from methane, carbon monoxide, and carbon dioxide to formaldehyde, along with water and ammonia, combined with a "vital spark," a high-energy source. This energy source broke down and re-formed the chemical bonds of these simple ingredients into organic molecules of greater structural and functional complexity. These in turn must have formed the basis for a variety of self-organizing, self-assembling, dynamic, and evolvable networks capable of selecting, propagating, and diversifying molecular complexity and its associated functions.

Several strands in chemical research have explored how such intricate molecules could have developed into the basis for life, such as the growing understanding of the covalent bond between atoms and the development of synthetic chemistry. Contemporary research into chemical structure and reactivity supports the development of a technology that could construct the complex molecular architectures of life. This marvelous accumulation of chemical capabilities can serve as a lens through which to view the antecedent ideas of the golem as a "bottom-up" construction of life from purely inanimate materials, and may begin to actually realize that formerly fictional method of creating life by studying self-replicating chemical systems within modern synthetic and systems biology.[5]

THE PAST AS PROLOGUE

> *I do not know that the relation of my disasters will be useful to you; yet, when I reflect that you are pursuing the same course, exposing yourself to the same dangers which have rendered me what I am, I imagine that you may deduce an apt moral from my tale, one that may direct you if you succeed in your undertaking and console you in case of failure.*
> —Victor Frankenstein to Captain Walton,
> who has rescued him in the polar wastes,
> in Mary Shelley, *Frankenstein*, letter 4

Frankenstein is a cautionary tale, built around our use of knowledge and told at the dawn of the Industrial Revolution, about the creation of a monster that destroys his creator. Left unresolved is whether Dr. Frankenstein could have made different choices about the implementation of his knowledge or whether the monster survives for good or evil in the world. One modern version of a man-made monster that could turn toward either good or evil is the growing possibility of manipulating the human genome through means such as CRISPR/Cas9.

Victor Frankenstein's hunger for knowledge and mastery in Mary Shelley's novel suggests a wider warning as well. We have grown in our knowledge and technical sophistication over the last two hundred years, allowing us to inhabit diverse niches and access practically all of earth's resources. And we have, unwittingly, created a "monster" not on a genetic but on a geological scale, a new epoch we call the Anthropocene—the age of humans, and earth's sixth major extinction event. Our species, where creator and monster are one and the same, is taking such control of the planet's resources as to threaten the viability of the entire biosphere. We have created a Frankenstein-like monster of instability, that we must come to terms with as it threatens our very existence.

And so after reading Mary Shelley's cautionary tale, we might ask, what would she say today about our progress in science and what it means for humanity? Would she discuss our remarkable developments in genetics, in computation, in alternative and artificial intelligence, and in other technologies, and whether these will shape the future in predictable ways? Would a broader knowledge and understanding of her narrative message change our behavior, better position us to control the monsters we are making or even prevent their genesis? Would she say that our ability to colonize Mars and the moons Enceladus and Titan, as well as the discovery of even more distant exoplanets, give us the opportunity to wash our hands of our creations and leave behind the monsters we have made? Or would she suggest that our discovery of alternative chemistries of life gives us new pathways to survive and even flourish in the face of global changes?

While contemporary storytelling increasingly reflects modern science, these stories also influence the science we do and how we do it. In many ways this virtuous cycle, acknowledging the spiritual, philosophical, ethical, and moral questions placed in context with our scientific and technical competence, privileges us to learn from the past while looking into the future. Over these past two hundred years, we have created the technology to view history at the very edges of the universe, and to define the foundational components of the atom. We also have the ability to prepare virtually any molecular structure we might imagine, even the ability to make synthetic life, but we cannot survive without stories, imagining our past, present, and our future. The choices we have made now threaten more than the nature of humanity as it might be changed by our new genetic capabilities and other technologies; they threaten the very existence of our biosphere. Is this the proverbial straw that breaks the back, or will reason and more ethical choices prevail? How might Mary Shelley weave this tale?

The research was supported by grants from NSF CHE-1507932 and NSF/DMR–BSF 1610377, and NIH Alzheimer's Disease Research Center P50AG025688.

EPILOGUE

THE NEXT TWO HUNDRED YEARS OF *FRANKENSTEIN*

C an a story that has survived and remains relevant after two hundred years continue to do so in the future? The answer would seem to be yes. Like Frankenstein's prodigiously durable monster, Shelley's story has shown itself to be a consummate survivor, able to be adapted and reinvented to fit new times and circumstances, continuing to inspire creative works even as new media and modes become available to express them.

We have glimpsed in these pages some of the richness of the story. We have touched on the advance of science and the ethical questions that raises, about how *Frankenstein* confronts individual morality, how it illuminates the relationships between parents and children, and much more. But there is so much more yet to explore. For instance, as our society continues to grapple with how to deal with the "other," in the form of immigrants, refugees, and other newcomers from different cultures, or of the disabled and the handicapped, or of existing minority groups, we can see in Victor Frankenstein's creature a model of the ultimate "other." How this hapless being is wounded and morally deformed by the incomprehension, hostility, and rejection he encounters should give us pause. Further consideration of the creature's thoughts and actions may help us, within this neutral literary arena, to see how to deal with the real issues of "otherness" we now face in our world, often none too successfully.

At the other end of the spectrum, Victor, too, may be worth another look. In a world in which the chasm between the haves and have-nots seems to gape ever wider, and in which we are becoming more acutely aware of the problems of privilege, Shelley's entitled, self-absorbed scientist seems a very familiar figure. Educated, indulged, and gifted with intellectual curiosity, an abundance of resources, and a costly education, Victor Frankenstein is monstrous in his own way, a monster made not in a laboratory but in a domestic and social system that may be for all its advantages dangerously deficient. Like science, politics and economics can unleash forces that have far-reaching and devastating consequences.

The aesthetic and artistic potential of *Frankenstein* also seem inexhaustible. Filmmakers, stage and TV directors, cartoonists, and authors will undoubtedly continue as well to re-create and revise these indelible characters, and restage the compelling clash of creature and creator. Not only is *Frankenstein* a great horror and science fiction tale with plenty of violence, dread, and shock value, but there is deeper, human drama here, too. The story is also about the tragic fallout of ambitions unchecked, children mistreated, and responsibilities ignored, about the promise of the present undone by a dark and ultimately inescapable past. At a level even more primal, as Jaime Paglia's "Life After Death" reminds us, *Frankenstein* tells the story of a man's quest to create life out of death. Shelley's story may not say so explicitly, but at bottom it is about the human desire to defeat death. That desire can never be satisfied, and it will always provide an irresistible draw to the story.

In the same vein, though the new science of gene editing is not today explicitly aimed at defeating death, its potential to improve the health of the human race is a step in that direction. But as the relevant chapters in this anthology show, science still has a long way to go. Which may prove fortunate, since so many important and difficult questions remain about the benefits that science may bring and who should get them when they became available, as pointed out by the National Academy of Sciences and National Academy of Medicine report *Human Genome Editing: Science, Ethics, and Governance.*

EPILOGUE

It will take us as a society a long time to answer these questions if indeed we ever do. That quest alone will give *Frankenstein* continued relevance as the genius of Mary Shelley's story reminds us of the stakes when we manipulate ourselves to create, we hope, not monsters but our own better selves.

Sidney Perkowitz
Eddy von Mueller
Atlanta, Georgia

EDITORS, CONTRIBUTORS, AND INTERVIEWEES

EDITORS

Sidney Perkowitz is Charles Howard Candler Professor Emeritus of physics at Emory University. During an active research career, he produced well over one hundred peer-reviewed research papers and books supported by significant government funding. Now he presents science for nonscientists through eight books, from *Empire of Light* to *Hollywood Chemistry* and *Universal Foam 2.0*, which have been translated into seven languages and Braille; print and web articles and essays in numerous outlets, including *Discover, Aeon, Nature, New Scientist,* and the *Los Angeles Review of Books*; theatrical works produced in Atlanta, New York, and Chicago; and appearances at varied media outlets and venues such as CNN, NPR, BBC, NASA, and the Smithsonian Institution. His latest book in progress is *Physics: A Very Short Introduction* (Oxford University Press). He is a Fellow of the American Association for the Advancement of Science and the recipient of a Lifetime Achievement award from the Society for Literature, Science and the Arts. http://sidneyperkowitz.net/, @physp.

Eddy Von Mueller, PhD, is a writer, scholar, and filmmaker based in Atlanta, Georgia. He has taught at Georgia State University and at Emory University, where he cofounded the unique Film and Media Management program for students pursuing careers in media and entertainment. His scholarly work examines the history of the entertainment industry and the intersections of technology, economics, and aesthetics in screen media, with publications that explore varied subjects: silent adaptations of William Shakespeare's works, Akira Kurosawa's samurai films, the police procedural genre on film and television, the use of science fiction to communicate and teach science, nature documentaries from the Walt Disney Company and the epic miniseries *Planet Earth*. He was invited to contribute to the entry on Walt Disney for Oxford's definitive series of bibliographies. His book *Synthetic Cinema: Aesthetics, Visual Effects and the Impact of Animation on Contemporary Cinema* is under review for publication. His film, television and book reviews, interviews, and commentary have been published in a wide range of regional and national publications, including *The Bloomsbury Review, Creative Loafing,* and *Jezebel*. His most recent film, the all-puppet film noir feature *The Lady From Sockholm* (2007), played over forty film festivals worldwide.

CONTRIBUTORS AND INTERVIEWEES

Stuart Beattie is an Australian screenwriter and film director. His credits include *Pirates of the Caribbean: The Curse of the Black Pearl* (2003), *Collateral* (2004), for which he received a BAFTA award, *G. I. Joe: The Rise of Cobra* (2009), *I, Frankenstein* (2014), *Tarzan* (2016), and *3001:The Final Odyssey* (in production).

Mel Brooks is an American film director, screenwriter, comedian, and actor. He began his career in early television as a comic and writer for *Your Show of Shows*. His successful and well-known Hollywood films include *The Producers, Blazing Saddles, Young Frankenstein, Silent Movie,*

High Anxiety, Spaceballs, and *Robin Hood: Men in Tights.* Three of these appear in the American Film Institute list of the 100 funniest comedy films of all time, and *The Producers* became a smash hit Broadway musical. He has won an Emmy, a Grammy, an Oscar, and a Tony.

Carol Colatrella is professor of literature and cultural studies at the Georgia Institute of Technology. Since 1993 she has served as the executive director of the Society for Literature, Science, and the Arts (SLSA). Her publications include *Evolution, Sacrifice, and Narrative: Balzac, Zola, and Faulkner* (1990); *Literature and Moral Reform: Melville and the Discipline of Reading* (2002); and *Toys and Tools in Pink: Cultural Narratives of Gender, Science, and Technology* (2011). Her essays have appeared in journals and anthologies, including *Cohesion and Dissent in America* (1994), which she coedited, and *Technology and Humanity* (2012), which she edited.

Alexis Gambis is a filmmaker and visiting assistant professor of biology, film, and new media, New York University Abu Dhabi. His work in film has been featured by the *New York Times*, TED, *Nature, Science, Huffington Post*, the *Village Voice*, and *Studio 360/*WNYC. As founder and artistic director of Imagine Science Films, a nonprofit, he fosters dialogue among scientists, artists, and filmmakers through an annual film festival and other events. His films blur documentary and fiction genres, creating hybrid narratives and depictions of science on-screen. He repurposes recorded laboratory footage and frequently casts animals as actors to provide visceral, multifaceted perspectives into the scientific process and its players.

Dwayne Godwin is professor of neurobiology and anatomy at Wake Forest University, and **Jorge Cham** is a cartoonist and creator of the comic strip series *PHD Comics,* http://www.phdcomics.com/. The two have collaborated on scientific comics for ten years, beginning with comics created for the Stanford design magazine *Ambidextrous* in 2007.

Since 2009 they have been regular contributors to *Scientific American Mind* on neuroscience-themed topics that show how the brain works and how we came to know it. The topic of *Frankenstein* was a natural outgrowth of the process they undertook to integrate basic scientific insights with historical and pop culture touch points. Their goal, like Dr. Frankenstein's, is to bring inanimate concepts to life.

Jay Goodwin is a senior research fellow in chemistry, and **David Lynn** is Asa Griggs Candler Professor in chemistry and biology, at Emory University. Their research interests include biomolecular chemistry, molecular evolution and chemical biology, the evolution of biological order, and the origins of life. They are also active in communicating science to the general public in such areas as synthetic biology and evolutionary theory, and in science/art collaborations.

Steven J. Kraftchick is a professor in the Candler School of Theology, Emory University. He teaches courses in the New Testament, and his research focuses on the epistles of St. Paul and how we can interpret biblical language to be meaningful today. His connection to the Frankenstein story arises from his current research about the intersection of theology and technology, especially as it relates to conceptions of the "techno-human" found in the philosophies of trans- and post-humanism. He is the author or editor of three books and regularly presents around the world.

Kevin LaGrandeur is professor of English and director of technical writing programs at the New York Institute of Technology and a Fellow of the Institute for Ethics and Emerging Technology. He specializes in digital culture; artificial intelligence and ethics; and literature and science. His writing has appeared in professional venues such as *Computers and the Humanities* and *Science Fiction Studies,* and in the popular press. His most recent works are essays on the ethics of creating emotion in artificial intelligence and a book, *Androids and Intelligent*

Networks in Early Modern Literature and Culture (Routledge, 2013), which won a 2014 Science Fiction and Technoculture Studies Prize Honorable Mention.

Evan Lieberman teaches media arts and technology at Cleveland State University. He has worked as screenwriter, writer, producer, director, or director of photography for various studios and for dozens of commercials, music videos, documentaries, and feature films. He has published on a wide variety of subjects, including situation comedies and cinematography. His book *The Moving Image,* coauthored with David Cook, is forthcoming from Oxford University Press.

John Logan is an American playwright, screenwriter, and television writer and producer. His theatrical writing has won awards such as a Tony in 2010 for his play *Red*. His film credits include *Gladiator* (2000), *The Aviator* (2004), *Sweeney Todd* (2007), and *Skyfall* (2012). He created and was the showrunner for the television series *Penny Dreadful*, which premiered in 2014 on the Showtime Channel.

Catherine Ross Nickerson is an associate professor of English and on the faculty of the Institute of Liberal Arts, Emory University. Her book *The Web of Iniquity, Early Detective Fiction by American Women* (Duke University Press, 1999), was nominated for an Edgar, the Edgar Allan Poe Award, by the Mystery Writers of America. She has edited two volumes of early detective fiction by women, also for Duke University Press. Her latest work is as editor and contributor to the *Cambridge Companion to American Crime Fiction* (2010).

Laura Otis is Samuel Candler Dobbs Professor of English at Emory University. With an MA in neuroscience and a PhD in comparative literature, she compares the creative thinking of scientists and literary writers. Otis is the author of *Organic Memory, Membranes, Networking,* and *Müller's Lab*; the translator of Santiago Ramón y Cajal's *Vacation*

Stories; and the editor of *Literature and Science in the Nineteenth Century*. Her book, *Rethinking Thought*, analyzes the different ways people use words and images in their thinking. For her interdisciplinary studies of literature and science, she received a MacArthur Fellowship in 2000.

Jaime Paglia is an American film/TV writer and co-creator/executive producer of *Eureka*. This is the record-setting longest-running original series ever on the Syfy Channel. He is executive producer/co-showrunner of MTV's *Scream*, from the film franchise released by Dimension Films and The Weinstein Company. He was recently co-executive producer of *The Flash* for The CW, and has developed projects with Universal Cable Productions, New Line Cinema, Weed Road Pictures, The Canton Company, ABC Studios, TNT, MGM TV, and others.

BIBLIOGRAPHIES, FILMOGRAPHIES, AND NOTES

1: "HIDEOUS PROGENY": TELLING A TALE OF MONSTERS IN *FRANKENSTEIN*

Bibliography

Gilbert, Sandra M., and Susan Gubar. *The Madwoman in the Attic: The Woman Writer and the Nineteenth-Century Literary Imagination*. 2nd ed. New York: Oxford University Press, 1984.

Hunter, J. Paul, ed. "Frankenstein": *Norton Critical Editions*. New York: W.W. Norton, 2012.

Knellworth, Christa, and Jane Goodall, eds. *Frankenstein's Science: Experimentation and Discovery in Romantic Culture, 1780–1830*. Aldershot, UK: Ashgate, 2008.

Malchow, H. R. "Frankenstein's Monster and Images of Race in Nineteenth-Century Literature." *Past and Present* 139, no.1 (1993): 90–130.

Marshall, Tim. *Murdering to Dissect: Graverobbing, "Frankenstein," and the Anatomy Literature*. Manchester: Manchester University Press, 1995.

Mellor, Anne K. *Mary Shelley: Her Life, Her Fiction, Her Monsters*. New York: Routledge, 1990.

Radcliffe, Anne. "On the Supernatural in Poetry." In *Gothic Readings: The First Wave, 1764–1840*, edited by Rictor Norton, 311–316. London: Continuum, 2000.

Sedgwick, Eve. *The Coherence of Gothic Conventions*. New York: Routledge, 1986.

Shelley, Mary Wollstonecraft. *Frankenstein* (1831). http://tcpl.org/community-read/Frankenstein/mary1831.pdf.

Smith, Johanna M., ed. "Frankenstein": *Case Studies in Contemporary Criticism*. Boston: Bedford/St. Martin's/MacMillan, 2016.

2: FRANKLIN TO *FRANKENSTEIN*

Bibliography

Brown, Alan S. "The Science that Made Frankenstein." *Inside Science* (Oct. 27, 2010). https://www.insidescience.org/news/science-made-frankenstein

3: *FRANKENSTEIN*: REPRESENTING THE EMOTIONS OF UNWANTED CREATURES

Bibliography

Bowlby, John. *Attachment and Loss*. Vol. 2 of *Separation: Anxiety and Anger*. New York: Basic Books, 1973.

Chester, David S., and C. Nathan DeWall. "Combating the Sting of Rejection with the Pleasure of Revenge: A New Look at How Emotion Shapes Aggression." *Journal of Personality and Social Psychology* (2016): 1–17.

——— *The Concise Oxford English Dictionary of Current English*, 7th ed., s.v. "wretch."

Dostoevsky, Fyodor. *Notes from the Underground*. Trans. and ed. Michael R. Katz. New York: Norton, 1989.

Frazzetto, Giovanni. *How We Feel: What Neuroscience Can and Can't Tell Us about Our Emotions*. New York: Doubleday, 2014.

Gilbert, Sandra, and Susan Gubar. *The Madwoman in the Attic*. New Haven: Yale University Press, 1979.

Goethe, Johann Wolfgang von. *Faust*. Trans. Walter Arndt. Ed. Cyrus Hamlin. New York: Norton, 1976.

Harper, Douglas. "Emotion." Online Etymology Dictionary. http://www.etymonline.com/index.php?term=emotion.

Hazan, Cindy, and Phillip Shaver. "Romantic Love Conceptualized as an Attachment Process." *Journal of Personality and Social Psychology* 52, no. 3 (1987): 511–24.

Kirkpatrick, Lee A., and Cindy Hazan. "Attachment Styles and Close Relationships: A Four-Year Prospective Study." *Personal Relationships* 1 (1994): 123–42.

Lakoff, George, and Zoltan Kövecses. "The Cognitive Model of Anger Inherent in American English." In *Cultural Models of Language and Thought*, 195–221. Cambridge: Cambridge University Press, 1987.

Li, Amy. "Monstrous Rage: Unnatural Bodies and Their Discontents." Unpublished essay, 2016.

Mandal, Eugenia, and Anna Latusek. "Attachment Styles and Anxiety of Rejecters in Intimate Relationships." *Current Issues in Personality Psychology* 2, no. 4 (2014): 185–95.

Milton, John. *Paradise Lost*. Ed. Scott Elledge. New York: Norton, 1975.

Norona, Jerika C., and Deborah P. Welsh. "Rejection Sensitivity and Relationship Satisfaction in Dating Relationships: The Mediating Role of Differentiation of Self." *Couple and Family Psychology: Research and Practice* 5, no. 2 (2016): 124–35.

Shelley, Mary. "Frankenstein, or The Modern Prometheus": *The 1818 Text*. Ed. Marilyn Butler. New York: Oxford University Press, 1998.

Shih, Terence H. W. "Bodily Pain: Romantic Neurology and *Frankenstein*." Roundtable presentation for the Society for Literature, Science, and the Arts, Atlanta, GA, November 2016.

4: WHO IS A MONSTER, WHEN?

Bibliography

Bartlett, Andrew. *Mad Scientist, Impossible Human: An Essay in Generative Anthropology.* Aurora, CO: The Davies Group, 2014.

Bissonette, Melissa Bloom. "Teaching the Monster: *Frankenstein* and Critical Thinking." *College Literature* 37 (Summer 2010): 106–120.

Botting, Fred. *Making Monstrous: "Frankenstein," Criticism, Theory.* New York: Manchester Press, 1991.

——— "Frankenstein and the Language of Monstrosity." In *Reviewing Romanticism,* edited by Philip Martin and Robin Jarvis, 51–59. London: Macmillan, 1992.

Brooks, Peter. "Godlike Science/Unhallowed Arts: Language and Monstrosity in *Frankenstein*." *New Literary History* 9, no. 3 (Spring 1978): 591–605.

Cantor, Paul A. *Creature and Creator: Myth Making and English Romanticism.* New York: Cambridge University Press, 1984.

Cohen, Jeffrey Jerome. "Monster Culture (Seven Theses)." In *Monster Theory: Reading Culture,* 3–25. Minneapolis: University of Minnesota Press, 1996.

Collings, David. *Monstrous Society: Reciprocity, Discipline, and the Political Uncanny, c. 1780–1848.* Lewisburg, PA: Bucknell University Press, 2009, 3–25.

Cooper, Melinda. "Monstrous Progeny: The Teratological Tradition in Science and Literature." In *Frankenstein's Science: Experimentation and Discovery in Romantic Culture, 1780–1830,* edited by Christa Knellwold and Jane Goodall, 87–99. Burlington, VT: Ashgate, 2008.

Freeman, Barbara. "'Frankenstein' with Kant: A Theory of Monstrosity, or the Monstrosity of Theory." *SubStance* 16, No. 1, Issue 52 (1987): 21–31.

Friedman, Lester D., and Allison B. Kavey. *Monstrous Progeny: A History of the Frankenstein Narratives.* New Brunswick, NJ: Rutgers University Press, 2016.

Haggerty, George E. *Gothic Fiction/Gothic Form.* University Park, PA: Penn State Press, 1989.

Ketterer, David. *Frankenstein's Creation: The Book, the Monster, and Human Reality.* British Columbia, Canada: University of Victoria Press, 1979.

Mellor, Anne K. *Mary Shelley: Her Life, Her Fiction, Her Monsters.* New York: Methuen Press, 1988.

Notes

1   The seminar was part of the Great Works Series, sponsored by the Fox Center for Humanistic Inquiry. Emory University, Atlanta, GA.

2   All textual citations are from the original 1818 edition of Mary Shelley, *Frankenstein.* 3rd ed., ed. D. L. Macdonald and Kathleen Scherf (Ontario, Canada: Broadview Press, 2012).

5: *FRANKENSTEIN* AT THE BOUNDARIES OF LIFE, DEATH, AND FILM

Bibliography

Burch, Noël. *Life to Those Shadows*. Berkeley: University of California Press, 1990.

Cawelti, John. "*Chinatown* and Generic Transformation in Recent American Films." https://filmgenre.files.wordpress.com/2010/08/generic-transformation.pdf.

Doherty, Thomas Patrick. *Pre-Code Hollywood: Sex, Immorality, and Insurrection in American Cinema 1930–1934*. New York: Columbia University Press, 1999.

Gorky, Maxim cited in Walter Murch, "Black and White and in Color." McSweeney's website, The Convergencies Contest, Contest Winner #36, October 3, 2007. https://www.mcsweeneys.net/articles/contest-winner-36-black-and-white-and-in-color.

Halberstam, Judith. *Skin Shows: Gothic Horror and the Technology of Monsters*. Durham: Duke University Press, 1995.

Jacobs, Stephen. *Boris Karloff: More Than a Monster*. Sheffield: Tomahawk Press, 2011.

Karasek, Hellmuth. "Lokomotive Der Gefuhle." *Der Spiegel* 52 (1994). http://www.spiegel.de/spiegel/print/d-13687466.html.

Littau, Karin. "Arrival of a Train at La Ciotat (1895–1897), Lumière Brothers" in *Film Analysis: A Norton Reader*, edited by Jeffrey Geiger and R. L. Rutsky. New York: W. W. Norton & Company, 2013.

Loiperdinger, Martin. "Lumière's Arrival of the Train: Cinema's Founding Myth." The *Moving Image* 4, no. 1 (January 2004): 89–118.

Paul, William. *Laughing Screaming: Modern Hollywood Horror and Comedy*. New York: Columbia University Press, 1994.

University of Maryland. *Romantic Circles*. https://www.rc.umd.edu/.

Vieira, Mark A. *Hollywood Horror: From Gothic to Cosmic*. New York: Harry N. Abrams, 2003.

6: *FRANKENSTEIN*, YOUNG AND OLD: AN INTERVIEW WITH MEL BROOKS

Notes

1 BoxOfficeMojo.com. http://www.boxofficemojo.com/people/chart/?id=melbrooks.htm.

2 "List of People Who Have Won Academy, Emmy, Grammy, and Tony Awards," *Wikipedia*. https://en.wikipedia.org/wiki/List_of_people_who_have_won_Academy,_Emmy,_Grammy,_and_Tony_Awards.

7: SINCE *FRANKENSTEIN:* EXPERIMENTAL SCIENCE AND EXPERIMENTAL FILM

Bibliography

Bendor, D., and M. A. Wilson. "Biasing the Content of Hippocampal Replay During Sleep." *Nature Neuroscience* 15 (2012): 1439–1444.*Chimera Experiments*. http://chimera experiments.com/.

Imagine Science Films. http://imaginesciencefilms.org/.

Jabr, Ferris. "Bluebrain: Noah Hutton's 10-Year Documentary about the Mission to Reverse Engineer the Human Brain." *Scientific American*, Nov. 9, 2012. https://www.scientificamerican.com/article/bluebrain-documentary-premiere/.

Lindsay, Jay. "Study: Rats Dream About Mazes." *Washington Post*, Jan. 24, 2001. http://www.washingtonpost.com/wp-srv/aponline/20010124/aponline170158_001.htm.

Tufte, Edward R. *Envisioning Information*. Cheshire, CT: Graphics Press, 1990. Zebrafish Heart Movie Light and GFP. https://www.youtube.com/watch?v=Py9zAUOYYLk.

10: THE FACE OF THE FIEND: MEDIA, INDUSTRY, AND THE EVOLVING IMAGE OF FRANKENSTEIN'S MONSTER

Bibliography

Brunas, Michael, John Brunas, and Tom Weaver. *Universal Horrors: The Studio's Classic Films, 1931–1946.* Jefferson, NC and London: McFarland & Company, 1990.

Forry, Steven Earl. *Hideous Progenies: Dramatizations of "Frankenstein" from Mary Shelley to the Present.* Philadelphia, PA: University of Pennsylvania Press, 1990.

Friedman, Lester D., and Allison B. Karvey. *Monstrous Progeny: A History of the "Frankenstein" Narrative.* New Brunswick, NJ and London: Rutgers University Press, 2016.

Hitchcock, Susan Tyler. *"Frankenstein": A Cultural History.* New York and London: W.W. Norton & Co., 2007.

Meikle, Denis, and Christopher T. Koetting. *A History of Horrors: The Rise and Fall of the House of Hammer.* Lanham, MD: Scarecrow Press, 1996.

Scott, Allen Nollen. *Boris Karloff: A Critical Account of His Screen, Stage, Radio and Television and Recording Work.* Jefferson, NC: McFarland & Company, 1991.

Spadoni, Robert. *Uncanny Bodies: The Coming of Sound Film and the Origins of the Horror Genre.* Berkeley: University of California Press, 2007.

Wiebel, Frederick C., Jr. *Edison's "Frankenstein."* Albany, GA: Bear Manor Media, 2010.

Select Filmography

Frankenstein (J. Searle Dawley, 1910)

Frankenstein (James Whale, 1931)

Bride of Frankenstein (James Whale, 1934)

Son of Frankenstein (James Whale, 1939)

Frankenstein Meets the Wolf Man (Roy William Neill, 1943)

Abbot and Costello Meet Frankenstein (Charles Barton, 1948)

The Curse of Frankenstein (Terence Fisher, 1957)

The Munsters (Allen Burns, Chris Hayward, 1964–1966)

Spirit of the Beehive (Victor Erice, 1973)

Frankenstein and the Monster from Hell (Terence Fisher, 1974)

Mary Shelley's Frankenstein (Kenneth Branagh, 1994)

11: FRANKENSTEIN'S CREATURES: THE PLEASURES OF TOYS, GAMES, AND COSTUMES

Notes

1   Excerpts from Friedrich Schiller's *On the Aesthetic Education of Man* (1794), compiled by John Zerzan in his book *Against Civilization*. Excerpts from pp. 27, 29, 33, 35, 43, 107, reproduced at http://www.primitivism.com/schiller.htm. Accessed November 22, 2016.

2   Braudy is cited in Gregory McGuire, "In Time for Halloween, a Taxonomy of Monsters." *New York Times Book Review*, October 30, 2016. Accessed November 2, 2016. http://www.nytimes.com/2016/10/30/books/review/haunted-leo-braudy.html?_r=0

3   "Frankenfood." http://www.imdb.com/title/tt3231534/. Accessed October 29, 2015.

4   "The Other Frankenfoods: Delicacies Brought back from the Dead," *New York Times Magazine*, November 1, 2015: 71. Examples include Olympia Oyster and Mangalitsa Pig.

5   According to "Frankenstein Video Game," *Wikipedia*: "*Frankenstein* is a standard text adventure with static graphics in some locations to set the scene. It is similar to the earlier game *Dracula*, which was produced by the same author. It is divided in three parts; the player takes the role of Dr. Frankenstein in the first two, and of his monster in the third." The game was published by CRL for Amstrad CPC, Commodore 64, ZX Spectrum Platforms. https://en.wikipedia.org/wiki/Frankenstein_(video _game). Accessed November 25, 2016.

6   "Mary Shelley's Frankenstein (video game)," *Wikipedia*: "The player controls Frankenstein's monster as he stomps through the streets of Ingolstadt, Bavaria, in the year 1793 seeking revenge against a certain man named Victor for rejecting him." https://en.wikipedia.org/wiki/Mary_Shelley%27s_Frankenstein_(video _game). Accessed November 25, 2016.

7   Silenig. *Mary Shelley's "Frankenstein."* Sega Mega CD Longplay. https://www .youtube.com/watch?v=n0RJTYTzkk0. Accessed November 1, 2015.

8   Sasha A. Barab, Melissa Gresalfi, and Adam Ingram-Goble, "Transformational Play: Using Games to Position Person, Content, and Context," *Educational Researcher* 39, no. 7 (October 2010): 525–536.

9   Cynthia A. Hoffner and Kenneth J. Levine, "Enjoyment of Mediated Fright and Violence: A Meta-Analysis." *Media Psychology* 7 (2005): 207–237, 207.

10   Examples of figures available from Amazon (for ages 14–18): http://www.amazon .com/Diamond-Select-Toys-Universal-Monsters/dp/B004TD3RX6. http:// www.amazon.com/Mezco-Toyz-Universal-Monsters-Frankenstein/dp/ B007T6C5C4. Accessed November 22, 2016.

11   Joanne Kaufman, "A Makeover, With Monsters: Gilbert Gottfried's Chelsea Apartment," *New York Times*, March 6, 2015. http://www.nytimes .com/2015/03/08/realestate/gilbert-gottfrieds-chelsea-apartment.html?_r=0. Accessed November 25, 2016.

12   Ty Burr, "A Few Words in Defense of Swag," *New York Times*, May 2, 1999. https:// partners.nytimes.com/library/film/050299film-tie-ins.html. Accessed December 1, 2016.

13 YouTube video demonstrating the toys: https://www.youtube.com /watch?v=5mIPplY6PDM. Accessed November 3, 2016.

14 "Frankenstein Crafts," *Pinterest.* https://www.pinterest.com/explore/frankenstein -craft/. Accessed November 3, 2016.

15 Puppet show Fri 3rd Apr 2015 offered by Lempen Puppet Theatre Company, Rothes Halls, Isle of Skye. http://www.onfife.com/whats-on/detail /puppet-animation-festival-little-frankenstein.

16 Jeanne Claire van Ryzin, "Trouble Puppet Theater stages its edgy version of 'Frankenstein'," *American-Statesman.* October 29, 2015. http://www.mystatesman .com/news/entertainment/arts-theater/trouble-puppet-theater-stages-its-edgy -version-of-/npBmj/. Accessed November 25, 2016. "Frankenstein is reborn as puppet theatre at BGSU," Bowling Green State University, March 2014. https:// www.bgsu.edu/news/2014/03/frankenstein-is-reborn-as-puppet-theater-at-bgsu .html. Accessed November 25, 2016.

17 *Dr. Franken, Wikipedia.* https://en.wikipedia.org/wiki/Dr._Franken. Dr. Franken was released on Game Boy in 1992. A sequel, *Dr. Franken II,* was released in 1997. Patrick Elliott's review of *Dr. Franken,* October 8, 2010, describes the action: "The player explores a vast castle as Dr. Franken to look for body parts of his girlfriend"; she is called Bitsy. Finding parts and putting them together means the player can bring the sewn-up girlfriend back to life. http://www.nintendolife .com/reviews/2010/10/dr_franken_retro. Accessed November 25, 2016.

18 Jennifer Schuessler, Top of Form "Bottom of Form 'Frankenstein' Comes Alive in the App Store," *New York Times,* June 8, 2012. http://artsbeat.blogs .nytimes.com/2012/06/07/frankenstein-comes-alive-in-the-app-store/. Accessed November 25, 2016.

19 "Classic Sesame Street—Dr. Frankenstein (body parts)." *YouTube.* https://www .youtube.com/watch?v=HXwTOmCTqFQ. Accessed November 26, 2016.

20 "Classic Sesame Street animation—Monster learns F words." *YouTube.* https:// www.youtube.com/watch?v=JvSfItZ2umo. Accessed November 26, 2016.

21 "Sesame Street: Back and Front Frankenstein." *YouTube.* https://www.youtube .com/watch?v=HjAClMcC7vY. Accessed November 26, 2016.

22 Adam Rex, *Frankenstein Takes the Cake.* New York: Harcourt Brace, 2008.

23 Ludworst Bemontster, Rick Walton, and Nathan Hale. *Frankenstein: A Monstrous Parody.* New York: Feiwel and Friends, 2012 (first page and inside front flap).

24 Patrick McDonnell, *The Monster's Monster.* Hachette, 2012.

25 Etienne Benson, "Toy Stories." *Observer.* Association for Psychological Science. https://www.psychologicalscience.org/index.php/publications/observer/2006 /december-06/toy-stories.html.

26 Scott Barry Kaufman et al. "The Need for Pretend Play in Child Development." *Psychology Today,* March 6, 2012. https://www.psychologytoday.com/blog /beautiful-minds/201203/the-need-pretend-play-in-child-development.

27 Jeffrey Goldstein, "Contributions of Play and Toys to Child Development." *Toy Industries of Europe* (December 2003): 15. file:///Users/cc60/Downloads/contributions_of _play_and_toys_to_child_development-2.pdf. Accessed November 1, 2015.

28 A film clip appears on *YouTube*: "Gene Wilder-Young Frankenstein (1974)-Puttin on the Ritz." https://www.youtube.com/watch?v=w1FLZPFI3jc. Accessed November 22, 2016.

29 Plot Synopsis of *Young Frankenstein* (1974), *Internet Movie Database*. http://www.imdb.com/title/tt0072431/synopsis?ref_=ttpl_pl_syn. Accessed November 25, 2016.

30 "The High to Present New Work by Thomas Struth," R&A Press Release by High Museum. April 12, 2016. http://www.resnicow.com/client-news/high-present-new-work-photographer-thomas-struth-fall-2016. Accessed November 25, 2016.

31 "Meet Jason Freeny, Custom Toy Sculptor." https://www.youtube.com/watch?v=nWxWyA9Z41E. Accessed September 28, 2017.

32 *Urban Dictionary* has a number of entries: http://www.urbandictionary.com/define.php?term=Frankenpets&defid=2363736. http://www.worth1000.com/galleries/frankenpets. http://www.picmonkey.com/blog/halloween-contest/.

33 Amazon description of Nicholas Rogers's book *Halloween: From Pagan Ritual to Party Night* (Oxford: Oxford University Press, 2003). https://www.amazon.com/dp/0195168968/?&tag=livescience01-20. Accessed October 27, 2016.

34 HalloweenCostumes.com http://www.halloweencostumes.com/frankenstein-costumes.html?q=frankenstein. Accessed October 27, 2016. The image used to promote a UK site known as Halloween store is that of Frankenstein's creation: https://images-eu.ssl-images-amazon.com/images/G/02/uk-toys/2016/Halloween/Fancy-Dress-Storefront/Halloween_Fancy-Dress_993x515_halloweenstore._V279808484_.jpg. Accessed November 26, 2016.

12: *FRANKENSTEIN* AND SYNTHETIC LIFE: FICTION, SCIENCE, AND ETHICS

Bibliography

Asimov, Isaac. *I, Robot*. New York: Gnome Press, 1950.

Auslander, Simon, and Martin Fussenegger. "From Gene Switches to Mammalian Designer Cells: Present and Future Prospects." *Trends in Biotechnology* 31, no. 3 (March 2013): 155–168.

Ball, Philip. "Man Made: A History of Synthetic Life." *Distillations* 2, no. 1 (Spring 2016): 14–23. https://www.chemheritage.org/distillations/magazine/man-made-a-history-of-synthetic-life.

Baltimore, David et al. "A Prudent Path Forward for Genomic Engineering and Germline Gene Modification. *Science* 348, no. 6230 (Apr 3, 2015): 36–38. http://science.sciencemag.org/content/348/6230/36.

Boeke, Jef D. "The Genome Project–Write." *Science* 353, no. 6295, (July 8, 2016): 126–127. http://science.sciencemag.org/content/early/2016/06/03/science.aaf6850.

Callaway, Ewen. "Plan to Synthesize Human Genome Triggers Mixed Response." *Nature* 534, no. 163 (June 9, 2016). http://www.nature.com/news/plan-to-synthesize-human-genome-triggers-mixed-response-1.20028.

Cohen, Jon. "The Birth of CRISPR Inc." *Science* 355, no. 6326 (Feb 17, 2017): 680–684. http://science.sciencemag.org/content/355/6326/680.

Dick, Philip K., *Do Androids Dream of Electric Sheep?* New York: Ballantine Books, 1996.

Egli, Dieter et al. "Inter-homologue repair in fertilized human eggs?" http://www .biorxiv.org/content/early/2017/08/28/181255.

European Commission. *Synthetic Biology. Applying Engineering to Biology.* Luxembourg: European Commission, 2005. http://www.synbiosafe.eu/uploads/pdf/EU -highlevel-syntheticbiology.pdf.

Fell, Jade. "Frankenstein Redux: Is Modern Science Making a Monster?" *Engineering and Technology* (June 14, 2016). https://eandt.theiet.org/content/articles/2016/06 /frankenstein-redux-is-modern-science-making-a-monster/.

Freud, Sigmund. "The Uncanny." http://web.mit.edu/allanmc/www/freud1.pdf.

Gibson, Daniel G. et al. "Creation of a Bacterial Cell Controlled by a Chemically Synthesized Genome." *Science* 329, no. 5987 (Jul 2, 2010): 52–56. http://science .sciencemag.org/content/329/5987/52.

Harmon, Amy. "Human Gene Editing Receives Science Panel's Support." *New York Times*, February 14, 2017. https://www.nytimes.com/2017/02/14/health/human -gene-editing-panel.html.

Hotz, Robert Lee. "Scientists Create Synthetic Organism." *Wall Street Journal*, May 21, 2010. http://www.wsj.com/articles/SB1000142405274870355900457525264 70152341984.

Huxley, Aldous. *Brave New World.* New York: Alfred A. Knopf, 2013.

Iowa Public Television. *Explore More: Genetic Engineering.* "Recombinant DNA: Example Using Insulin." Iowa Public Television. http://www.iptv.org/exploremore/ge /what/insulin.cfm.

J. Craig Venter Institute website. http://www.jcvi.org/cms/home/.

Kaiser, Jocelyn. "U.S. Panel Gives Yellow Light to Human Embryo Editing." *Science* (Feb. 14, 2017.) http://www.sciencemag.org/news/2017/02/us-panel-gives -yellow-light-human-embryo-editing.

Karas, Bogumil J. et al. "Designer Diatom Episomes Delivered by Bacterial Conjugation." *Nature Communications* 6 (April 2015): Article 6925. http://www.nature.com/articles /ncomms7925.

Karel, Capek. *R. U. R. (Rossum's universal robots).* London: H. Milford / New York: Oxford University Press, 1925. http://preprints.readingroo.ms/RUR/rur.pdf.

Katsnelson, Alla. "Researchers Start Up Cell with Synthetic Genome." *Nature* (May 20, 2010). http://www.nature.com/news/2010/100520/full/news.2010.253.html.

Kozubek, Jim. *Modern Prometheus: Editing the Human Genome with CRISPR-CAS9.* Cambridge and New York: Cambridge University Press, 2016.

Ledford, Heidi. "Court Rules on CRISPR." *Nature* 542 (Feb. 23, 2017): 401. https:// iatranshumanisme.files.wordpress.com/2017/02/nature-2017-21502.pdf.

Le Page, Michael. "First Results of CRISPR Gene Editing of Normal Embryos Released." *New Scientist* website. Daily News (March 9, 2017). https://www.newscientist.com /article/2123973-first-results-of-crispr-gene-editing-of-normal-embryos-released/.

Liang, Puping et al. "CRISPR/Cas9-mediated Gene Editing in Human Tripronuclear Zygotes." *Protein & Cell* 6, no. 5 (May 2015): 363–372.

Lussier, Germain. "NASA Says '2012' Is Most Absurd Sci-Fi Movie Ever; 'Gattaca' Most Plausible." *Film.* http://www.slashfilm.com/nasa-2012-absurd-scifi-movie-gattaca-plausible/. January 6, 2011.

Mirchandani, Aneela. "The Original Frankenfoods: Origins of Our Fear of Genetic Engineering." Genetic Literacy project. https://www.geneticliteracyproject.org/2015/02/10/the-original-frankenfoods/. Feb. 10, 2015.

Mori, Masahiro. "The Uncanny Valley." *Spectrum* website of the IEEE. June 12, 2012. http://spectrum.ieee.org/automaton/robotics/humanoids/the-uncanny-valley.

National Academy of Sciences and National Academy of Medicine. *Human Genome Editing: Science, Ethics, and Governance.* Washington, DC: The National Academies Press, 2017. https://www.nap.edu/catalog/24623/human-genome-editing-science-ethics-and-governance.

National Library of Medicine, NIH. "How Did They Make Insulin from Recombinant DNA?" web page. https://www.nlm.nih.gov/exhibition/fromdnatobeer/exhibition-interactive/recombinant-DNA/recombinant-dna-technology-alternative.html.

NIH National Human Genome Research Institute. "All About the Human Genome Project" web page. https://www.genome.gov/10001772/.

NIH Research Portfolio Online Reporting Tools (RePORT). Human Genome Project. https://report.nih.gov/nihfactsheets/ViewFactSheet.aspx?csid=45.

Nobelprize.org website. "The Nobel Prize in Physiology or Medicine 1962" web page. https://www.nobelprize.org/nobel_prizes/medicine/laureates/1962/.

Nobelprize.org websie. "The Nobel Prize in Physiology or Medicine 2015" web page. https://www.nobelprize.org/nobel_prizes/medicine/laureates/2015/.

Norrgard, Karen. "Human Testing, the Eugenics Movement, and IRBs." *Nature Education* 1, no. 1 (2008):170. http://www.nature.com/scitable/topicpage/human-testing-the-eugenics-movement-and-irbs-724.

Pauly, Philip J. "The Invention of Artificial Parthenogenesis." Chap. 5 in *Controlling Life: Jacques Loeb and the Engineering Ideal in Biology*, 93–117. New York: Oxford University Press, 1987. http://10e.devbio.com/article.php?id=72.

Perkowitz, Sidney. Digital People. Washington, DC: Joseph Henry Press, 2004.

———. "Digital People in Manufacturing: Making Them and Using Them," *The Bridge* (National Academy of Engineering) 35, No. 1, Spring 2005, 21–25.

———. "Resistance Is Unnecessary: Accepting the Cyborg in our Midst." *Literal* 19 (Winter 2009–2010): 26–27.

———."Cuerpo y Mente Unidos Por un Chip (Body and Mind Joined by a Chip)." *Quo* (Nov. 2014): 40–44.

———. "Removing Humans from the AI Loop—Should We Panic?" *Los Angeles Review of Books*, Feb. 18, 2016.

———."How to Understand the Resurgence of Eugenics." *JSTOR Daily*, April 5, 2017. https://daily.jstor.org/how-to-understand-the-resurgence-of-eugenics/.

Plumer, Brad. "Scientists Can Now Genetically Engineer Humans. A Big New Report Asks Whether We Should." *Vox*. http://www.vox.com/science-and-health /2017/2/15/14613878/national-academy-genome-editing-humans. Feb. 15, 2017.

Pollack, Andrew. "Scientists Announce HGP-Write, Project to Synthesize the Human Genome." *New York Times*, June 2, 2016. http://www.nytimes.com/2016/06/03 /science/human-genome-project-write-synthetic-dna.html?mwrsm=Email.

Roosth, Sophia. *Synthetic: How Life Got Made*. Chicago: University of Chicago Press, 2017.

Sample, Ian. "Craig Venter Creates Synthetic Life Form." *The Guardian*, May 20, 2010. https://www.theguardian.com/science/2010/may/20/craig -venter-synthetic-life-form.

Science News Staff. "And *Science*'s 2015 Breakthrough of the Year Is . . ." *Science*, http://www.sciencemag.org/news/2015/12/and-science-s-breakthrough-year. Dec. 17, 2015.

Service, Robert F. "Synthetic Microbe Lives with Fewer than 500 Genes." *Science*, http://www.sciencemag.org/news/2016/03/synthetic-microbe-lives-less-500 -genes. Mar. 24, 2016.

Servick, Kelly. "Genome Writing Project Confronts Technology Hurdles," *Science* 356, no. 6339 (May 19, 2017): 673–674. http://science.sciencemag.org/content /356/6339/673.

———. "Embryo Editing Takes Another Step To Clinic." *Science*, 436, no. 6350 (Aug. 4, 2017): 436–437. http://science.sciencemag.org/content/357/6350/436.

Shelley, Mary Wollstonecraft. *Frankenstein* (1818). https://archive.org/stream /Frankenstein1818Edition/frank-a5_djvu.txt.

———. *Frankenstein* (1831). http://tcpl.org/community-read/Frankenstein/mary 1831.pdf.

———, edited by Johanna M. Smith. "Frankenstein": *Complete, Authoritative Text with Biographical, Historical, and Cultural Contexts, Critical History, and Essays from Contemporary Critical Perspectives*. Boston: Bedford/St. Martin's, 2000.

Snyder, Carl. "Bordering the Mysteries of Life and Mind," *McClure's Magazine* 18 (2 March 1902): 386–396. http://tinyurl.com/j87hscc.

Synthetic Biology Project website. "Synthetic Biology 101" web page. http://www.synbio project.org/topics/synbio101/definition/.

The Center of Excellence for Engineering Biology website. "Introducing GP-write" web page. http://engineeringbiologycenter.org/.

The *Economist* website. "Playing Demigods." Aug. 31, 2006. http://www.economist .com/node/7854771.

Tracinski, Rob. "The Future of Human Augmentation and Performance Enhancement." *Real Clear Science*, April 4, 2017. http://www.realclearscience.com /articles/2017/04/04/the_future_of_human_augmentation_and_performance _enhancement.html.

Travis, John. "Germline Editing Dominates DNA Summit." *Science* 350, no. 6266 (Dec 11, 2015): 1299–1300. http://science.sciencemag.org/content/350/6266/1299.

Twist Bioscience blog. "Synthetic Biology Assures Global Access to a Vital Nobel Prize Winning Malaria Medication." Nov. 23, 2015. https://www.twistbioscience.com /dr-jay-keasling/.

Wade, Nicholas. "Scientists Seek Moratorium on Edits to Human Genome That Could Be Inherited." *New York Times*, December 3, 2015. http://www.nytimes. com/2015/12/04/science/crispr-cas9-human-genome-editing-moratorium.html.

Watson, James D. *The Double Helix*. New York: Scribner, 1998.

Filmography

Blade Runner (Ridley Scott, 1982).

Forbidden Planet (Fred M. Wilcox, 1956).

Frankenstein (James Whale, 1931).

Gattaca (Andrew Niccol, 1997).

Metropolis (Fritz Lang, 1927).

Star Trek: The Next Generation (Television series, 1987–1994).

The Day the Earth Stood Still (Robert Wise, 1951).

13: WHAT WOULD MARY SHELLEY SAY TODAY?

Bibliography

Darwin, Charles. *On the Origin of Species by Means of Natural Selection*. London: John Murray, 1859.

Shelley, Mary Wollstonecraft. *Frankenstein* (1831). http://tcpl.org/community-read/ Frankenstein/mary1831.pdf.

Notes

1   Julian Savulescu quoted in Ian Sample, "Craig Venter Creates Synthetic Life Form." *The Guardian*, May 20, 2010. https://www.theguardian.com/science/2010 /may/20/craig-venter-synthetic-life-form.

2   Gibson, Daniel G. et al. "Creation of a Bacterial Cell Controlled by a Chemically Synthesized Genome." *Science* 329 (2010): 52–56. DOI: 10.1126/science.1190719.

3   Goodwin, J. T., and D. G. Lynn. *Alternative Chemistries of Life—Empirical Approaches*. Emory University, 2014. ISBN: 978-0-692-24992-5. http://alternativechemistries .emory.edu/.

4   Ibid.

5   Ibid.

ACKNOWLEDGMENTS

We would like to thank our agent, Laura Wood of FinePrint Literary Management, for her faith in our idea of an anthology celebrating the 200th birthday of Mary Shelley's story, and for connecting us with Pegasus Books. Jessica Case at Pegasus has also completely grasped our goals in the book. She has greatly contributed to achieving them and has been constantly helpful. We also appreciate the careful copyediting and other pre-production work carried out by Pegasus staff. Like Victor Frankenstein's helper Igor, they have ably brought this our monster from the slab to the shelves.

None of this would have been possible without our many contributors, who have enriched the book through their expertise and insight across so wide a range of fields.

SP offers his personal thanks to Pat Marsteller at Emory University, who shared her knowledge of genetics to improve the book; and to the organizers of the Frankenstein Bicentennial Workshop at Arizona State University that he attended in 2014, where he became inspired with the idea of a bicentennial Frankenstein anthology.

Sidney Perkowitz
Eddy Von Mueller